CRITICAL ACCLAIM FOR *JOHN DOLLAR*

"Much of her writing has the feverish mysteriousness of a vivid dream.... Wiggins tells her story in a prose as feathery-light and rhythmical in movement as it is weighty in symbolism.... *John Dollar* succeeds best at projecting a mood of woman on the move: adventuring into the unknown, stumbling all the while, yet constantly seeking to make the world anew."
—Dan Cryer, *Newsday*

"A stunning new novel... *John Dollar* is a feast for the reader. In scene after scene, Wiggins' prose explodes from the page.... Mesmerizing. You won't be able to read *John Dollar* once; you'll want to read it at least one more time."
—Charles Larson, *USA Today*

"The book is, finally, a circular experience, and oddly healing. When you set aside *John Dollar,* what hangs on is not the horror of the story but the pleasure in the way it was told, and an abiding respect for a next-to-impossible task most elegantly accomplished."
—Anne Tyler, *The New Republic*

"One of the most disturbing new novels I've read in years.... Wiggins' prose has a quirky brilliance...a prose simultaneously spare and lush, as precisely opulent as a diamond solitaire—darting, telegraphic, cutting quickly from one scene, one tense, one point of view to another. That style gives the novel an almost cinematic speed and objectivity."
—Michael Gorra, *New York Times Book Review*

"A richly imaginative novel.... Wiggins' vividly physical, feminine approach is fresh and interesting. *John Dollar* is pure adventure."
—Tanja Zimmerman, *San Francisco Chronicle*

"A superb novel, hypnotic, disturbing and artful...so good that most readers will want to devour it in one gulp.... The writing throughout is masterly.... Wiggins' humor and her understanding of people, especially lonely women, both shine in *John Dollar.*"
—Michael Dirda, *Washington Post Book World*

"No better writing is being done nowadays.... The story of eight girls marooned on an island off Burma is all but unbearable in its horror, the more so, because its beauty leaves us almost without defenses."

—Richard Eder, *Los Angeles Times Book Review*

"Wiggins' most compelling, unnerving work... *John Dollar* has a strange, cracked beauty, the result of a first-rate imagination and a daring pen.... In a decade that has produced one too many soft, small novels that entertain without disturbing or challenging the reader, *John Dollar* is quite an achievement."

—Denise Gess, *Philadelphia Inquirer*

"A truly horrifying story... wrought with an elegant style."

—Peter S. Prescott, *Newsweek*

"A tense, dark novel that will keep you turning pages... a beautifully written examination of the dark side of the human spirit. It is a novel you will want to read and read again."

—Dave Hendrickson, *Milwaukee Journal*

"Wiggins has come upon the kind of elemental narrative that seems to have been resting in the collective unconscious waiting for the right author.... *John Dollar* is a cruel story of ritual and impulse.... It inhales and exhales the harsh air of the wildly possible, the possibly wild."

—David Finkle, *New York Post*

"A powerful story that not only pulls you through to its final pages but also propels you back to the beginning again, where you find you want to follow her descent into hell a second time."

—Christopher Lehmann-Haupt, *New York Times*

"Marianne Wiggins sets out to rivet, thrill, unsettle, dismay, scare and sadden the reader. She is successful.... But as well as telling a story vividly, violently and often shockingly... Wiggins is also capable of moving us to great sadness.... Charlotte's love story, like that of most human beings, is a tragedy."

—Peter Reading, *Times Literary Supplement*

ALSO BY
MARIANNE WIGGINS

Babe
Went South
Separate Checks
Herself in Love

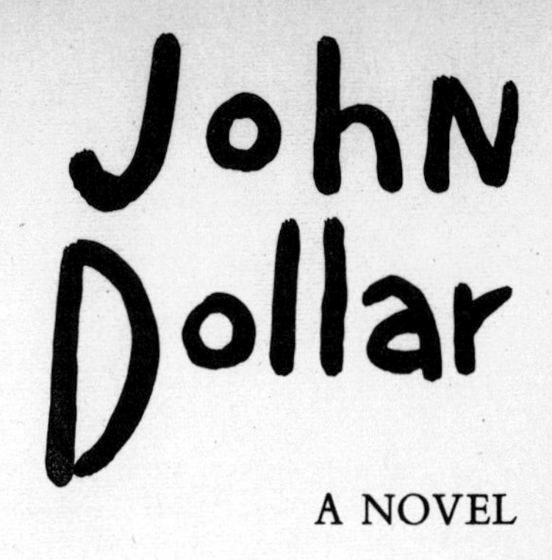

A NOVEL

MARIANNE
WIGGINS

Harper & Row, Publishers, New York
Grand Rapids, Philadelphia, St. Louis, San Francisco
London, Singapore, Sydney, Tokyo, Toronto

The poem which appears on page 17 is an abridged and freely translated version of "Ithaka" by C. P. Cavafy, based on the translation by Edmund Keeley and Philip Sherrard in the *Collected Poems*, Princeton University Press, Princeton, New Jersey, 1975.

Four lines (not consecutive) of Rudyard Kipling's poem "Mandalay" are quoted on page. 28.

The list of "Evil" and "Good" on page 70 is from *The Life and Adventures of Robinson Crusoe* by Daniel Defoe (Penguin Classics Edition, 1985).

The essay on page 78 ("On Water") is from *The Notebooks of Leonardo Da Vinci*, selected and edited by Irma A. Richter. Oxford University Press: World's Classics Paperbacks, 1986.

The essay on page 97 ("The Eye") is from *The Notebooks of Leonardo Da Vinci.*

The quotation on page 168 is from *The Notebooks of Leonardo Da Vinci.*

A hardcover edition of this book was published in 1989 by Harper & Row, Publishers, Inc.

First PERENNIAL LIBRARY edition published 1990.

Designed by Karen Savary

The Library of Congress has catalogued the hardcover edition as follows:

Wiggins, Marianne
John Dollar

I. Title.
PS3573.I385J64 1988 813'.54 88-45538
ISBN 0-06-016070-5

ISBN 0-06-091655-9 (pbk.)
90 91 92 93 94 FG 10 9 8 7 6 5 4 3 2 1

for
beloved
Salman

1

CHARLOTTE

LAST ACT OF THE APOSTLE

They appeared with the sun at their backs on the crest of the hill after daybreak, black figures, threading their way toward the sea through the gray rocks and heather into the town of St. Ives.

The old Indian descended first, leading the donkey on a tether; Charlotte rode across the donkey's back. Charlotte's hair had gone from gold to white when she was rescued from the island years ago, and it fell around her now, wild and full and loose, because the Indian had thought it looked its best that way. The Indian had rinsed the long white hair in tea she brewed from flowers of the English chamomile, then she had anointed it with almond oil, but hadn't found the courage nor the faith to bind it up. Neither had she closed the eyes, folded the arms, entwined the fingers, nor wrapped the body with cloths soaked in linseed oil to stanch its putrefaction. She had known her mistress to have died before so this time she sat vigil, not daring for a full day to disturb the body from what she thought could be a deep but only temporary sleep. She had waited, watching, holding a makeshift wake to discover if this death was going to be irrevocable in the way that some deaths are, or if this death was going to be a sleight of hand like Christ's or like the seasons. This was not the first time she had watched a person die and this was not the only time this person, in particular, had died; so she was not bereft so much as she was chary in the several hours of severe and awful silence that descended over Charlotte's body. Finally three things happened—not so much occurred as seemingly accumulated—which proved that death this time was lasting and irrevocable. The first proof surfaced on the corpse's skin: Charlotte was an old woman, two decades older than the Indian, and for the last ten years her skin and her aroma had been those of dry old age, two powdery sensations, like the wings of lepidoptera. But after she had fallen silent in the night her skin had started to turn waxy. The second proof was soon to follow with the daylight. Charlotte's eyes—one blue, one green: the independent signs of her two natures—had always signaled youth, but with the light of the next day they grew murrhine and clotted, vitelline as yolks and lastly, thirdly, she began to stink.

The Indian had been alone but once in life and so, exploring that condition, she began to sing. While cleansing Charlotte's hair in chamomile, the Indian surprised herself in song. It was not a pleasant noise at first, arising as it did from grief, but after several sounds of pure lament, the Indian found music, half-remembered, from her childhood and she sang, nonstop, as she groomed the corpse and set out on her journey with it into town. A tin miner's daughter, on her way to school that morning near St. Ives, was frightened by the sound and ran to town to warn her friends a witch was walking down the hill, but sightlines over Cornwall ravel. The land buckles and it troughs and although the children of St. Anselm's school in St. Ives strained at the window, they couldn't catch sight of the demon. The witch and its victim had vanished.

The Indian wove 'round the valley, avoiding its roads, cutting through pastures where lambs for the slaughter ran, innocent. She saw several men in succession, wearing caps and rough jackets. She gave them wide berth. She was unused to men. She was unused to people. Charlotte and she had lived for six decades on high land where rock was the backbone just under the earth. They had done nothing. They looked at the sea. The Indian knitted and planted her gourds and potatoes. Of all of God's fruits she best loved potatoes, loved holding them, planting their eyes. The Indian cooked: unleavened bread, thick soup, thin stews. They never ate at a table. On a mat on the floor, side by side, back to back, they took single meals never breathing a prayer of thanksgiving. At night before going to bed they drank bowls of goat's milk and looked at the sea. When they spoke, if they spoke, they were careful of saying not much. Birthdays were always forgotten. The seasons were never rejoiced. The summers in Cornwall were never too hot to remind them of where they had come from, or Hell. They lost their religion to silence, they lost their forbearance to fear. Year after year they refused to forget, to look forward, look inward, look anywhere, but to sea. The Indian loved the blind eyes of potatoes. She rubbed them. She set them eyes-down in the rock-riddled earth. Each year she grew the same number. Nothing progressed. Nothing changed. Except Charlotte was dead and soon, the Indian knew, she herself would die, too.

Only first she had come into town to make peace with the englishman's devil.

The man in the black dress had spoken.

Madam, he said, *Madam,* he thought, was the best he could do. "Madam," he said, "I must ask you most kindly to see my position."

"I will see it, yes. Ask."

"You must see that it's not every day."

"Very good. Yes, it's not."

"It's not every day one is called on to deal with a matter like this."

"Yes, it is not."

"You do speak, you are fluent, conversant in English?"

"I am a Subject."

"Of course, well, the rules are quite clear. The rules are quite strict on the subject."

"She is One. A Subject."

"On this matter, I mean. Holy ground. There's a question of Rites. Holy unction. A question of—do you know—was she—*baptized?*"

"Yes."

"She was—*properly* baptized?"

"Yes."

"When and where?"

"A long time ago. In a church."

"But I mean, before we consider, we need the baptismal certificate."

"Yes, very good, I will pay."

"You don't understand. There has to be proof that she's Church of England. . . ."

"Yes, very good. She is English."

"Sor-ry?"

"The proof. She is English. The Church of England. Same-same."

The man in the black dress waved the back of his hand toward the donkey. "Look," he said. He was not meeting her eyes. She looked where he looked. "Go over there," he instructed. A sign read, "Police." "They can help you."

" 'Police'?"

"Yes."

"For Heaven?"

"What?"

"Properly buried?"

"I'm sor-ry—?"

"You won't make the business?"

"Look—"

"You won't say the prayers?"

"I *am* sor-ry. . . ."

"You won't put her down in this ground?"

"It's out of the question."

"The 'question'?"

"Forbidden."

" 'For-bidden'?"

"Verboten. Défendu. Non licet, interdit. Vetitum est."

Was he mad? Was this hokus?

The Indian took two steps backwards and put up her hand. She showed her palm to his eyes to signify she, too, could translate. The english makes laws. He makes one law for men. He makes one law for women, a law for his children. Laws for his dogs. A law for bats. This law, exclusive, ecclesiastic, for keeping the dead from the dead, under ground. Very good, she translated. The english would never fill rivers with corpses, he hides them instead in the ground. He eats with sharp knives. He chews with a knife and a fork. He buries his dead so the other white castes will not cook them and eat them. Worms and the maggots are better than teeth of one's enemies, that's why the white caste is always at table. He eats and he eats. He eats mountains and ore. He eats diamonds and rubies, blue sky. He eats cities, chews names. He eats people. Her name was something a long time ago that the english had chewed from its whole state of "Menaka" into a word they said "Monica" into the status of "Monkey", for short. He translated her person, he chewed and he chewed. The Indian knew a translation, though, too. She translated his laws into liquid, into the likely suspicion of outlawry, floating face-up on her being, pretending a surface, a sea: she could bury, *o yes.* She had buried before. She could translate while smiling, bow down and back up, take the donkey with Charlotte across it to wait by the gate of the high wall till darkness, till he and his brothers all slept. It would be pocus, a bother, the words, but she'd have to remember. She'd said them once, many times, many ages ago. *Blessed be the root of our desiring,* no, no. *May that come upon him which comes upon a drum at times of feasting,* yes. A beating. No one would deny her right to mourn. No one would prevent her doing right by Charlotte's soul.

She sat down on her haunches in front of the wall. The donkey slept, standing. She sang, while she sat and watched Charlotte. She held Charlotte's hand. Charlotte's hair moved in the wind, as if living.

After dark they stole in. There was a moon and the graves were all light. Some spirits assembled. *Diggery dig,* Monkey said. In her heart she felt slight as a girl. Against the wall, by a shed, there was a shovel, a bucket, a single-wheeled handcart. Monkey tethered the donkey. How many years ago, Charlotte, did they do what they did on that shore by the light of this moon? *Dig here, you crazy old woman,* the Indian ordered herself.

She dug.

She threw her weight into the breaking of ground. Sixty years, or a lifetime, just digging, she judged. She and Charlotte had killed them, not Monkey so much, although Monkey had beaten their heads with a stone, after their hands had stopped moving. Then Charlotte and she had dragged their two bodies down to the sea for the vultures and sharks. Then Charlotte had said, *'I want you to bury him.'* Charlotte was crazy by then.

Monkey had dug a big hole, digging alone in the sand with her hands. Charlotte had stood by, just watching. 'Is it ready?' she'd said. Monkey was blinded by tears. *How big must it be?* she had wondered. *When should I stop?*

Charlotte had picked up his bones. The arms and the legs and the head. Then she and Monkey had puzzled them out in the earth till they looked like a man. Place his head facing Hell, Charlotte said. Monkey twisted the skull. 'Place him eyes-down in the earth.'

Then Charlotte had wept and Monkey covered the bones. Night had come fast. Charlotte tamped the earth with her feet and the moon had come out. Under the moon she kept tamping and tamping, stamping his grave as if tamping a fire, stamping and stamping, a march going nowhere. When she came to a halt she fell to her knees and said, 'Say it with me. *Man that is born of a woman is full of misery Amen.'*

—Misery, amen, Monkey said. She got down on her knees next to Charlotte.

He's cut down like a flower he fleeth as shadow and never continues one stay Amen.

—In one stay, amen, Monkey said.

Thou knowest Lord secrets of our hearts but spare us O God most mighty O holy and merciful savior Thou worthy judge Suffer us not at last Amen.

—Yes, Monkey said.

Say after me: *Earth to earth ashes to ashes.*

—Ashes. Two ashes, Monkey had said.

Dust to dust.

—A Dust. Two dusts.

As it was in the beginning is now and ever shall be world without end.

'Without end,' Monkey said.

CHARLOTTE

Charlotte had gone to Burma in the fall of '17, when God and history took her there.

Before the War she never thought she had a calling, never thought that life was such a fragile thing it needed to be patched together with a purpose. Before the War she'd been a girl with no extraordinary prospects—a pretty girl, but never beautiful; a level-headed member of her social class whose single claim to the exceptional was the fact that she had one blue eye, one green one. The green one was the larger. She went to Burma in the way that single women go to foreign places by themselves—she went because there were, and there will always be, women who will nest *parfois* like papermoths, women who will try to cling on paper legs to the primeval.

She arrived 8 November 1917, on her birthday, at Rangoon, in the dry season, via Gibraltar, Marseilles, Malta, Port Saïd, the Suez Canal, the Red Sea, Aden, Bombay and Calcutta. She was twenty-five years old. Her knowledge of the Bible was considerable, her knowledge of the world was less. Her knowledge of the East was sketchy, based on Kipling and a desultory reading of descriptions of the tenets of Islam and the myths of Hinduism, which were required for the personnel of schools receiving grants-in-aid from Government in Burma, even though the Burmese were devotees of the Buddha. One eastern religion was much the same as any other in the minds of the Home Office and the missionaries of Christendom: they were all massed as exotic, their distinctions being nullified by the process of the British mind which separates the heterodoxy out of things as if it were a substance in the daily milk. Besides, Charlotte was not sent to proselytize among the Natives. She wasn't a missionary—she never took the pose of having been called upon by God to Christianize the Pagan souls. She worked for The Government. She was there to teach the British Youth. Sent to foster and preserve the standards of the Empire in English children. Her task was godly, yes. But under the Raj the differences between working for one's God or working for one's Country were very subtle and most of them were things to do with how one wore one's wealth or how one exercised her right to sexuality.

In neither of these categories had she owned a genius.

She'd been poor, without a family income or a dowry.

And she'd been unsexed.

She'd lived in a room along a corridor in a house without coal fires owned by Mrs. Crowley, a nervous woman with three children who coughed all night, a recent widow, like herself, owing to the War. The halls were painted dark green and the stairways smelled, alternatively, like two currents lacing through a sea, of fish and disinfectant. The house was cold and welcomed wind through useless flues and wormy shutters. It sat along a narrow street of red-brick buildings whose fronts were all the same. To defray her costs, Charlotte taught the younger Crowleys sums each night, and the oldest Crowley penmanship and "Literature." For this she earned two baths and a supplementary daily tea, the latter being only somewhat darker than the first. She owned two dresses, four shoes, five woollen stockings and a coat. Her fingernails were riven and her hair was falling out. At her temples, near her thoughts, there was a frost of white among the roots, the coming of a glacier. Every day she walked from Mrs. Crowley's house two miles to her clerkship in the City to save money. At night she wrapped her feet in hansom rugs, the only things her father, a cab-driver, left her. She didn't own a feather pillow. Everything around her showed its edge. Nothing that she owned was soft, or comforting, or bright. At night she lay, a mummy in coarse wool, and wished for candlelight, its play of life around her walls. She dreamed of warmth, the rising or the falling of bright stars, a conscious or unconscious bonedeep dream of embers.

In her mind she saw her own heat dying. It was very strange. It was not the same as being old and facing certain death, it wasn't that, she'd seen that look, that fading, in her parents' eyes when they were sick and dying and the only point of focus in their faces was a distant bright light burning in the centers of their pupils. She wasn't dying, she knew that. A forward-moving consummating death would have meant a passion, and her life was passionless. That's what she saw. A person without passion owns a different kind of fear: a fear of emptiness, a length, a sentence. Dying, its progression, is revolt, a rage, a passage, exodus, migration, exclamation, and she wasn't dying. She wasn't falling headlong into life, her heat was going, very strange, she watched it, watched her endless days, *poor thing* she sometimes thought about herself as if she'd passed a strange girl in the street in early dark, the damp, the cold, she hated

London but her hatred wasn't anything. Her hatred was another ghost, another shadow of a thing she used to know. She wanted death. She didn't think herself a coward. She wanted death, she wanted substance. She wanted death, that death that takes a person somewhere else. She wanted transport. What she had was death that was a tenant.

She could have borne it, borne this death a little better, if everywhere she looked she didn't see her misery repeated in the women on whom loss of love showed like an anemia: War showed on them all. Sometimes in the street their faces read like place names on a map: *Ypres, Marne, Verdun.* Her own face, she assumed, read *Somme.* That's why she hated looking at herself, turned her mirror to the wall, turned away from anything or anyone who might reflect an image of herself. Before the Somme she'd seen the War on women's faces but they hadn't haunted her. So long as Henry was alive she could close her eyes and see his face, replace immediate reality with visions of their past or future. So long as Henry's letters still arrived she knew life as she imagined it, whether real or not, was shared because he wrote to tell her that her dreams were his dreams, too. Somewhere, in a place that each one visited, as real as France or England, they went on making love to one another. Their love progressed. Equally and mutually, by dreaming, their love deepened. It was outside possibility that he would not return. It was impossible. For two months after he was killed, after the day they said he'd died, his letters written from the trench continued to arrive. A dead man can't send letters, Charlotte knew. She also knew that they'd been written months before, but she pretended. She went on hoping against hope it was another woman's husband, some other Henry Lewes, whose heart had been exploded by a Lewis gun as in the dark he ran, mistaken for a jerry by a green recruit. His kit arrived and Charlotte signed for it, believing she could fool herself as long as it remained unopened. But then the letters stopped. A month went by without a word from him and one night with a paperknife she pried his locker open, and she knew. From that box as if from a cave there escaped eternity. It was going to be forever winter. The things she found were not enough to help survive him: buttons, needle, thread, a cup, her letters and her wedding band. When he'd gone they'd kept each other's ring. Charlotte wore his on a thread between her breasts, she was stunned to find he hadn't died with her ring somewhere on him. Now she had them both, when even one was one too many. Sometimes she put them in her mouth. She put them on her tongue, one inside the other. She bit down on them. Sometimes she smoothed the paper of the letters that he'd written like shrouds over her face as she lay still. Sometimes she tried to hear his voice. She missed his face. She longed to know what it was doing. She held his shaving brush, she tried to touch her stomach with it but she couldn't feel a thing beyond the cold. She tried to keep the locker closed so it would hold his smell but then she longed to hide herself away inside it. She couldn't see his face. She fell from dreaming to a sort of stupor in which she was the victim of a loss of every sensory perception. She longed to put in her possession some talisman which could relieve her body of its stupefaction, of its insentience, its strangeness to itself, but everywhere she went she saw the other widows, windows onto one another's sensory deception. They could not look the others in the eyes. Wherever grief stopped them, on street corners or on trams or in tea shops, these women looked but didn't look, looked ghostly, couldn't see, sought with awful emptied glances faint extremes of what was set before them, women looking always to a distance, to the ragged edges of existence, single threads of cloth, for instance, snapped plait on a cane seat, wayward hair, a crumpled leaf, a crack in a glass globe, but never *eyes* and never closeness to another because one of them might start to speak and then the telling would begin to welter, ravel, never cease. *Do not admit that you remember love,* their faces seemed to say. Hide your passions in thin wash. Grow sour, never sentimental. The British are supposed to be that way: A passionless, perfective people. She wanted to be dead. She hunted for him in the books they'd read together and found that, even there, she'd lost him. What had previously defined her world now served to torment her—she went searching through their old books looking for some words of comfort and heard herself screaming in her mind at stupid heroines instead. Through *Clarissa,* through Jane Austen, through the Brontës, through Flaubert, she hungered for a different sort of story, one to reinvent the world she knew. "At twenty-five," she read one night in Henry's copy of *Un Coeur Simple,* "she was often taken for forty. . . . Like everyone else, she had had her love-story."

That night she turned the mirror outward and saw that she, too, looked older than her years—she looked abandoned, untended, deserted and unloved.

That same week she bought, and read, different authors, Americans, Henry James, Edith Wharton, Stephen Crane. She stole, on an impulse, from a bookstall on Charing Cross Road, two issues of the journal *The Egoist,* in which she discovered Ezra Pound and Joyce and Stephen Hero: She started reading myths.

She applied for a posting to Burma.

She grew restless and dreamed she had lost her acquaintance with conscience.

She lost her old habit of thinking to God.

At the end of the month the letter arrived which confirmed her worse fears.

It gave her a date of departure.

It gave her the place of asylum:

Rangoon.

"ITHAKA" Only later did it seem the love affair was instantaneous.

She was seasick, for a start. Two days out of Portsmouth on the *Viceroy of India* they sighted the French Finistère and met the Bay of Biscay the way Charlotte imagined she would greet a savage bear while walking through Hyde Park. Of the stormswept pitching week that followed, Charlotte would recall only a putrid smell (her own), cold tea and a voice repeating through her bolted cabin door, "It won't be long now, Miss. It'll all be over soon's we can take Lisbon."

Taking Lisbon seemed to be the cure.

After that there were a series of calm glasslike days, and then Gibraltar. The voice that she recognized as having spoken to her through her cabin door belonged to Seaman Slash, a Yorkshire boy in a white steward's jacket whose sleeves were too long. The cuffs were discolored and only his fingertips showed. "Pillar of Hercules," he told her, pointing with the tip of the fingers of one hand from the deck toward the Rock. "Other one's over there." He turned 'round, each sleeve extended to extreme and added, "In Africa." Charlotte smiled and raised her eyebrows. "It's called the 'Djebel Musa'," he explained. "Chap called Hercules was supposed to plant a foot on each peak, stradlin' these two conty-nents. 'At was the size a' *him',"* he told her. His voice cracked. He was only sixteen or fifteen years old and Charlotte was beginning to find that she thought he was amusing, when she realized that the seaman's jacket he was wearing must belong to someone bigger, perhaps older, someone else whose job this boy pretended at, a man in France or Belgium or an unmarked grave so she stopped. She didn't like the sudden thought that he was finding her attractive.

"I suppose your lot are told to chat up women passengers," she said not kindly, intending to inform him, Don't think I'm a fool for *that,* but he blushed so deeply with confusion, she felt brittle and schoolmarmish and leaned against the rail and tossed her head and breathed the salt air in a way that she hoped would seem more winsome. She looked down at her wedding band and twisted it, then felt for Henry's on the thread beneath her dress. "Oh, my," she said. Something had just played beneath the surface.

"Pretty, ain't they?"

"My, yes," Charlotte said. "What are they?"

The boy smiled and Charlotte noticed how his teeth were ruined. "Ain't you never seen a dolphin, Miss?"

Charlotte looked with wonder, then she tried to laugh. She hadn't, actually. She'd only ever seen them on Greek friezes.

"Me Dad said these ones who habitate the Straits are ghosts of them Phoenicians."

"Your 'Dad'—?"

"*The whole world ended here,* that's what me Dad would say about these Straits. He would say the world went back from here to Syria an' all, an' that was it, that's where it ended. Them Phoenicians sailed around here all their lives, for centuries, not knowing it was one great pond. Sad, ain't it, when you think about it, don't you think so, Miss?"

Charlotte looked at him and said, "You're wearing your Dad's jacket, aren't you?" but nothing came of what he answered because half the crew, including him, shipped off on another transport bound for Casablanca when they put in that night to take on stores at Malta.

At Malta there boarded a group of the most appalling types, all bound for *N*'dya who wheezed about the *M*'pyre and hurled fruit at the flying fish and cups and saucers at the German *Unterseeboot* which surfaced like an accidental insult against their protocol, off Crete.

After Crete came Port Saïd where they stopped to bring on coal and Charlotte heard her first muezzin. She went ashore, to Cairo, in tow with other English (the Maltese) and was set upon by Greeks and Arabs selling pornographic pictures of young girls. One especially zealous eager wallah pinned her to a nook in the medina and displayed before her eyes a series of prints of boys, which she was forced to look at, eventually, though not too quickly, forcefully, although she liked them, there were one or two that were exceptional in terms of light, their shadings, shadows on their skin, their thighs, their feet, their ardent eyes, and so she bought them: nine. Too much money, yes, but never to be looked at, and back on board she found a strange Australian, a man, who had bought the same ones, who showed them 'round at dinner.

"Cavafy," he said, later, when he saw her the next morning.

"Lewes," she said, acknowledging the introduction, and offered him her hand.

"No. I mean: the poet."

He had pity on her ignorance and shoved a pamphlet in her hand.

" 'Ithaka'," he said.

"Charlotte," she persisted, in response.

That's how, anchored at Egypt, she came to read,

As you set out for Ithaka
hope your road's a long one,

full of an adventure, a discovery.

Arriving there is what you're destined for.

Don't hurry,
better if your journey lasts for years
so you're old by the time you reach the island

Ithaka gave this journey to you

Without her you'd have never dreamed her

If you find her poor, she won't have fooled you:

Wise as you'll become,

so full of ports,

You'll have understood what "Ithakas" are for.

THE END OF STRIFE

Lucky you, she was told one night at dinner by a woman with pale lips and nervous fingers. "If Patrick had been posted to Rangoon instead of to the wretched Punjab, I'd have been allowed to keep my babies."

With this, the woman lost her self-control and left the dining room and later in the evening Charlotte pieced together that this woman was, in fact, the woman in the cabin next to hers whose weeping had kept her awake every night since they'd sailed from Cairo. At Aden, where they stopped once more to take on coal, this same woman attempted to defect by running down a gangplank over which the coolies were delivering the coal in baskets on their heads, but succeeded only in falling at the feet of a deck officer who stopped her, begging him to help her find a way to England.

"See it every time," the purser shook his head and said to Charlotte.

" 'It'—?"

"This hysteria. Duty failin' in a woman. Hobson's choice."

"Hobson's is the choice between taking what there is or taking nothing. I don't see how this—"

"You're the one's going out to be the teacher, ain't 'ya?"

"Yes."

" 'Ya wear it."

"Thank you."

"Pleasure. What I was sayin' was she has to choose between the little ones and wifely duty. You know. Call it what you will. Hobson's, Jobson's, stayin' with the husband when the babes are sent for school to England. Don't suppose you'd have that choice?"

"Why not?"

"Well you ain't married for a start."

"Widowed."

"The truth? You hide it nicely."

"Thank you."

"Pleasure. Babies?"

"I—?"

"Did you have some? You an' him."

"There wasn't time."

"There's always *time.* Want one?"

"Baby?"

"Bedtime visit."

No she didn't want one though she watched the visits between the single men and women occur with mounting frequency the nearer that they came to India. One particularly starry-eyed and stupid couple actually got married by the Captain after having met on board and danced together all night off Gibraltar. They were married on the Red Sea in a ceremony all the first-class passengers attended as if they'd known the couple all their lives. Charlotte traveled second, so she hadn't been invited but she watched the bride throw flowers from the "A" deck. The groom wore his regimental uniform but the bride was in a full lace gown and veil. The woman standing next to Charlotte on the deck said the girl had planned to marry *someone* when she'd had it made for her in England the week before she left for India. It was so new it hadn't had a chance to crease its folds. *"Ah! Marriage,"* the woman said; *"Ah! Monongahela."* This woman's name was Tim, a name she had adopted for herself fifty-seven years ago when she was old enough to argue with her mum and dad when they called her by the name they'd chosen, Daisy. "If I'd a choice I'd do it all again," Tim said, at some point, about marriage. "Though I'd wait a bit before I'd marry Tel a second time. He was a good man, Tel, don't take me wrong, for all that he was Irish. Lovely hands. They gave him a fine funeral."

Tim ran a tea plantation and had been in India for forty years. She spoke a singsong cadence, Irish English burled with Urdu. She'd been back to Blighty to bury her last son and to take the mercury for what she called her "Borodino." ("I made a costly conquest one time, dear, which ended my campaigns for good.") When she heard Charlotte was going out to Burma she offered her companionship from Bombay to Calcutta, where she lived in the Cold Weather, and Charlotte happily accepted. Later, Charlotte couldn't imagine how she would have made it across India without Tim. The first thing to alarm her was the Heat. It started on the ocean. Daily, after Aden, days seemed longer with no land in sight and Heat in viscous layers on the water. Tim said, "This is nothing." She was right. Although they landed in October at the start of the "cold" season in Bombay, Charlotte found the heat a sheath, a suffocating sheet around her. "You'll acclimatize," Tim commiserated. "I have an eye for those who won't: You will. Just keep away from gin. Too many think the gin will help them, something in its color. And the idiots who drink claret in this weather get the early death that they deserve."

Of Bombay Charlotte would remember little because from the Heat there flowed the Lassitude. Her blood felt waxen. Docks, the mossy decadence of balconies and buildings, steamy streets, the beach, every detail of her landing and her passage through the city to Victoria Terminal coagulated, the very moments that she'd dreamed of with excitement came to her through Lassitude as one whole single-sheet, flocculent mass, a woolly, fleecy, opaque, blurred surrounding.

After Lassitude there was the Sudden Loss of Language. Tim was talking talking, lecturing to her about the architecture, the timetables and diseases. "Always seek the shade," she thought she understood Tim saying, but then Tim was saying something else in another language to some bearers in the station while announcements barked from speakers on the platforms NEXT SERVICE IS DISORGANIZED and trains, like clocks, ticked in syncopation to requests *five rupees only missus* and a goat chewed at her skirt, a sleeper woke, *hullo! hullo!* and Tim was pulling at her arm, she thought, and shouting This way, Charlotte, you and I are first-class on the male, that one over there, Calcutta male.

On the journey, four days, Charlotte slept, or thought she slept, although she dreamed a boy was fanning ice in her direction. She woke, or seemed to wake, as if from fever, several times, although each time she seemed to surface from the loss of language, heat, the lassitude, she fell again into a deeper panic, that of having made a fatal error, she dropped through time into abyss, no absolution. Days went by wherein she couldn't bring two thoughts together, there were moments when her mind no longer functioned to include itself in the reality around. At Calcutta she got off the train, a trunk was lost, she spent a week with Tim, her trunk was found, she boarded the small packet steamer for Rangoon as Tim pressed books, names and addresses, foolproof remedies on her. It was November. On the water once again she succeeded in regaining her lost balance but still she couldn't shake a sense of doom. She listened with no sympathy to someone at her side along the rail describe the Burmese ("unlike those testy *Indians,* you see") as "merry easygoing brightly-festooned natives who give themselves with passive ease to our English kind of squirearchy." *Help me,* she silently petitioned as they came in sight of the first rice mills, I've come halfway 'round the world to spend my life inside a land of *merchants.*

It was true, the love affair was never instantaneous, rice brought the white man to Rangoon—rice, mahogany and teak—and their mills, like exclamation marks, stressed her first impressions of Rangoon. Farther north in Mandalay and Mogôk there were ruby mines and fortunes to be had in sapphires and rubber but nine-tenths of the land in cultivation was in rice and teak and all of it passed down the Irrawaddy through the customhouses in Rangoon where it was milled, refined and traded several times before it reached the world by way of the Andaman Sea. The men who owned the trade were British. For them, and for their wives and children, England was a myth and memory, a place more real in microcosm, in its re-creation, than in any actuality. For them, there may as well have been no Kitchener's Army nor a war in Europe. There was instead a sort of faded picture, a sepia-tinted life superimposed on a teeming colorful locale beneath. When the locale did not conform to the image that they needed to conserve, the British acted as if it didn't matter, they ignored it, as if fantasy and fact, image and reality, truth and fiction were, inseparably, the same. Against this, more than against the Heat, which cooled, and the Lassitude, which lifted, Charlotte made her small rebellion. She started, first, with Language. First, she started, silently, by seeing. She wanted words to match the things she saw. English failed the hundred different shades of red she saw in flowers and in spices. She didn't know the names of trees she saw, of birds, or fruits. She couldn't find the names for things within the lexicon she was familiar with, there was no English word which could approximate what *hti* was, for example, the umbrella-like-shaped-thing-on-top-of the pagodas from which shivered tiny bells which trilled their silvery tintinnabulation on the wind throughout the night. Plain solid meaning seemed dissolved by ignorance and she rebelled: the English words for trousers, coats and skirts could not describe the fluid garments that she saw, but, then, neither could the words *sam foo* describe them in those first months, either. The street signs were transcribed in English—Merchant Street, Canal Street, Tiger Alley Road, King Edward Road, Judah Ezekiel Avenue—but the streets themselves bore traffic which was everything, but never English. Riding in a rickshaw on her first day there she passed an oxcart full of purple prawns the size of bishops' miters and saw prawn eggs clustered like expensive diamonds on their bellies while blue ravens dove at them in frenzied hunger and the susurrated prayers of penitents were carried on the wind from the pagoda while vermin, lice, whatever they were called, living in the horsehair of the rickshaw seat were massing on her buttocks making meat of her beneath her poplins: and what she wanted, what she needed, what she sought was language that described it *all.*

What she didn't know, what the Lassitude disguised, was that she was waking from insentience. It would take a long long time. It takes time, a long time, and the element of surprise, to reawaken love. In the meantime, at the end of March, the scorching winds began and then the rain came on the first of May. One would think that all one's years in England could prepare one for the rain but there's no English word that estimates the seamless press of a monsoon on one's existence. Its sound inside a room becomes a constant presence like a mother's heartbeat in a womb. There's no escape from it, no drier place, no fireside, no walnuts, no crisp apples, nothing flinty, no dry pages, nothing cracks, not even bones. Charlotte drank her first monsoon as if she were turned earth. She stood in it and let it wash her. She walked in it, making laughing eddies 'round her ankles. The other memsahibs cautioned sternly of *the worm* a monsoon parasite which enters like a thistle through a bare foot and nestles in one's bloodstream at some length, but Charlotte left her wellies in her trunk and refused the pretense of a brolly in such downpour. She liked to feel she was amphibious, swimming through a double life. She was neither one thing nor the other, not a gill-fitted English woman who'd gone troppo nor an indiginous inhabitant of the native land. The feeling that she lived somewhere between known boundaries, extraterritorially, was enforced by those around her. Among the Chinese, Indians and Burmese she was made to feel that she was from a different Heaven, they were deeply superstitious about the colors of her eyes. People would bring other people in from the villages to wait outside her house to ask to look at them. She was offered rice and fish and bits of colored string, all kinds of presents from the Buddhists. Others were afraid of her—the Hindu women hid their children's faces from her gaze. She was said to have a second head she kept somewhere (beneath her *longyi!*) which held the matching eyes to this one. She was said to sleep with one eye always open (the green one! which could watch the spirits of the dead!). She was said to have been born without the aid of parents, to exist on a higher plane of humanity, to be luminous at night, to be free of sensual desire, to feed on no known food except the crystal distillation of pure joy, to be nearer to *nirvana* than a monk: she was said to be half-man half-woman. Among the Burmese she was something never seen before. Among the British she was *odd.* They interpreted her dedication to her work as one more admirable example of the ethic of self-sacrifice in the female of their species and never entertained the shadow of a doubt that what she really came for, what she'd come around the world for, was a husband.

No self-respecting single woman ever traveled to the Raj alone for any other purpose, in their view. A séjour with a relative or in a missionary service only served as thin disguise of the laudable, and necessary, trade in British brides for British bachelors in the Civil Service and the Army, plus it guaranteed the Empire's racial purity. A single English woman on the social scene was a thing imported like the bonded gin, a bit of home to aid morale, old thing: Her first summons into matrimony arrived a mere month-to-the-day after she had landed in Rangoon. It was delivered by a Mister Macgregor ten o'clock one morning after he had shaved, before he'd had his breakfast and his gin.

"One knows of course," he said, "what the word *Rangoon* means in the native lingo."

The web of ruined capillaries on his nose collapsed somewhat as he exhaled. Charlotte stared at them. They seemed to be a seine through which he fished for breath. "No," she said, "in fact one doesn't."

" 'End of Strife'," he solemnly pronounced.

She smiled politely. *Fitting,* she was thinking, then he used this definition to suggest that since they were both single and together in a place so aptly named there appeared to be no reason why they ought not make it lasting, perforce, and become a man and wife.

"Except that I'm in mourning," Charlotte offered.

"Twattle," and he waved his hand.

He was twenty years her senior, seriously loyal to the Crown despite his being Scottish, and careless in his bearing. He had been in Burma fifteen years. She knew nothing more about him, not even his first name. She thought he'd been described to her as some long-established *sirdar* in the sapphire trade but she wasn't sure because she'd met so many indistinguishable types in the last month he might very well have been the *apke-wasti* in the ICS who still lived with his mother. She was certain he was not the father of a child or, at least, of any of the children under her tutelage, or she would have met him at the school. In fact, now that she'd considered it, she couldn't say for certain that she'd met him previous to this and the thought of ever being touched by him was ludicrous in the extreme. She wanted to forgive his arrogance as a thing acquired from the climate like a jaundice, forgive his attitude toward her as owing to the fact he'd been away from England for too long, or that he'd been outside the company of women for too many years and formed the habit of addressing them as *exotics* from whom he had to bargain cheaply with a minimum of fuss. But it didn't take her long to learn his attitude toward entering on marriage was the British attitude in force in Burma about everything, as if the English there weren't conscious of the current century. Most of the men and all the women were retrogressive in their prejudices and opinions. Even while her senses had been captive to love, before the War, she had never failed to notice that the world had moved into the modern age, that books were being written and inventions made, ideas flown from cafes, sidewalks, auditoria—but the British who were out in Burma were not engaged by *new* ideas, *new* books or *new* ways of being men and women. Nor were they interested in the strange and contradictive wonder of the country which surrounded them. They were interested, to the extent their interest was exercised, in justifying a selective point of view, in demonstrating by example to the world that they were privileged by the nature of their birth. Perhaps they, and she, had always been that way—mannered, preemptive, supercilious—but she drew, in those first months, farther and farther away from the people who believed they were her own. With no sense of shame at her rebellion she began to find the English far more foreign than the foreign weather, heat and lassitude. Burma and its weather happened, to extremes. Rangoon happened, teeming with extremes. The Irrawaddy River happened—and yet nothing of its floods, its traces, caused the slightest perturbation in the course of British life. Red-brick monumental office buildings were constructed. Clubs were organized. Petunia seeds were planted where the former frangipani grew. Ice cubes were cultivated and conserved in straw. Buddhist monks with begging bowls, their shaved heads blue below the skin, passed the British by, unnoticed. The Russian Revolution happened, and the Third Battle of the Aisne. The Germans held a line thirty-seven miles northeast of Paris. In Rangoon they held a tea dance at the club and the men played cards while the women discussed goods on sale from catalogues. The rains came early, flooding out the paddies at the season of transplanting. Gold leaf on the Shwe Dagon Pagoda furred blue-green with fungus. The Czar of Russia and his family were assassinated. The Second Battle of the Marne occurred. In Rangoon a Mister Stewart struggled to find pleasure one night on the verandah and was stabbed (between the fourth and fifth metacarpals of his right hand while his palm played at her breast) with the jade and abalone dagger Charlotte bought herself in the bazaar. Soon after that an elephant rampaged on the docks destroying rice stores and Charlotte was the only English person who spoke out against exterminating it. By then the love affair was started. At night, for sleeping, she wore colored silk as thin as air, or nothing, never cotton. By day she dressed as Burmese men and women did, in a *longyi-eingyi* and a long-sleeved jacket. She walked in the bazaar alone and smoked native tobacco in the dark in bed. She was tempted often and profoundly by both oriental men and opium but still felt unentitled to test pleasure and, besides, she felt as certain saints have claimed to feel, that she was being guarded, watched, approved for something else. She went less and less to club affairs, and when she did she went alone, said little, never drank, left early, unescorted. After a while the English, as they often do, bestowed on her the status of a social invisibility. The Treaty of Versailles was signed. Parliament in London passed the Government of India Act, excluding Burma. The Irish Free State happened. Italian Fascists seized the government in Rome. In Rangoon the annuals surpassed themselves, petunias blossomed large as cabbages. Boxing Day was celebrated and the rice export was at its peak. Polo rhythms echoed on the maidan. The ice was as the ice had been, invisible. The men played cards, the women gave what little time they had outside their homes to worthy Christian charities. They read the London papers, two weeks late. They ate off English bone and starched their Irish linen. They took their quinine like religion, like the eucharist it was. They imported Life As They Thought It Was, with confidence. They kept their children at their sides unlike their counterparts in India, imported Schooling with all else, and gave their daughters, blindly, to the teaching and the waking of the widow, Charlotte Lewes.

"EK BURRA BILLA DA."

There were eight of them—nine, if they included Monkey, which they only ever did to dig for water *diggery dig* dig for rags and bones. They were a varied lot.

Shauna, Ruby. Sloan & Sybil.

Amanda, Norris, Gabriella, Jane and "Monkey."

Some of them were sisters—two of them were twins. All of them had known each other all their lives or all the span of life they could remember, certainly as long as each of them had known her parents, maybe longer, definitely as long as every one of them had lived in Burma. In other words: forever.

By day they went to school and learned their lessons about England, and the sky was an umbrella, silk blue canopy. They learned from Mrs. Lewes that England had a sky and that its sky was two or, at most, three sure colors. These colors were white and gray and sometimes blue. Her eyes were always two (colors) and it was hard to tell which one was telling them the truth.

From their ayahs they had learned their pidgin nursery rhymes. From their parents they had learned to say a lot of things that own no meaning, how to proclaim words that fall like hymns upon the ear but fail to render any sense of what one's feeling. From their fathers' *chokras* they had learned the names of snakes and from the *dubashes* and *gorawallahs* they had heard the sounds of fervent praying. On the chests of *chin chin boys* they'd seen tattoos, the smiling faces of the demons. From their mothers' Chinese cooks who fed them *hingyo* and rice noodles in the kitchen while they talked they'd learned about the Zodiac and planetary posts of the pagodas (how devotees should walk clockwise, keep the object of their worship at a fixed point off the bones of their right shoulders).

By day, they did much *pooja* of the union jack. By night, they organized their magic on an abacus of stars.

They employed their hands in what they prayed as syncretism even though they didn't know its meaning: played at witchcraft. They believed in *nagas* and *garudas* and the sixteen planes of *Rupa-Loka.* They believed in Father Christmas. They'd been born within a spitting distance of the *bo* tree and they laughed at Alice's dilemmas in her Wonderland because they thought they were all silly. They liked drawing letters of the foreign alphabets, all mixed up, as codes.

They liked watching Charlotte, night and day.

They liked looking at the cards their fathers bought from Malay sailors in from Indochina.

By day they memorized the lines of poetry needed to assist their English accents:

> On the road to Mandalay,
> Where the old Flotilla lay . . .
> Bloomin' idol made o' mud—
> Wot they called the Great Gawd Budd—

By day they listened and recited perfectly, in perfect English, English poetry for Mrs. Lewes.

By night they listened to the boy they paid to watch her tell how Charlotte stood on her verandah in the moonlight in her silk pajamas, smoking, and bent down, and brushed her pale long hair.

CHARLOTTE AND THE DOLPHIN

Charlotte's house was built on stilts and stood across the inlet from the steamer jetty on a little spit of land on Monkey Point between Pazundaung Creek and the Rangoon River.

In the rains the waters flooded to within an inch beneath her floor, but in the heat pariah dogs and stray cats from the riverboats dug hollows in the dirt beneath her house and slept there through the long days and roused themselves at night to prowl for sex and scavenge meat and bones.

At night Charlotte could see lanterns on pearl fishers' boats leaving on the morning ebb for Mergui. She could hear the divers singing to themselves, a trick, like dolphins sending sound through water, that they used among themselves to help them navigate the harbor. Most nights she slept only a few hours, waking in the dark to river sounds that came to her through open salts of her jalousies. She woke when the market woke, when the boats came back, and set out in a silk sarong and plaited sandals through the city toward the Shwe Dagon pagoda.

The pagoda opened every morning before sunrise, while the British city slept. From her house Charlotte walked along the jetties where the fishermen from Diamond Island unloaded turtle eggs and swifts' nests into baskets strapped to coolies' backs for transport to the Chinese market in the center of Rangoon. The nests were sold, still wet from the sea, to the women who made vats of birdnest soup, the steam from which trailed through the streets spiced and hot and reeking of the limestone where swifts nested at low tide.

From the Strand, north to Merchant and Bandoola Streets, the traffic from the river proceeded toward the markets. On Lan Ma Daw Road there was a songbird market, then the fish markets of Chinatown, then *Thein Gyi Zei,* the Indian spice and cotton market. Closer to the Shwe Dagon pagoda there were the stalls that sold *nirvana* goods—scent sticks, candles, flowers, puppets, rosaries and prayer flags. Next to them were vendors of sweetcakes wrapped in bright rice paper—vendors of the most perfect fruit. The Buddha was a connoisseur of all things beautiful, Charlotte had learned—People on their way to worship carried simple things, a gift of spices, for example, beautifully displayed. People brought whatever offering they could afford. The wealthy, praying for their future lives, brought money; the poor brought grains of rice. Some people brought lacquer boxes containing their shorn hair. The monks brought nothing, only prayers. They had vowed renunciation of possessions in the service of the Buddha and could offer nothing material, not even a flower petal. Because she was a woman, Charlotte was not allowed to speak to them. She was not allowed to touch their alms bowls when she gave them alms or come within a certain distance of their prayer mats on the floor of the pagoda. Still, despite the distance, she was drawn to them. She identified herself as one with them in abnegation. She envied them their received cosmology, their canonically fixed purpose. She, too, longed to live in a non-world, outside existence of the law and literature, of the King's Own Version of the text. Nightly, she saw these young men, these priests with golden bodies in orange robes moving through the market stalls, the traders and the prostitutes, toward the pagoda and she followed them. She tried to come as close to them as possible. Sometimes, in the crowd, she could touch one of their robes. She tried to smell them and imagined they would smell metallic, or like saffron, but that imagined sense was probably owing to the color of their robes. She longed to put herself before their notice but she knew they couldn't see her. They were blind to her existence. They owned nothing of the physical except their robes, a needle, razor, belt, an alms bowl and a strainer to ensure no living thing was swallowed when they ate. They had pledged themselves to injure nothing and offend no one. They were young and beautiful; and they were celibate. On them celibacy glowed, a phosphorescence. On her it showed, like pain. By day she created a behavior that conveyed acceptance of her role of unsexed woman. By night she lived an anguish of a soul without religion, love or sex. She convinced herself that there is merit in the solitary life. Her work was, if not a passion, enough to give her life a meaning. But she had never meant to spend her days in the exclusive company of children, so she roamed the streets at night with the passport of a pilgrim. By day she was that apparition of a self that each adult is made to be when he or she is captive to a tribe of little people whose opinions are informed by pasts of less than thirteen years. By night, she was another sort of ghost—she was invisible by race, by reason of extreme minority among a crowd in whom she was the one exemption, minority of one.

As the months passed, Charlotte grew accustomed to not being seen. She lost all sense of ever being watched. She took the steamer packets to Pagan and Moulmein on days she wasn't teaching. She began to sketch and paint—awkwardly, at first—with no eye for rendering the human face or figure—but then she found her own expression in the tradition of the naturalist afield. She began by drawing flowers. The logic of their form was a line her hand could follow and soon she found that she was painting with a heightened sense of the particular, as if their parts were objects of intense desire. She kept her paintings to herself but took her sketchbook with her as a way of disappearing whenever social contact with the parents of her girls was inescapable.

Which is how she came to be leaning on silk cushions in a longboat on the Inle Lake, sketching, while a man named Ogilvy rowed and five others chatted, when the white face of a dolphin appeared in the water beside her.

(*What they heard:*)

Charlotte—bloody!—*sit still!*—you'll capsize us—

But there's a dead man—

Dead man—

Are you certain?

Harry, *stop rowing,* for godsake—

Let's go back—

But a *dead* man—!

Charlotte's had a bit much sun, I'd say.

What did it *look* like, Charlotte?

—seeing things.

I only saw his face.

See? Sun. Seeing faces. . . .

It was laughing.

Oh I say. . . .

Laughing? Not *grinning?* Charlotte—?

Harry, stop it. And *stop rowing*—

Not to worry, Charlotte, thing. We get our dolphins up here, now and then. Should bring luck, I'd think: or so they say.

Dolphins?

Right-i-o.

It was a *dolphin—?*

Blind one at that. Whole breed's as blind as bats. Gangetic River type. Bloody rare this side of Assam.

Oh, I say, we know that breed, don't we, Geoff? We had them in the Ganges I remember. Swam right up and rubbed against the nig-nogs at their baths. Blind as bats, as I recall.

As bats. That's what I said. . . .

Bloody awful tasting, too, as I recall.

Yes. Gamey. . . .

Absolutely foul. . . .

Yes, that's what I hear. I've heard the meat's so foul a Jap won't even eat it.

The Japs. My, yes. Now *there's* a country. . . .

They were rowing in a longboat under silk umbrellas in hot weather on the Inle Lake where the Intas live. The lake was twenty miles long, four miles wide, surrounded by pine forest. At its southern end the British had established a hill station with a part-time District Office and a store to serve the families from Rangoon who built large bungalows amid the trees to retreat to in hot weather.

When they went they took their servants and their children with them.

They took their children's teacher.

Charlotte despised the pretense of being "in the country." She missed the city, she abhorred croquet and badminton.

She rowed out on the lake each day with them and cultivated silence while she drew the details of the sex organs of water hyacinths. She tried to draw the way the Inta men and women in their boats floated in the middle of an optical illusion, appearing to be several feet above the water, shimmering *fata morganas,* as they fished and gardened in the lake, but she failed. She was an imagist, at best, never an illusionist and what she saw across the lake was more like a dream than anything she'd ever seen—The Intas built floating islands woven from the stems of hyacinths over bamboo poles where they lived and cultivated cauliflower, peas, tomatoes and green chilies. The women gardened the lake while the men fished for carp and eels from flatboats, balancing on poles while rowing with their legs. The effect of watching them across the water was that they were angels taking flight, running through a band of gold above the water.

Charlotte tried to capture that hallucination in her lines on paper but what she drew, instead, was a laughing dead man floating from the bottom of the lake to haunt her.

The dolphin, if, in fact, that's what it was, had vanished. Every morning before sunrise she set out as she was used to doing in Rangoon, to search for it. There was a dinghy hidden down the shore which she used for rowing to the center of the lake before the others woke. She had had the girls write papers on "Animal Behavior in the Higher Vertebrates" last year and the oldest girl, Amanda, had produced a first-rate study of the dolphins so for a week she rowed out with the knowledge that a dolphin cannot fathom while it sleeps, it sleeps while circling, the way she did through the markets in Rangoon, close to the surface. She rowed, drifting for long intervals, listening for a sound, the parting of the water, the noise that something makes when breathing.

Then one night she saw them.

She was standing on the shore beside the dinghy, preparing to push off, when she saw them cresting on the water, playing with the mirrored moon across the lake as if it were a puck of mercury.

From shore she saw a sudden shadow fifty feet away from her beneath the surface. Then she saw its shimmering white face.

When she moved toward it, it moved an equidistance toward her, too. If, in fact, it was a blind thing or if, in fact she was invisible, nonetheless, she absolutely knew that it perceived her. When she walked, diagonally, across the waterline, it came in on a slant which mirrored hers.

They seemed to dance an elegantly cautious minuet a while and then she found to her surprise that she was swimming after it.

She swam to where she thought it was but she lost sight of it. She treaded water for a while. She searched as best she could in the moonlight but at this depth the water was too dark so she swam on, hoping it would find her, until she grew too tired. When she stopped to catch her breath she saw it leap into the air under the moon far across the lake from her. Then another dolphin leaped, and then another, four, five, seven, she lost count. One and then another one and then another, higher and still higher, until she felt the water beat against her with their rhythm.

Soon they were around her.

She had never seen such sweet expressions. They swam around her, clicking through their smiling beaks, then one dove and came up right beside her. It floated on its back and made clicking noises that sounded like a dozen hollow sticks falling down a flight of stairs, and then it touched her with its flipper on her thigh.

A second dolphin swam beneath her, lifting her along its back. She held on to its dorsal fin and let herself be carried and the school, she couldn't tell how many, began a long slow cruise around the lake, displaying Charlotte.

As they swam it seemed they made a single body. The dolphin that she held to took its air in rhythm with her breathing. As they swam they rolled and Charlotte let her body press along the animal's whole length. She was longer than it was, a discovery which pleased her. In a fold of skin along its belly she found two nipples.

Then, as if the dolphins were a sleep a dream was threaded on, she lost all sense of time.

They swam miles and miles around the lake, around the floating islands in the moonlight till the sun came up. When the light broke on the water and day began to mass she seemed to wake to find herself near a floating island on the far side of the lake from where she started.

One by one the dolphins pressed their beaks against her and then they dove and disappeared.

The dolphin she was holding onto slipped into the depths and pushed her from it with its flippers. She held on until her lungs forced her to surface. She breathed then dove, then surfaced, dove again, but she had lost it.

The light above the water was quite suddenly intense.

She searched across the surface for some sign of them but light made every plane a galaxy of prisms. Then along the floating island nearest her she thought she saw the dolphin running through a band of light.

Through the light which lifted off the water she was sure she saw the dolphin running upright, taking off his shirt and running toward her on his legs, a vision of a man who ran toward her across a field of light, this man who rushed to her as if he lived for nothing else but running to her, on the water.

JOHN DOLLAR

No one knew where he had come from.

He seemed to be a man of thirty-five or so but Charlotte wasn't sure he wasn't younger. His eyes were hard. His hands were used to halyards but not unused to women and he kept his silence with assurance, as a person who's survived a lot of nights outside alone.

It was his command that made him seem so old, she thought. He was distinctly scientific and he understood how things should work. He read. He read everything in English he could find because he said books in English had been hard to come by where he'd been. Landed people took books with them, sailors couldn't. Three books in a canvas bag were all he could afford to carry—*three books, only*—so when he read he read for life. He memorized. It was something in his memory that made his eyes so hard, she thought. Somewhere, she suspected, he had watched men die. Or he had been a coward. Something, somewhere, had been done to him that he would not permit again.

She'd never thought herself the sort of woman who deserved a handsome man or that her body offered anything that any handsome man could want so the suddenness of her submission to him shocked her.

All the things she thought that Love should be, John wasn't. He was sudden, never subtle; immediate, but never restive; restful, never insufficient.

He was a sailor.

Everything about him spoke the sea and there were only three extreme adventures in its service that he'd never known:

He'd never drowned.

He'd never found a ghost ship.

And he'd never fucked a mermaid until Charlotte.

Castellated

abnegation

2

ABOARD *THE CHARLOTTE*

WHAT THE SNAKE SAID

On the morning they were set to sail a snake slid through the window in the room where Oopi slept.

It was a yellow snake with amber scales that looked like fingernails of old men in the market. It had a black head and a pearly throat and when it spoke its eyes gleamed amethyst and gold. *"Ssscream,"* it said, *"and I shall ssslide inside you."*

Oopi stared into its eyes as best she could. A snake is not an easy thing to stare at.

"*Whole,* you mean?"

"Whole," the snake concurred.

It smiled and Oopi saw it held a heron's egg between its fangs.

Its smile was meant to let her know that it could hinge its thorny mouth on anything, the earth, the sky, her tiny heart.

Its smile was meant to let her know that it could slither in and *eat her* inside-out.

She thought: if it does then I'll be dead at seven-and-a-half years old, which was not as young as some girls die, but it was younger—*much*—than she had ever planned.

Still, she must not scream or it would slither in and coil inside her belly like a rope and she'd be dead, that much was certain.

Screaming was a not-fit thing for a person of her race to do. One could scream at dogs, at servants—scream out a command. One could scream at beggars, hindus, arabs, negroes, moslems, insolents and frenchmen but one could never scream at prussians or at *snakes.* A prussian, he will *slap* you but a snake will smile and *kill.*

Against a snake, she had to draw on faith and her superior intelligence.

A girl must call upon her inbred nation if she's to hold her own against the vagaries of nature, her Dad said, be it here in Burma, on the high sea or in the bunt of the Sudan. A snake is just an ugly thing without an angel on its shoulder or a sense of civil duty so she should not scream she should *outnation* it:

"Would you like to hear a *nursery* rhyme?" she said. *"I'll tell you a rhyme and then you'll go away."*

It smiled at her again.

"I've heard them all," it said. "I am The *Naga,* Dreaded *Nagh.* There is nothing you can tell me that I haven't heard. I exist in minds of little girls like you in places, *far-off-frozen-places,* places where no real snake has ever lived."

"So are you *real* then?" Oopi asked and the snake inched toward her in an awful way.

"Ek burra billa da!" she said.

(The words meant, "Once upon a time there was a *big cat!*" and she almost screamed them:) They were Magic Words she'd pledged the other girls they'd never use without permission (along with all their other Magic Words) but *a snake's a snake* and now she didn't have a curse left, nor a weapon, nor any hope of Magic and she blushed a rubyred which she often did because her father was a ruby miner and she had red hair and Ruby was her Christian name: meanwhile the snake poured through the window and was going to bite her belly. It would sink its foul curved teeth in her like a winged dart sucked into a bull's-eye and she would die from snakie bite at seven-and-a-half years old without a Will and Testament, in Burma, before she'd been confirmed into the Holy Church or even had her breakfast.

"Shauna! Wake up!" she decided to cry out.

"Git away wi' ya—"

"It's a snakie! Shauna!"

"Beg off't, I told ya—!"

Oopi scrabbled toward her sister's side of their shared bed and Shauna kicked her because Shauna woke up mean and hated everyone, especially Ruby.

Oopi made a little gasping sound and their ayah, sleeping outside on the balcony, called, "The missies—*baba,* what? The *baba* want . . . ?"

Beneath the bedsheet, in the breach, Oopi felt a dampness and she smelled an outlawed smell. She kicked the sheet off and the snake was laughing at her and its tongue was red. "It's bited us!" she yelled. "We're dead! It's bited us and now we're dead!" Shauna sat up with her fists against her eyes. "Shut up, Ruby pig!" she cried. Her nightdress, from the waist down, was splattered with a sticky stain.

Oopi hated blood because it looked like something that should never actually be *seen* so she started crying and the ayah came, her hands all serious and her eyes big and lamenting, then her mother came and then their Scottish terrier Mister Hobbs ran in and truffled at the sheets and then their father burst in with his two revolvers.

GOD ALMIGHTY he exploded. He was the sort of man who opened windows; he was a violent man. He'd never been completely calm since his malaria.

"It's not my fault—it's Ruby's, Dad!" Shauna—that

pig!—started to explain but as she stood before him he assessed her state and turned his face away in haste, having first permitted both his daughters to consume his absolute distaste.

Another disappointment, Shauna thought. But, "You should have seen it, Dad!" Oopi put forth. "A snakie, twelve feet long he was! Look! He bited us, the both of us, right here on our stomachs—!"

Her words fell on their father's back.

He was always turning 'round and going somewhere where the air was better when they spoke.

Their mother, Mrs. Fraser, closed the door behind him and ordered, *"Tunda pani, ayah—chelo!"* Then she started stripping off the sheets.

"Let the *dhobi* do that, Mum," Shauna, who was masterful with servants, told their mother.

"*You* should do it," she was told. "It's *your* soup, Miss High-and-Mighty."

"It was the snakie," Oopi piped. "He made a mess of me as well. . . ."

At this, she was inclined to peek and pulled her nightdress up.

"I don't feel sick," she heard her sister saying.

"You will," their mother said.

"I can still sail on *The Charlotte*, though," Shauna put forth.

"In a month of Martinmas' ye' might—"

"Mum—?"

"No."

"Mummy—?"

"No!"

Oopi heard her older sister say, "If I can't, Ruby can't!" so she searched for evidence of snakie bite along her belly.

Her belly looked unscathed, her little button looked the same as it had always looked.

She pushed her knickers down.

And then in her impenitence, she peed.

. . .

THE PRINCIPLES OF FLIGHT

On the morning they were set to sail a brown dove flew into the teak tree outside Gabriella's window and began to *kukuru.*

Then it flew up to the dovecote on the roof and tried to fuck Grandfather's pigeons.

Grandfather ran at them in his altogether and began to shout his native Portuguese topspeed wherewith he cursed the brown dove's father mother future generations dangling balls et cetera. Gaby was accustomed to his execrations and his nakedness as partandparcel of his being. Keeping Grandfather decent and/or dressed had long since been abandoned by her family, though her mother still required that he free his penis from his left hand, please, while eating.

Like Grandfather, Gabriella, too, was ambidextrous.

Everything she knew about the principles of flight she'd learned from him, who learned it all from Leonardo, even though he kept his pigeons less for study than for shit and lime to grow tomatoes. His tomatoes, olives, grapes and nakedness all helped him to remember how to think of Portugal, *sem pensar não podemos protestar,* he said. Without to think not we be able to protest. *Pensamos com o cerébro, que se acha na cabeça:* we think with the brain which is (found) in the head but his (brain) had been addled by cholera and yellow fever and produced less thought than a tomato; still, Gaby loved him—not only because he made kites.

He made mythical kites from bamboo and he taught her how to fly them from the jetties out on Monkey Point.

His kites were so light they lifted themselves—the tug of the string from the sky in her hand was sufficient for flight, she thought, if only she jumped.

Sideslipping rolling and yawing, Grandfather's kites were well known in Rangoon, and Gabriella was his apprentice.

From him she had learned how to lash the rattan for the spars, tie the half knots, build the bridles. She learned by watching and by doing—but chiefly she learned by *flying,* mastering speed, mastering lift, drag, velocity, impetus, without ever flying, herself.

Only one other person knew as much about kites as Grandfather did. *O capitão* knew about wind and the weather and how the ships sailed. *O capitão* had appeared on the jetty one evening, bringing a kite of his own, a crimson eight-pointed star of *Hakkaku* design which he'd brought from Siam and although Grandfather had not had a friend except Gaby for so many years *Dólar* and he became friends in an instant.

This pleased Gabriella a lot.

The two men included her in adventures—kitefishing for whitebait from Dólar's boat . . . kitefighting with glass shards attached to the spars to cut the enemy's kitestring . . . flying kites in the dark with fireworks fixed to their tails. Best of all was to see Grandfather flourish under the *capitão*'s friendship, to watch his designs and inventions. For Gaby to take with her on *The Charlotte*, Grandfather had made the best kite she'd ever seen *reclamar o luz dessa a lua,* he said. While he was flying his pigeons on cords from the roof to exercise them, he shouted *Eiyyyy! This kite I have make! She have a crix tied on top!* (A *crix?* Gaby wondered.) He ran over the roof to his workshop, flapping his arms, and came back, naked as always, carrying what was, in her eyes, the most beautiful object of flight in the world.

É sua, he said: it is yours.

É a nossa, it's ours, she replied.

Then he said too many things at topspeed she could not understand about *O Rei Momo* (King Momo?) and *sua beleza e graça* (your beauty and grace?) and *O Capitão João* and the kite she can fly her twelve miles into heaven *o próximo Deus* over *o mar* where he (*Deus,* Grandfather?) will see it from so far away and know with his eyes (points to heart) she is safe wherever *Carlotta* (*The Charlotte*) might take her.

. . .

THE GIRL THAT GOD CREATED TWICE

The morning they were set to sail two girls lay curled around each other on the bed on the verandah the same way they had curled around each other in pre-life.

Half of them loved hunting, stalking, imitating natives, playing deaf and digging up bones in the garden:

She was Sloan.

The other half loved saving *annas,* patting out *chapattis* with the *bobaji,* telling lies and making maps of lands that can't exist:

Her name was Sybil.

They owned a sibling, age three, name of Malcolm, whom they treated as a pet or an impostor, and despised.

He was posing as a baby brother. He was incontinent and smelled.

"Let's drown Malcolm," their two halves agreed.

Neither half could understand the use of pronouns so, "Let's get rid of *his,*" they chorused.

Neither half was nasty. Each was practical, and crafty, devising ways to make the world, in general, more amenable to their specific.

They were twins, although they didn't know it, and they knew the world by halves.

So identical were they, so complete in replication, that their mother, Mrs. Ogilvy, could not distinguish who was which. From the moments of their birth they inspired awe among the natives and distress in her. She was afraid she'd never keep them straight or that she might begin to love one not the other, fail to praise them equally. Never having been a mother she was now a mother twice and because she had a fragile nature she felt like a neurasthenic swimmer in a riptide sea. She was not constructed for childbearing, as some women are. She was small, small-boned, and she withstood the long slow maturation of her female duty with the thought that she was bringing forth a single angel, a small bud, a snowdrop like herself whom she could dress in crinolines and ribbons. But then she brought forth not only one but two enormous babes who conspired to prolong her suffering by rejecting girlish things, identically. Even as infants they conspired to look idiotic in organza and by the time they mastered walking, it had become impossible to keep them dressed. *Heathens* was how she thought of them; *heathens* was what they had become. Whereas in the past she had distrusted servants, as soon as they could crawl she learned distrust of them. She imagined every time she saw them bent together at their play they were conspiring against her so she kept them separated days on end until the obvious occurred to her and she suspected the domestic staff of interchanging them behind her back. In secret she imagined scarring one, or branding both. Then one day in the heat under the dark look of a servant she took a pair of paper shears which rested on the table near her as she read the London weeklies and cut Sybil's hair off at its roots when she burst in in the middle of her tea, so she could tell one from the other.

"It's cut off all our hair!" the one who wasn't Sybil screamed.

The servant who witnessed this was the estimable Ma Bwa, "Miss Grandmother," who had hatched a couple *(twenty!)* children of her own but showed no threads of age across her face. She was faultlessly devout and believed the five great sins to be (1) the killing of a flea, (2) the killing of a father, (3) the killing of a monk, (4) the hurting of a child, and last) the raising of a bump on Buddha (Who could not be murdered like a flea or hurt, but merely *bumped*). She chewed betel nut and drank a bitter curry for her ailments. She believed in the calming uses of the poppy. Under her tutelage starting that same day, Mrs. Ogilvy (whose name was Kitty) learned to smoke the pipe. Reluctant at first, she soon found she possessed real genius, a true talent, a natural gift for the addiction.

Over the years most people guessed, but, on the whole, the British denied that any of *them* used the drug.

Her husband guessed from the start. He could see it and smell it and he was outraged—but he was seduced by it too, as a spectator, tempted by its effects on her, by her languor. When he timed it just right, when he was several gins down and he timed his arrival back home form the club to those moments when she was just slipping toward torpor, then he could make her thin body taut, he could make her breasts hard and her kindling limbs made no objections. It was, after all, a relief with one's wife in a way nothing else could fulfill. *By God,* he was known to say (and not just to himself): It's *bracing* to screw one's own wife dammit, to *shag* one's own children's mother. . . .

Kitty spent her inevitable Next Term in bed, away from her menacing daughters. She accepted them into her room once a day, receiving them vaguely and telling them she was baking them a new sister. *Something to eat* they at first thought—a *little sister,* to their mind, meant one more of *them.*

They expected a new replication, full-grown, identical. A Late Arrival, yes, but still a *sister* from the Source. But then a thin passive *boy* arrived who slept all day and all night with their mother. His curls grew unchecked to his shoulders and their mother arranged him in linen and lace. Her other two children grew fused, her world fused, to a sort of a shimmer, a halo. Her other two children, by now indistinct, wavered like sunlight on water. Finally, blissfully, they became perfect. *God,* she cautioned them, *answers one's prayers.* Sometimes she leaned toward them saying *God, God.* Sometimes she reached for her husband. *Darling,* she said. To the silence she told him or them *God has given me my perfect daughter.*

JANE

As she did each morning since her brother's death, on the morning they were set to sail Jane went to the stable to tack up her father's stallion.

Since her brother's death, her father had been taking

longer rides, mounting before breakfast, not returning until evening, *Kraft,* his stallion, frothing at the bit with thirst.

Sometimes by staying out on the horseback her father managed to avoid the sight of her for days.

That's why Jane went down to curry *Kraft* before dawn, in advance of him.

The first few times she'd done it she'd surprised him.

Who goes there? he'd called out in his regimental manner.

Jane,! father,! sir! she'd answer sharply.

Sometimes he seemed surprised to find he owned a daughter.

Who goes there? he'd require. "Is that *you,* James, boy—?"

When she handed him the reins he seemed to look straight through her.

Her brother was a hero.

His name was James, he'd died in the War.

He'd been away at school in England most of her life.

Before the Army transferred them to Burma he'd come to stay with them in India one month every year.

Jane had seen him ten times in her life, and she remembered seven of them:

James was always stepping from a train and she was always waiting on a platform at a hill station. It was always the same month same light same time of day and very hot and yet he always wore his uniform to please their father, looking larger each successive time; more handsome.

Their parents acted different in his presence than they acted other times because, Jane knew, they loved him better.

Well, she thought. *They should:* He held a sort of radiance. He was their hope. What she was was *jane,* something that came after "Hope"—an afterthought; a lapse.

After James was killed in the Third Battle of the Aisne, Jane's parents couldn't satisfy their loss in any ordinary way.

It was not enough to mourn, to be bereft—*Blame* was needed, as a comfort, as a clear example of accountability and what her father came to blame were Germans.

What her mother came to blame was Life.

A grieving parent is a fool of nature, a vacuum most abhorred.

A grieving parent is a quantity which self-devours.

When children disappear the text foreshortens, the conclusions prove themselves:

There is a Maker who unmakes the world.

Each thing and every moment derives a meaning from a context one is meant to understand.

One's life is voluntary.

Excuses cannot serve.

Jane's mother killed herself soon after; Jane was never told.

For two years Jane has lived alone with her father in his regimental exile in Rangoon. Like his leathers and his medals she's a shadow of his former days. When she looks into the mirror, which she seldom does, she is surprised to find she owns a body. *It's I who go here, sir,* she often needs to say. just jane.

WHY THE BROWN MAN MADE BLUE GODS

Menaka was woken that morning by her mother whom she loved more than any girl had ever loved her mother, and while she drank the *chai* her mother brought to her *charpai* she watched the little bird inside her mother Ammi's throat jump up and down as Ammi finished telling her her favorite story.

"And then he died?" Menaka asked when it had ended.

"Yes."

"It is something I remember."

"It is good that you do so."

"I was very sad."

"You will never have a day when you are sadder."

"Then you will never die, Ammi?"

"Oh, yes, I'll die, you'll see."

"He was handsome?"

"Yes, he was."

"But you are beautiful."

"In his eyes, I was."

"I am ugly."

"Who says this lie?"

"They do."

"What is this 'they'?"

"These girls."

"Their names?"

"You know the ones."

"Their *names?*"

"Shauna, for one."

"Full name, first-and-last, in English—"

"Shauna Fraser."

"*Spotted pig!* Who else?"

"Norris."

"This is a *girl*'s name—?"

"Norris Petherbridge."

"*Another pig!* Who *else*—?"

"Amanda."

"I think this one an eel, what is her family name—?"

"Amanda Sutcliffe. . . ."

"*Eel!* I told you so! What other names—?"

"The sisters, Sloan and Sybil. Twins. . . ."

"Two rats!"

"Gaby. Ortíz. Her name is Gabriella."

"Dog!"

"Jane Napier."

"A bat!"

"A girl called 'Monkey'."

"There is a girl called 'Monkey' in this school?"

"Yes."

"She is an English girl?"

"She is half a loaf."

"The other half—?"

"They laugh at her . . . they call her ugly."

"And *is* she?"

"Yes."

"I see. She has great claws—?"

"Hands like these. . . ."

"A face of sores?"

"A face like mine."

"A broken body, leprosy?"

"Brown skin."

"O yes, o *I* see, yes: she must be truly ugly then. . . ."

"They say so—"

"Because they're devils."

"I don't want to go with them! I'm afraid of water! They're so clever, they know how to swim—I want to stay with *you . . .!"*

"When are we apart?"

(No answer.)

"This is nothing," Monkey's mother says. "Not a parting. Three days."

". . . *and* two nights."

"A blinking. . . ."

"But I'll be afraid—I should stay with you and do what Father said. Father said I should take care of you, and I should listen to him—Did you ever have a father—?"

"Yes. . . ."

"*See?* And he told you things to do?"

"He did."

"You *see?* And then you *did* them, right—?"

"I did not do them."

"No—?"

"I did not."

"That was very bad."

"He thought so."

"What was it that he told you you should do—?"

"He told me to be pleasant to the members of my family and to the cattle we possessed."

"And you couldn't do that?"

"He told me to give birth to heroic children."

"And *that* you couldn't do?"

"He told me never to miscarry and never have an empty lap and to obey my husband."

"That was wise. . . ."

"He told me he was made ashamed the morning of my birth and that my husband's father was not ashamed the morning of my husband's birth. So I disobeyed him."

"Did he beat you?"

"No man is allowed to beat a woman."

"Did he turn you into stone?"

"The proof that he did not is here."

"What did he do?"

"He pretended I was dead."

"And what did you do?"

"I did not pretend that I was dead."

"You jumped up?"

"In bright colors."

"And you flew?"

"Far far."

"And this was possible?"

The bird inside her mother's throat jumped up and down and Monkey hoped the bird was blue, like Krishna. Ammi's skin, its smoothness, was impeccable and Monkey knew she'd never be a woman like her mother, beautiful. Her parents had succumbed to an insanity they thought was Love, white man, black woman, and they'd made a hybrid child. Her teacher Charlotte Lewes had taught her that the reason ordinary men paint gods with blue skin or with halos is that blue skin or a halo are *impossible,* so hoping against hope, Monkey asked her mother, "Do I look like him?"

"Do you look like Mister Lawrence?"

"Yes. Like Father. . . ."

Not knowing how her words destroyed each hope, the person that the Monkey loved the best in all the world confirmed, "Of course not! Not at all—!" and thinking it had spoken wisely, the bird inside her mother's throat lifted through the room on wings of laughter, red, not blue, and flew away, out toward the ocean.

THE KING'S BIRTHDAY

There were three boats putting under sail from Monkey Point that morning in a working breeze—Mister Fraser's diamond-mining cutter-yacht *The Ruby Girl,* Mister Sutcliffe's spice-running sloop, *The Cinnabar* and John Dollar's lateen-rigged dhow, *Charlotte.*

On the dock the military trooped, a band played and Reverend Petherbridge invoked God and prayed for His injunction against Storms, High Seas, Et Cetera. He was a florid and stentorian sermonizer of the Lollard School, but incapable of stirring souls, even his daughter's, who stared rigidly through his clichés at a spot of breakfast on his chin and counted backward from five hundred to keep from fidgeting until he finished—On and on he went, reciting from The Book of Common Prayer every form of Prayer To Be Used At Sea including, to everyone's confusion, several which were supposed to be reserved for singing Thanksgiving After a Storm, *Jubilate Deo* and *Confitemini Domino:*

> *"That they would offer unto him the*
> *sacrifice of thanksgiving:*
> *and tell out his works with gladness!"*

What is he *on* about? Nolly thought and lost her count around three hundred:

> "*. . . They that go down to the sea in ships:*
> *and occupy their business in great waters;*
> *These men see the works of the Lord:*
> *and his wonders in the deep. . . .*"

Mister Fraser chorused, "Hear, hear!" and Nolly plainly saw John Dollar look at Charlotte with a smile:

> *". . . For at his word the stormy wind ariseth:*
> *which lifteth up the waves thereof.*
>
> *They are carried up to the heaven, and down*
> *again to the deep:*
> *their soul melteth away because of the trouble.*
> *They reel to and fro—"*

Someone giggled:

> *". . . and stagger like a drunken man:*
> *and are at their wits end . . ."*

"Oh, *shut up,* father," Nolly whispered, as Grandfather, confused between a sense of religion and droit de seigneur, appeared on the dock wrapped in a bright linen towel and gave John an armful of tomatoes and made obscene gestures at the sea for good luck.

The weather was fresh and clear, proving once more God was English.

This was a day for celebration—the King's Birthday—and the sky was faultlessly, royally blue.

The day had lived in their imaginations for three months, beacon to their future, an event they could look forward to with patriotic dedication, like a coronation, or the Ascot. The War was over and they needed celebration—the world had come too close, it was repeated, to becoming permanently Kingless. In Europe there were only four monarchies remaining. Of them, England's was the most esteemed, the never-ending one, they told themselves. Something needed to be done to mark the Royal Birthday, something proper, apt and perfect. A Dress Ball was thought too frivolous even though Missuses Sutcliffe and Fraser lobbied for it on the basis that it would provide a good excuse for refurbishing the ballroom at the Club which was being used, at present, as an indoor playing field in the monsoons. Word came from Lucknow that *there* they had commissioned a bronze statue to commemorate The Birthday, to be forged from twenty-one ancient Mughal cannons, weighing several tonnes, no less, and the British in Calcutta sent news that they planned to name a regiment of native conscripts and a hospital for lepers after him. *Not to be outdone* became the spirit in Rangoon; still no Plan was born until the night John mentioned to the men that he was drinking with in the Gymkhana Club that he'd like to chart the Andamans.

Oh good-o: And then why not be the first to chart the coast of Devon, too, while you're out there with your theodolite, John—?

(Sutcliffe answers:)

Devon has been charted for two thousand years, John said.

Well, of course Devon has been charted since the Romans, that's the point. So have the Andamans.

I beg to differ with you, sir.

Steady—Sutcliffe knows his water, John. We've got people there, men and women quartered with the penal colony at Port Blair—you don't think we'd put them down smackdamn in the middle of a place we hadn't charted, do you? I've seen the Royal Survey of those islands with my own eyes—you need to bring your dreaming up to date, John, or at least into the current century. . . .

(Colonel Napier defends another white man's ignorance:)

The Survey, John replied, that the Colonel spoke of, had been made in 1888 by a drunkard with one eye and a quill dipped in invisible ink. The contours of the islands in the archipelago were curiously undifferentiated, as if they had been sighted from afar, like stars, and never visited. In all his years of reading charts he'd never seen a chain of coral islds. whose appearance on a map came as close to looking, as these did, like seeds broadcast from a single pod each one the doppelgänger of the others. Besides, he argued, the Andamans were still-evolving islands, their contours always changing. Even if the survey had been accurate in the

(John sips a whiskey.)

beginning, which it wasn't, forty years was too long between charting expeditions. He had first-hand knowledge that at least one deep-water channel between un-named islands on the survey was now a solid field of coral and that two sister atolls marked as *N. and S. Brother Islds.* had submerged entirely into shoals. Earthquakes raked the area two or three times every year, heaving brand new atolls and lagoon islands from what were previously shallow fringing reefs—

(*The men adopt A Plan:*)

Hang on:

Brand new, you say?

Islands—?

Uncharted, you say—

Atolls—?

Are there any *big ones,* John?

The way it happened, Sutcliffe took the credit for The Plan.

(That was fine with John—he wasn't a royalist and it made no difference to him whether the King lived long or died or had a dance named after him or a rare species of civet or indeed a desert isld.)

But, in fact, when it came to presenting the King with an island for his birthday, the members of the club were forced to honor him not with the discovery of a new one, but by re-naming one already known. Out of several hundred islands in the northern chain they chose a sixteen-square-mile solitary one called by Marco Polo *L'Isola dei nostri sogni proscritti* or *The Isld. of Our Outlawed Dreams.* Its size was seemly as gift-islands go, they thought, and the name was begging to be changed so they informed the King that on his birthday they, his loyal and obedients, his most resp. servants, the Eng. of Rangoon, would sail in full regalia (their women and their children inc.) to the Aforesaid-to-be-Renamed-Shore and plant his standard on what would thereafter be referred to as *King George's Island,* happy birthday.

The fulfillment of The Plan, then, as it developed on that sterling day was this:

The Ruby Girl

Fraser's cutter-yacht, the fastest and most ardent, led the fleet out of Rangoon harbor with Fraser's hired man, Captain Matlock, at her helm. She carried, as her crew, Matlock's two bearers; Fitzgibbon the headmaster and boys' don of the school; and seven lads, sons of England, ranging in age from six to seventeen, every one a *Scout* in a *Scouting uniform* and each one with a badge in Knots, Celestial Navigation or Semaphore at stake. Trailing to her lee a half a mile behind was Sutcliffe's sloop with Sutcliffe on the bridge and Ogilvy as mate. She carried with her, in addition to the expedition's stores, Mrs. Sutcliffe, Colonel Napier, Mr. and Mrs. Fraser, five servants, harpoons for turtle sticking, rifles of assorted bores, several hundred rounds of ammunition, a Royal Geographic Society Land Mark, Mr. Sutcliffe's water spaniel, the King's colors, the union jack and the ensign of St. George. Behind these two, hoisting a dipped Pilot Jack from her foresail peak and flying three boxkites off her taffrail—one white, one red, one blue—there ran John's boat, sailing large, with her distinctive earth-red canvases. She carried John, Charlotte, eight girls, two bearers and John's jackboy, a fifteen-year-old Bengali jolly known as Jib. All the girls had been on boats before—the oldest ones, Nolly and Amanda, had come by ship from England and even the younger ones like Monkey could remember crossing from Calcutta on a steamer to stay with her mother's brother in Rangoon when her father died. But only Oopi and Amanda, whose fathers owned the other boats, had ever *been under sail,* and, anyway, no other vessel in the water for a hundred miles around was anywhere as sheer and wondrous and as beautiful as Captain Dollar's dhow. John had her frame and keel built in Goa by Portuguese shipwrights, but he'd had her timbers stepped and

The Cinnabar

The Charlotte

her rigging made to order by an oriental genius in Rangoon. It was said of John's boat that not since Noah's Ark had any more improbable creation taken to the water—quirky, distinctive, built to maximize the talents of its master, *Charlotte* looked and handled like no other sailing vessel. Her sails were cinnamon—a color John devised for being sighted easily in any weather—and her poop raked sharply high above the water. She was fitted for economy and ease and every inch of her was put to one of those two uses. Logic was the form in all her details, therefore she was beautiful and quick. John lived on her when he wasn't staying nights with Charlotte at her house by the river out on Monkey Point. He had lived on her for years, before they'd met, when he was shipping contraband between Bangkok and Rangoon on this beauty of a boat which he called nothing, then, in English.

(Charlotte has some peppermint she says will help, Monkey says, consolingly, to Jane.

Jane is all one color, powdery.

"Captain Dollar says it helps to stare at land. Don't look down into the water," Monkey says. She waits for Jane to notice her, or answer. While she waits, she wonders what it would be like if Jane ever would look at her. She wonders what it would be like to touch her.)

Astern, the spine of Monkey Point diminished. Where the sky came down and touched the water the vestige that was Burma rolled away and dropped off the horizon. Behind them for as far as they could see there was sky and water only, nothing else, a hundred hues of all one color: blue.

"Get a pail for her," Amanda ordered.

She put an arm beneath Jane's shoulders and helped her from the rail.

"Well—?" she snapped at Monkey when the Monkey didn't move.

Monkey got the bucket and Charlotte and Amanda carried Jane below.

"*It*'s feeling very bossy," Sloan and Sybil said.

"It's jealous," Gaby whispered.

Is it—?

"Yes."

"Who *of—?*

"Shauna," Gaby told.

Why?

"Guess."

"You *tell!*

"All right: the *es-en-ay-kay-ee . . . .*"

. . . *When—?*

"This morning."

Where—?

"*Guess* where."

You mean—?

"Yes. Oopi saw it."

—*Bit* her?

"In *the place,"* Gaby announced, "and you know what *that* means. . . ."

The queen is dead, they knew; god save the Queen.

NAME-CALLING

Oopi was the first to sight it—John had hoisted her aloft inside a basket and her voice rang out *Land ho!* *Land ho!* *Land ho!*

She pointed off port bow and they all ran forward to the watch. "It doesn't see him!" Sloan complained but Oopi gestured furiously, bobbing in her basket, shouting *hi! hurrah! hiho!*

On the *Ruby Girl* the Scouts sent up three cheers, and on the *Cinnabar* Mr. Fraser discharged twenty-one revolver shots into the sky to the accompaniment of "God Save the King" sung a cappella by the women and the Burmese bearers.

Everyone experienced Landfall as emotion—though they'd passed a dozen islands in the chain, this one stirred their feelings in a patriotic way. The Scouts, especially, could not contain their thrill. Matlock, watching them cheer wildly toward the shore, told Fitzgibbon, "It's the blood, sir. Sons of England. In the blood, sir. *Island* people."

Charlotte led the fleet into the wind for their approach and Sutcliffe brought the *Cinnabar* to starboard and lay aboard and Ogilvy shouted through his megapone,

REQUEST TO LIE TO, JOHN—IS THIS *THE PLACE?*

REQUEST GRANTED—LIE TO, MATE! John called into the tunnel he formed with his hands against the wind.

They brought the vessels 'round into the leeside of the island where two finger reefs remained of what had been the barrier formation—the reefs promised sheltered bay inside the rip, so John signaled to drop anchor. They had sailed nine hours on a west-by-southwest course, running a degree before the sun which hung behind them now above the sea as they stood, on the tide, with their heads to the island and hauled in their sails. It was eight bells, six hours till dusk. Moonrise came late at this latitude—daylight was long but they were thirty-five people (and a dog) in five punts with plenty of stores to take in, in advance of the ebb.

"Reminds me of that riddle, *you know the one,*" Sutcliffe marveled as they argued how to best deploy the smaller boats, "about those missionary chaps who have to get across that river in a single boat with those flesh-hungry cannibals. . . ."

(Everyone except the servants and the seamen had repaired below to change their clothes when they'd dropped anchor. John thought the hour thus consumed would be put to better use if he and Jib and Matlock and some servants shipped supplies ashore, but Fraser argued the first footprints set upon the sand by anybody of this expedition ought to consecrate the ground for King and Country and not track crates of glass and china up the ebb-dry to high-tide mark. Compromise was struck between pomp and the circumstance when John suggested that the punts go in and disembark the servants and supplies within the high tide reach, and this was thought to be a sound and passable idea, unusurping in support of royalty because, as everybody thought they knew, a shore at ebb tide isn't actually any sort of nameable *land*. . . .)

John oversaw the transfer of supplies into the punts. There were: eight rugs, two crates of Royal Worcester fine bone china in the "Hyde Park" pattern, a casket packed with raffia containing Irish leaded crystal, a chest of silver cutlery, phials of powdered spices, three firkins of sherry, GIN, LIMES, FLOUR, EGGS, a dozen tins of Swedish fishballs, SUGAR, casks of wine, a caisson each of CHEDDAR and of STILTON, lemon curd, two dozen tent supports, five canvas canopies, umbrellas, mushrooms, WATER, celery onions, garlic, condensed MILK, tomato ketchup, RICE, TEA, papayas, TWO LIVE PIGS, eleven pots, three woks, bananas, mangoes, oysters, aubergines, sponge cake and water biscuits.

"No *spotted dick?*" John joked.

Fraser, in particular was without a sense of humor.

"In my day," he said, "if we went out with less than sixteen elephants we could hardly even call the thing a 'tiffin'."

"Absolutely," Sutcliffe confirmed. He was a tall horse-

faced Etonian who sailed for sport and was said to keep a Burmese adolescent for his pleasure. Rumors of his child wife had reached even his daughter, whose resemblance to her father was grotesque, as if the elder had shaved off his beard and slipped into a dress. "There is no such thing as what the Frogs would call *de trop* in the administration of an *m'*pire," he reminded them. "John, I know you're soft on this and I forgive you but the fact is We own everything. They don't own their own backsides. We own them. We own them because We're better. There isn't anything that we can't own in any corner of the world wherever we might want it. (Name your tastes, John. These people are our servants . . .) Why shouldn't we enjoy ourselves? So far this century's been ruled by *W*'s: The *W*idow of *W*indsor and the *W*ar—I say it's time for *w*ealth and *w*hips and *w*hoops! and *w*ine and—"

"*Chaque à son gôut,* Edward," Mrs. Sutcliffe put in sharply. (She was not as weak a person as her contribution to her daughter's looks suggested, even though her French was bad.)

Matlock, who was in Fraser's employ but knew everything about the present company, changed the subject (although awkwardly) to something he claimed every sailor knew, a gourmet's delight that he called *Riz océanique.* ("That's plain rice. Ocean-going, missus.")

Really? Mrs. Sutcliffe asked. Like her daughter, she was called Amanda. "You must tell me—then I'll tell our boys—how to prepare it."

"Well, it's not that simple, Missus. Requires years of practice."

"Yet you say that every sailor knows it?"

"Yes, m'am. I reckon Captain Dollar's put his hand to it and he can tell you, too. It's these essential steps. The first: boil water."

"*Rusty* water," John corrects.

"If you've got it. If not, bilge will do. Next: add rice."

"With roaches," John corrects.

"The roaches, m'am, is optional. Any type of hard-shelled insect can be used. Third: Boil 'til cooked. Four, Season it with anything. Fifth: Carry it on deck. Six: Throw it overboard. Saves your life, that last step. . . ."

"Matlock!" John shouts from one punt to the other as they row on the tide toward shore: "They don't appreciate your humor—!"

"Aye—why not—?"

"You're not that funny—!"

"Maybe not—but have you heard the one about the elephant who dies of laughter when he sees a tribe of pygmies *pissin'* in the river—?"

"No—!"

"The elephant—!"

"—?"

". . . sees a tribe of men—!"

"—?"

"Pygmies! By the river! Naked—!"

"—?"

"Dies laughin'!"

"—?"

"Couldn't see how anything could get enough to drink through trunks like those—!"

"Captain Matlock!" Jib calls from the other boat. "These bearers want to know if there are lions on this island—?"

"Ask Capt'n John—"

"Are there lions on this island, John—?"

"No!"

". . . The bearers want to know if there are *snakes*—?

"Yes!"

". . . Are there giant women with white breasts—?"

" 'Giant'—?"

"*Women!* With white breasts—?"

"Tell them 'No' The place they're thinking of's called 'Heaven'—"

The place where they landed the punts was a beach on the leeside of the reef. The sand was pink and green and coarse as sugar and traced throughout with lattices of *ipomenas,* the wild deep-purple morning glories, on which orange hummingbirds and crimson honeybees were gorging. The bearers made a temporary camp below the high-tide reach and sat down on the crates to wait until the boats returned with the official landing party. They watched the sandfleas jump between the tides and baited sanddabs with their toes and smoked, and one of them, the oldest one, stood watch, a "Made In England" Sheffield steelblade in his hand (his eyes fixed on the trees behind the beach), for snakes.

On the big boats, everyone prepared to go ashore. The men who had known military service (Sutcliffe, Fraser, Colonel Napier and Ogilvy) assembled in their regimental dress; the women put on hats, shoes, dresses, gloves and hosiery (except Charlotte, who went bare-legged, barefoot and hatless. She wore lace gloves, however, with her fingertips exposed, for eating.) They wore jewelry. Standing as they were along the port-side of *The Cinnabar* the four men and two women resembled guests fetched up before the village vicar for a country wedding. Seeing them thus, Fitzgibbon, on *The Ruby Girl* was seized by a passion to immortalize them "for the unborn generations!" and ran to get his Leica, waving madly that they not descend into the punts until he'd photographed them. In addition to his *Liebchen* (as he called his Leica—Fitz. was positively deaf to world affairs and had no ear for the offense a Teuton word could cause his fellow *Engländers,* especially the Colonel, so soon after the War), he had found an ancient although mint-condition dry-plate daguerrotype camera in a pawn shop in Rangoon from which he produced a series of mercury prints of the Burmese art of the tattoo, and to which he referred with no less adoration than to his Leica as *die Witwe.* John called him a madman with a tripod, "that hunchback Fitzgibbous," owing to the way he shouldered his equipment running with it in a stooped and loping gait. "Fitz," as Charlotte called him, was always in a mad rush, always passionate about some new discovery such as *bats* for instance. He was very keen on *bats* and had earlier that day (at dockside, actually) expressed his great enthusiasm to the Colonel as they waited for the Reverend Petherbridge to arrive to bless the fleet, by stating that he hoped to find some *bats* in natural habitat on this expedition, to which Napier, who had never been the keenest mind in Burma, responded that even if the isld. were inhabited (which he strongly doubted), it hardly seemed within a sane man's reason to expect the native population to have devised the game of *cricket,* independent of the British.

For posterity! Fitzgibbon now shouted as he photographed his Scouts aboard *The Ruby Girl.* They descended into two punts rowed by Matlock and a bearer and made for the tow line by *The Charlotte* where the girls began to climb down to the water on rope ladders. Fitzgibbon stood up in the punt and shouted *One more for posterity!* and tried to keep his balance while he focused. A titter ran among the Scouts as Charlotte backed down, her bare feet and legs exposed.

Stop right there, girls! Fitzgibbon shouted: "That's it! H-o-l-d it! One more! Charlotte, *please:* try to stay inside this one—"

"What are you talking about, Fitz—?"

"Please?"

" 'Inside' what—?"

"The picture! Get *inside*—"

"Well I'd like to, Fitz, but first you have to tell me where it *is*. . . ."

He looks up from the viewfinder, squints at her and says ha. ha.

They crowded into boats.

In Matlock's there were: Mrs. Fraser and four girls.

In John's: Charlotte, Sloan and Sybil, Jane (who was still feeling ill), and Oopi (who refused to get into the first boat with her mother because Mrs. Fraser said—in front of everyone—"You'll stop this nonsense *now,* girl, about Shauna kept at home with *snakebite*" . . .) Monkey had wanted to be with Charlotte and Jane, but Oopi had appropriated the last place in the boat at the last minute, so now she sat, rigidly, at the back of Matlock's, behind Gaby, Nolly and Amanda, catching spray from Matlock's oars across her face.

In the third and fourth boats, rowed by Jib and Matlock's bearer Gunama (they called him "Monday"), were Fitzgibbon, seven boys and Fraser. The boys' names were Edward, Edward, Charles, Charles, George, George and (Nolly's brother's:) Nigel.

In the lead boat rowed by Matlock's second bearer Pandi (whom they called "Thursday"), were the Sutcliffes, Colonel Napier, the Sutcliffes' water spaniel called "Nelson", the standards, ensigns, colors of King George, the Geographic Land Mark and Mister Ogilvy.

This was the boat they'd all agreed should make The Landing, plant the flag and name the territory and it cut a pretty figure and a straight course, coming in. On shore, the servants sitting on the crates of china watched it while they smoked. They talked, aware their voices wouldn't carry anywhere on the prevailing westerlies. Among themselves they called each other Kow Chow, Maung Ang, Ningyan, U Maung and U Thet. Other people called them

Sat,
Sun,
Tuesday,
Wednesday,
(and the old one:)
"Friday".

BOTTLES AND PLATES

Everyone who stepped ashore that day (except the bearers) had either read or heard the story of *The Life and Adventures of Robinson Crusoe* so there was that, that sense of exhilaration which comes when one's life bears a likeness to the fictions that one's dreamed; plus there was the weighty thrill of bringing light, the torch of history, into one more far-flung reach of darkness:

" 'Good' . . . and . . . 'Evil'," Fitzgibbon lectured at the boys as they came in. "First thing he did, really. Crusoe. Assessed the situation. Jotted down his moral ledger entries, weighed the doubts against the credits. Such an enterprising man, that Crusoe. Wonder what I'd do, really, in his situation—?"

"Sir! I know the answer, sir!" said the younger Edward, standing.

"I assure you, Edward, please sit down, it was a philosophical exercise. . . ."

"Signal dot dot dot full stop three dashes followed by three dots, sir, by radiotelegraphy," Edward recited, "or send up a rocket parachute flare showing a red light, or fire shells throwing red stars at no more than one-minute intervals, or build a smoke signal on a promontory giving off orange-colored smoke as per instructions in the *Boatswain's Manual of Scouting,* sir."

"And if there were . . . no radiotelegraphs, nothing to burn which made orange-colored smoke—?"

"Put a message in a bottle, sir."

" 'A message in'—?"

"A bottle, sir, then wait for Help, which would arrive."

"You're certain, are you, Edward, Help would arrive?"

"Within a month, sir, yes. It would."

"A *month?* Edward: how can you be certain?"

"The King's Navy is patrolling the world seas, sir—"

"Searching on the q.t. for messages in bottles, you think, Edward?"

"Yes, sir. That's the way the King's Navy rescued Robinson Crusoe off that wretched island in the South Sea, sir."

"When we return to Rangoon, you'll show me the exact line in Defoe from which you received this crime of misunderstanding. . . ."

"—in 'Defoe', sir?"

"Daniel."

" 'Daniel', sir?"

"As in the Prophet of Apocalypse."

"Oh right, sir—"

Robinson Crusoe's Household Account Book (His Ledger of "Evil" and "Good")

"EVIL"	"GOOD"
I am divided from mankind, a solitaire, one banished from human society.	But I am not starved and perishing on a barren place, affording no sustenance.
I am without any defence or means to resist any violence of man or beast.	But I am cast on an island where I see no wild beasts to hurt me, as I saw on the coast of Africa; and what if I had been shipwrecked there?
I have no soul to speak to, or relieve me.	But God wonderfully sent the ship in near enough to the shore, that I have gotten out so many necessary things as will either supply my wants, or enable me to supply my self even as long as I live.

. . .

(A peculiar thing arose, or, rather, fell, during the Naming Ceremony: The wind that brought them in and kept the ladies' hats precariously angled on their pins, fell, as soon as they had planted the King's standard on the shore in front of Fitz's camera, as if the staves thrust in the ground had sucked the air out of the early evening:)

Younger George and younger Edward climbed up on the Charleses' shoulders and held the drooping colors rampant on their rods so King George could see his symbols clearly in the photograph, along with Mrs. Fraser's blood-red uncut-ruby choker, Mrs. Sutcliffe's decorative lorgnette, the Colonel's ribbons and Sutcliffe's Irrawaddy River eelskin laces. ("What I do, see," he explained to Charlotte, "is cut the head off the eel along with a little piece of neck and then peel the skin back same as a banana, slice it lengthwise into inch-wide strips and stretch it in the sun. Wonderfully flexy, plus there's the added value that they're waterproof . . .")

In the stillness that resulted at the drop of wind, they were beset by a commotion of red butterflies.

O lovely just wonderful, cried Fitz, "Here I am without my panchromatic plates in the middle of a fuss of reds that will photograph as gray as last week's pudding—"

"Gray?" Mrs. Fraser seemed to shout behind the embroidered handkerchief which curtained her mouth to keep the butterflies from entering: "What about my *rubies—?*"

"Someone light a fire for godsake, create some smoke against this vermin!" Sutcliffe choked.

"Aren't they *beautiful,*" Charlotte marveled.

"One flew in my mouth—!"

"They're in our ear!"

"No, no, don't catch them, let them go—"

"Are they a kind of moth, Fitz, do you think—?"

"Hold still everyone! Let's have one for the unborn generations!"

"You don't really mean to say my rubies will look gray, do you—no, Oopi, you may *not* eat off a banana leaf at supper in your best dress—"

Wonderful! Now everyone hold still while I run around and get inside the picture, ready? On the count of three:

(1) ONE
(2) TOO
(3) MANY

Mrs. Sutcliffe, sitting on a carpet on the sand, her feet before her toward the sea, watched the servants fan the fire and told Mister Ogilvy, "It was always *one* of sour, *two* of sweet. *Three* of strong and *four* of weak."

"You're wrong again, Amanda," her husband said.

"I'm not 'wrong', Edward. It was juice of one ripe lime—not a lemon—that counts as the 'sour.' Cut it lengthwise, squeeze into a *tumlet,* toss the rinds in, too."

"A lemon would do just as well, Harry, take my word for it," Edward testified.

"*Two* teaspoons of best Jamaican syrup—we always used an unrefined one from Accompong Maroon Town—"

"West part of the isld., Harry, behind the John Crow Mountains. Do you know Jamaica—?"

" 'Fraid not, Edward."

"Pity. You, John?"

"Never sailed that road myself, I have to answer, Edward."

"Thought I heard an accent now and then."

"Sorry?"

"From those parts."

"Which parts?"

The Colonel Asks the Question:

"Yes, if you don't mind owning up at last—where *are* you from, John?"

"Born at sea, I'm proud to say, Colonel. So my legend has it."

" 'Legend'—?"

"That's a pun, I think," explained Fitzgibbon. "On his *map,* I think he means. . . . Is that one of *my* boys up that palm tree, Charlotte? (Excuse me:) CLIMB DOWN AT ONCE WHOEVER YOU ARE BEFORE YOU DO YOUR PERSON HARM. Why can't they occupy themselves collecting shells like your brood, Charlotte? WHAT?? O lovely wonderful. Now I'm supposed to go and rescue him. . . ."

"Then add *three* ounces of the best dark special reserve Jamaican rum," Mrs. Sutcliffe continued, "and top with *four* splashes of fresh Blue Mountain rain water. . . ."

"And you say it's called a 'Planter's Punch'—?"

"Yes."

"Well. . . ."

THE CRABS AREN'T INTERESTED IN YOU GEORGE THEY'VE RUN UP THE TREE TO EAT THE COCONUTS

". . . I must say *my* favorite jungli pani is a decent saké, plain and simple. Heated. Splendid stuff when served by women. . . ."

"O the list is long—the *things* we didn't eat in those days! Matiti grubs—remember when we ate matiti grubs, my dear?"

"Tasted just like prawns, they did, you'd never know the difference but the one was slightly salty and popped when you bit down on it—"

"And python."

"Yes. Python. Well, it's impossible to eat a python properly without vermouth."

"Samuelson—remember him?—Samuelson used to manage Edward's forests in the Shan—you remember—kept snakes—you must remember—he's that one that Edward found was thieving. Kept a Russel's viper as a pet. When Edward found out he'd been robbing us he had the *khansama* cook the snake and serve it up to him for supper. . . ."

"He'd eat anything, that Sam. I once watched him coax the penis from a cobra with his thumb, then slice it off and eat it—"

"Well, when you think what snakes feed on, frogs and other snakes and lizards, insects and the like, they can't make such delicious eating in and of themselves—"

"(*I* didn't know reptiles had—)"

"(O yes dear. Male ones. They have two—one on either side. Reversible, they are. And in some breeds there are spines on them.)"

"*(Really? Where—?)*"

"(Well at the *end,* how else do you think they—?)"

"(Well I've never stopped to think about it before this, Fiona. It's not the sort of thing I stop to think about. But why do they have *two—?*)"

"(. . . Considering your husband's reputation I should think the answer is self-evident.)"

"What *are* you women rabbiting away about?"

"Snakes."

"*Poison,* if you want the truth. . . ."

"O God yes—*poison*—reminds me of that time I got wind of prospects for a vein of pigeon-blood rubies in the Naga Hills about ten years ago. My foreman at the Mogôk mine got word the Kachins had unearthed a strike of pigeon-bloods in Nagaland about fifty miles due east of the border so we took some ponies and some *baksheesh* up and a few sharp-shooters. *Head-hunters,* those Nagas are, *fierce* bastards, let me tell you—"

ALL RIGHT ALL RIGHT I'LL TAKE YOUR PICTURE FOR THE KING BUT THEN, GEORGE, YOU ARE COMING DOWN.

"—harboring rebel armies from China and the Musselmen: *deeply* animistic. So up we go, just we two and a dozen or so bearers into the wild and the first night they receive us we're to dine on sheep's head. Fine. It's your having said that word 'poison,' Amanda, that reminded me: *deeply* carnivorous, they are, otherwise they live off a kind of blue corn as their staple diet. . . . We were invited to observe the preparation: First the head was shaved with a straight-edge knife, rather like a razor. Then the horns were chopped off with a cleaver. Then the head was shaken, side-to-side, so the worms would fall out of its ears and mouth—"

DON'T BE AN IDIOT, GEORGE, I'M TELLING YOU YOUR EYES *WEREN'T* CLOSED AND I'M NOT TAKING IT AGAIN.

"—in half and then the brain was scooped out and cooked in ashes elsewhere. Then the head was steamed for several hours, wrapped in leaves and then the whole was put on exhibition on a brass tray in the forest so the Gods could gorge on the object's soul—I told you that these types are deeply, deeply animistic—after which, we ordinary men were welcomed to feast, if that's what one could call it, on their leftovers, which was the bloody head entirely as before as far as me and my companion could make out, and then, needless to say, these pagans' protocol demanded that the best bits be handed over to the two of us. Imagine sittin' down surrounded by these filthy people watchin' every move, expected to rejoice about the bloody *eyes*. . . . Bloody fools we were we didn't know enough to chuck the iris and the upshot of it was that we were made sick as dogs and robbed blind and I never found out if the rumor of those pigeon-bloods was true, or not. . . ."

"Well, I can tell you from my dealings with that type of people that it wasn't, Fraser. They always try to get you with that native food. Designed to make a civil human being gag—"

"We used to have pig's head on Christmas morning," Ogilvy announces.

Everybody turns to look at him.

"My grandmother was Swedish," he explains. "She used to let me brush the pig's teeth before boiling it. . . ."

"Did you use a toothbrush, Harry?"

"I used my *own* toothbrush, Amanda," he confesses proudly.

"(—If those men don't get that fire up those porks are going to take forever, sods, what are they burning—?)"

"(Coconut shells that they've collected,)" Charlotte answers, standing.

"Not good enough," says Mrs. Fraser. "What we need is proper wood, those are two grown pigs for God's sake—"

"I'll take the girls and go collect some. I'm sure there's plenty. These mangroves—"

"Absolutely not, they're in their best white dresses—*Fitzgibbon!*"

"Right: lovely wonderful. Of course, Fiona. Lord knows they could use some occupation ALL RIGHT THEN LADS FOLLOW ME OFF WE GO THEN—"

Charlotte sets her glass down on a lacquer tray. "I could do with a short walk, myself," she says.

"I'll come with you," John suggests, and follows her. They walk about a yard apart, not looking at each other, down the beach. When they're out of hearing from the others Charlotte says, "Did you hear their conversation about snakes?"

In response he touches her.

"Did you hear Amanda ask me if I thought they copulated in a horizontal position—?"

She skips ahead along the water's edge then turns to him. " 'Can you imagine them *copulating standing up—?'* I asked. . . ."

The girls are playing in the water, their white dresses tied around their waists.

Monkey sits up shore, alone, braiding *ipomenas.*

As they pass her Charlotte stops and asks, "What are you making, Menaka?"

"A flower necklace."

"Very lovely."

"Thank you. It's for Jane. Please take it if you like."

"No no it's Jane's. . . ."

"Are you going for a walk?"

Charlotte holds a flower to her lips and nods.

"Is the Captain going with you?"

Charlotte moves her shoulders.

Monkey puts the string of flowers around Charlotte and leans her face up close:

"Please?" she whispers. "Take me with you?"

For want of space, a man can take with
him upon this journey only three books
at a time.

For the first he takes the Travels and
Adventures of Shaykh Abú 'Abdalláh
Muhammad of Tangier known as Shams ad-Dín,
or, more commonly, Ibn Battúta.

As the second he has
Da Vinci's "Notebooks," in French, bound for
reading right to left, as was the original,
because the genius was left-handed;

But only with the third can he ever practice
frequent pleasures.

FROM LEONARDO'S TREATISE ON THE NATURE OF WATER

She had learned her French with Henry because the War had broken out. When he left, she had forced herself to try to think in French, to translate street signs, signs in London shopfronts into French street scenes: an exercise that couldn't, wouldn't work. She spoke it badly, as most English people do, but within three months she was capable of reading simple stories, and after half a year she was reading Henry's copies of Flaubert in the original. Now, from the copy of the "Notebooks" John has with him, she translates from the French out loud,

"Therefore it must be said that there are many rivers through which all the element has passed and have returned the sea to the sea many times.

"mordant"
"fort"
"aigre"
"amer"
"la peste"

"And so it is now sharp and now strong, now acid and now bitter, now sweet and now thick or thin, now it is seen bringing damage or pestilence and then health or, again, poison.

"laxatif"
"acerbe"
"sulfureux"
"sanguin"
"bas"
"en colère"
"oléagineux"

"And as the mirror changes with the color of its objects so, too, does the water change with the nature of the place it passes: health-giving, harmful, laxative, astringent, sulfurous, salt, sanguine, depressed, raging, angry, red, yellow, green, black, blue, oily, thick, thin.

"arracher"
"fonder"
"remplir"
"se vider"

"Now it brings a conflagration, then it extinguishes; it is warm and is cold; now it carries away, then it sets down, now it hollows out, then it raises up, now it tears down, then it establishes, now it fills up and then it empties, now it rises and then it deepens, now it speeds and then lies still, now it is the cause of life and then of death, now of production and then of privation, now it nourishes and then does the contrary, now it is salt and then is without savor, and now with great floods it submerges the wide valleys.

"Avec le temps, tout le monde se change."

SEAEGGS

Some of them were smooth and some of them were hedgehoggy—she liked the smooth ones better, and put them to one side. Some of them were castellated while others of them were as satiny as flower petals, fitting on her fingertips like castanets. Some of them were shaped like angels' wings, some looked like cups and saucers. Some had ruffled edges, some were patterned like giraffes. Some were packed in clusters on the sides of corals, some were solitary teardrops on the sand. Some had spiny arms while some aspired through a plaited cone of whorls. Some were incised, horny, corrugated. Some had flamings, patches of bright color. Some were spiraled like pagodas. Some were buttons. Some were clams and some were cowries. Some were wentletraps. Some resembled lichee nuts. Some were purple, some were green. Some were stippled, brown on yellow, blue on burnished orange. Some were thick and robust, some were sickly. Some were white, translucent, ovate, with a wide curved lip which seemed to smile and fitted snugly in her hand. Oopi knew that these were special. These were sea-eggs and she thought the fish had laid them, fish that she could see among the coral, moon-shaped fish of many colors.

She was gathering the eggs.

The sun was fading and the shells shone through the water like white roses.

"These are called 'money cowry,' " Gaby says. "Grandfather says that when the Portuguese—"

"*Shh!*" Oopi commands, braving yet another step across the coral. So far she'd gathered two and she could see another three.

"You can bleed to death," warns Gaby. "Coral—*éh!* How do you think it got its color—?"

"I'm going to get those eggs," says Oopi.

"*Shells.*"

"I'm going to get them."

"Goodbye, feet! Who cares—?"

Every step she takes at this depth is a formulation of an *if then,* an hedonic calculus—across the calcified anatomy of coral her little toes appraise the price of pain against the gain of pleasure: the sea was at her navel, she had ruined her white dress.

An asteroid, a starfish, siphoned by.

Sloan and Sybil were collecting cockles, clams; bivalves—throwing back to sea the single whelks and periwinkles, single halves of mussels, oysters, which had lost their twins.

Nolly and Amanda had gone off in opposite directions and had found what each one hoped would be the largest shell.

Amanda brought a ten-inch section of a Giant Clam.

Nolly found a twelve-inch Triton's Trumpet.

Jane, who hadn't tried at anything, had stumbled on a foot-and-a-half wide Horse's Hoof *(Hippopus hippopus),* grossly encrusted, which she tried to lift and couldn't lift and ran for help and tripped again and finally had to call on Monkey in the absence of a better person to help her carry it along to show her father.

"What the hell is that?" the Colonel shouted.

"It's a Horse's Hoof," Jane announced. "That's what it's called, I asked the Captain—Do you like it, sir? I found it—"

"Stinking seaegg! Crust! Execration—!"

"Young ladies," Mrs. Sutcliffe says.

She turns to where their places have been set. The moon is up. There are mosquitoes.

"It's time for dinner," she proclaims.

TURTLES *Die Fledermaus,* the opera. Strauss. Certainly you know *Die Fledermaus?* Certainly you must have heard of Strauss?

"Can't say I have," the Colonel tells Fitzgibbon. "Name's familiar. Generally I'm ace with names. German fellow, is he? Never took to opera. Poncey. Never took to Germans. . . ."

"—The Waltz King? You never heard— *'The Blue*

Danube Waltz'? Certainly you've heard *'The Blue Danube Waltz'*: pah rum pumpum-*pum* pum-*pum!* pum-*pum!*"

"Yes yes but what has that got to do with *them?*" The Colonel asks, waving his fork at the dark shapes flying through the twilight sky.

("The Indian Fruit Bat," the older Charles was telling Amanda where they sat together at the children's khana: *"Pteropus Giganteus."*

The older Charles was known to be meticulously boring on all matters zoological:

I *know* what a bat is, Amanda said, Something that drinks blood.

"You don't believe that childhood nonsense, do you?" Charles asked, tucking into his roast pig. Amanda noticed that she didn't like the way he ate. "I suppose you believe that rubbish about vampires as well—?

Yes in fact I do.

"It's pure rubbish."

We don't think so.

" 'We'—?"

Amanda pulled her high lace collar from her neck and let him see the two liver-colored marks beneath her skin, an inch apart.

"Oh, really, Mandy. All of us have done that with a pencil now and then, grow up. I bet your father would have something to say about that if he saw it—"

This and other things.

"What 'other things'?"

Amanda waited 'til he finished chewing.

What will you give me if I show you? she asked Charles.

"I don't play those sorts of games," he told her. "Have some more of this disgusting curry." A servant leaned between them with a platter and he heaped his plate with rice and vindaloo. "I'd rather hear the secrets you could tell about our friend Nolly's brother," he suggested and looked along the row of plates to where he could catch a glimpse of Nigel's legs and hands.)

"They're the only mammal that can fly, you know," Fitz was saying to the Colonel. "Flying squirrels and flying lemurs only coast."

"But certainly you're not forgetting angels?" Mrs. Sutcliffe asked, reducing the roast pig on her plate to dainty morsels with her knife and fork before consuming them.

All I know is that I had one once and it was richer than goose liver, said the Colonel.

Mrs. Sutcliffe hesitated, looking for the thread of conversation, then the Colonel told her that the legs, especially, were very tasty and could pass for gammon in his book.

"You . . . ate . . . a *bat?"* Fitzgibbon asks.

"A flying fox, sir."

" . . . but you *ate* one?"

"Bones and all. Can't think of a more complete food for the soldier in the field. Every part of it is edible except the gall bladder. The gall bladder will kill you."

"You don't say . . ." Mrs. Sutcliffe said. She wondered how one would identify the gall bladder among the other organs of a bat but she was of too sensitive a nature to enquire further while they ate. She had a sip of claret to relieve the odd taste that had risen in her throat. "And what about you, Mister Fitzgibbon?" she queried. "Do you have a decent cook? Edward and I have been so fortunate with our man Friday . . ."

("It's called the Bread Bag," Nigel was demonstrating to the girls on either side of him. "It's like the Reef Knot but the Bread Bag has the two ends coming out at opposing corners instead of both ends up or down. Here. You try it," he said. He gave the rope to Gaby and she tied it. "Excellent!" he said, "where'd you learn to do that?"

"—you just showed me," she answered.

"Yes, but," he insisted, "most girls can't—"

"Don't be an ass," Nolly warned him at his other side.

Someone called out, *First star of evening!* Look, everyone! *The evening star!* All you children make a wish!)

As they had known it would be when they sailed, the

moon that night was five days small of being full, and the tide was neap. The servants had lit torches at the sunset, as the bats and the mosquitoes took to air. There was nothing they could do about mosquitoes except employ two bearers, one at either side of their encampment, upwind, fanning smoke in their direction, creating a perimeter within which they were relatively safe from pests. The bats afforded them no danger and the fires kept away whatever other predators they might have had to risk. As night closed in they began to feel the satisfaction that was due them. Someone raised another toast to King George and Queen Mary and they stood their sovereigns yet another round. They were pleased, extremely pleased, to be among themselves—their self-satisfaction made them light, expansive as hot air. The day had been a long one, but it had been carried out with spit and polish. Now the night assembled and promised to be perfect; they relaxed. The boys and girls began to play a game of snakes and ladders while they waited for their pudding. Their parents and the others stood or stretched or lit their smokes and talked about the prospects for tomorrow's hunt, while three days of the week collected the soiled china from the banquet and the other two began to brew the tea and lay the places for the cakes and cheeses. Wednesday, sitting on his haunches at the water, rinsing pots, stood up. Either he was seeing things or there was lightning coming toward him just below the ocean's surface. Sutcliffe's water spaniel rushed the waves, then crouched and whined and looked at Sutcliffe for his orders. *What the hell is that?* Sutcliffe was thinking. His cigarette had fallen from his fingers to the sand.

"Dollar—?" he began to ask.

The phenomenon had silenced everyone.

In the offing, where the ships were anchored, the water was bright green, a lurid sort of yellow, in a band several hundred yards across, trailing half a mile and moving, like sheet lightning, outward, towards them. Charlotte slipped her hand around John's arm and whispered, "John—*what is it?"* Matlock moved toward them and he and John exchanged a look. "What do you reckon, John?" he ventured: "I'd say orcas but I haven't seen their blow."

"—it's not a pod of whales, Mat."

" . . . somethin' out there agitatin' all that phosphorescence. Could be dolphins mating, John. . . ."

" 'Dolphins'?" Charlotte echoed.

"I don't think so, Mat. Not the way they're traveling. . . ."

"Dollar, you're the expert here," Sutcliffe ordered, "what the devil's going on?"

"Turtles, I think."

"Turtles—?"

Matlock looked to sea and nodded. "Moon's right," he concurred.

("Why's the water shining?" Amanda asked.

"Phosphorescence," Charles the elder told her, "visible when atoms of the micro-organism *noctiluca miliarus* are disturbed."

"—you mean it's not a submarine? It's not the *Nautilus?* That's what I wished for on the evening star: that Captain Nemo and his crew would come. . . .")

"—but turtles, John? I mean: *turtles?"*

"Coming in."

"—to shore?"

"Yes."

"Here, you mean?"

"—to lay. Mat—we better haul those punts into the trees. Fitz—get the boys to ford our punts over the beach beyond those fires. Colonel—we'll need torches. . . ."

"—to lay?" Mrs. Sutcliffe interrupted. "To lay *what,* Captain?" but he was gone, running with Fitzgibbon toward the punts.

"Eggs, Amanda," Mrs. Fraser answered. "Whatever else would turtles lay—bricks?"

"Oh my," Amanda said. "This is going to be exciting—

Charlotte? What's your view on this: Is this something that the children ought to watch? Colonel—? Is this going to be the sort of thing that as a mother I should censor—?"

(The first two dragged themselves ashore to no one's notice, coming in in darkness before the crest of eerie light. Sutcliffe's spaniel charged the first one and then the other, nosing at their carapaces until, by chance, it tipped one over and pinned it to the sand, its forepaws resting on the turtle's plastron as the turtle writhed, flailing the air with its massive flippers and its stunted rudder-like hind legs. The spaniel rocked it back and forth and then lost interest in it as the first rank of female turtles were hurled through surf onto the shore and began to lumber up the gentle slope, seeming to lack energy to overcome the burden of their locomotion.

What Charlotte would remember was the silence.

They pulled themselves over the sand, fifty of them in a single rank, followed at an interval by a second rank and then a third, laboring up the wet slope, the dry sand acting as a magnet on their eggs as if they were iron filings in the female bellies.)

The sound of their communal struggle was a nothing, a silence like a hive of insects suffocating in a vacuum. In their wakes they left a tortured pattern on the sand around a central furrow where their tails pushed into ground to lever their bulks forward. The patterns interwove as hundreds of them came—the beach began to look as if a giant hand had drawn a complex diagram of an undecipherable system on the sand. Some of them knocked against a wok or brought a tentpost crashing down, the canopy then moving forward, centipodal, humpbacked, blanketing them across the sand.

The frenzy started.

Like a single locust in the vanguard of a swarm, the excitement of the air, the fury, started as a single flutter: sand, an agitation of it like a nervous eddy, flustered, suddenly erupted off their flippers as they pivoted their bodies on their spinal axes, throwing sand in a haphazard frantic way. A blizzard rose around them and their bodies disappeared then re-emerged in sight, partially submerged in sand. With their hind legs they sent up another spume and then a second deeper silence came as each one dropped her clutch of eggs into the arid well she'd dug in the infertile sand.

It was either Nigel or the elder George who was the first to say they looked like tennis balls.

Or it was either Colonel Napier or Fraser who expressed a taste for turtle soup.

Or it was Sutcliffe's spaniel, unable to control its instinct any longer, who mangled the first nest trying to retrieve the soft-shelled eggs in its pointy teeth.

Or it was the Komodo dragons, their throats enlarged with rage, intimidating Ogilvy as they strode upright, their tongues extruded, racing on their hind legs from the mangroves toward the clutches as he rushed at them, pathetically, with fire:

In the end no one could be said to have been guiltless, except the very young, who ran behind the fires in the shadows of the trees to hide. No one tried to stop it. Matlock didn't, nor Fitzgibbon, nor did John or Charlotte. Fitz. ran at them and then realized he'd have to restrain them physically to stop them so he drew back, sat down, cried. Matlock turned his back on it, concerned himself with making sure, despite them, they weren't going to be marooned god dammit, he established his ownself as keeper of the punts, the soul of calm, someone who could mastermind retreat, a safe return to reason, and Rangoon.

Charlotte in her terror thought, So this is how it happens, and she kept the girls behind her and away form it. She stood and watched John watch it. *Stop them, why aren't you stopping them?* she wondered.

In their boat, going back to ship, the boys were still rambunctious, singing, slinging bits of albumen and meat at one another.

The girls sat silently and watched John row. From a

distance, in that way sound travels over water with a clarity in calm conditions, they could hear the Colonel speaking with his blood up,

By God. I'll tell you nothing beats a turtle omelette in the field—

They could hear Mister Fraser answer:

Funny thing about these turtle eggs, though Colonel—When you cook 'em, see (I have this from my nigger cook at Mandalay), the yolks will set up after several minutes same as chickens' eggs but you can boil the damn things donkey's years and the whites will never set. . . . Strange, isn't it—?

"Yes," they heard a woman's voice accede, "like it's a flaw, wouldn't you say, a flaw in the way that God has planned them?"

FIRSTNIGHT

What are they doing? Gaby asks because they're not allowing her to look. There's room for only two to look each time.

Nothing, Nolly whispers.

Nothing? Let me see—

It's not your turn.

It hasn't been my turn *yet*—

Your turn is next.

It should have been my turn before the Sybs—

They got their turn because they found the peephole. They didn't have to tell, you know—

They *did.*

They *didn't.*

Code of Honor, yes they *did.*

Shh! They're talking.

Are they kissing?

All they're doing is talking, you're not missing anything, Amanda says.

Are they naked?

Shh . . .

They're naked, aren't they . . .?

"Yes, shut up.

Let me see—

Shh!

Is it true?

It's true.

I mean, is it true about—

Yes.

—tattoo?

I told you, *yes.*

I want to see it—

Shut up, will you? we can't hear what they're saying—

(The cabin was constructed to accommodate four drop-hinge pallets, two on either side of the middle timber. Two lesser berths—hammocks—were slung across the beam and in one of these slept Oopi who did not deserve a proper mattress, so her mother said, because she'd wet it; Monkey had the other. In the two top bunks there were the Sybs, together; and, also together, Jane and Gaby. Below, singly, because they were the oldest, were Nolly, starboard, and Amanda, port.

Monkey couldn't sleep because the hammock held her in a way that made her feel like she was falling. Oopi slept; she snored. The Sybs were sound asleep as well, entwined in one another. Monkey could tell Jane was still awake, she could see Jane's fingers moving. The others—Gaby, Nolly and Amanda—had crept out to spy on John and Charlotte. Suddenly Jane sat up and hit her head and fell back down against her pillow. Monkey slipped down from the hammock, stood up on the lower bunk and looked at her:)

"You're hurt?"

Jane moved her head a half inch from side to side, as if a fly had landed on her nose. She had the sheet pulled up around her throat.

"You're cold?"

This time she nodded, a sharp up-and-down.

Monkey pulled the cotton blanket from the hammock. "May I?" she asked.

Another nod.

Hoisting herself up, Monkey squatted at the end of Jane's bunk and smoothed the sides into an envelope around Jane's body. Jane was very thin.

"You hardly ate a thing," Monkey said. "You ought to eat. That's why you get cold. Your blood is thin. Food would make it thicker."

She dared to hold Jane's feet, to rub them through the blanket. Her heart was beating fast.

"Better?" she asked.

A nod. Then: "Your hands are warm."

"They are. My mother says I have the sun inside my hands."

"When I was cold like this before, when we were in Naini Tal in the North, my mother used to put a warming cushion in my sheets. It was a pillow slip that had a hot stone in it."

Was it nice?"

Another nod.

"It sounds like it was nice."

Then: "She's dead."

And then: "My mother."

"So's my father," Monkey said.

"Amanda says your father isn't 'dead.' She says he lives in England. She says he has a wife named Pamela and they have blond babies."

"Do you believe her?'

"Yes."

"Amanda says your mother killed herself."

"Amanda says a lot of things."

Then: "I'm still cold."

"Think something warm."

"I can't."

"You can."

"You do it."

"Make you warm?"

A nod. Then: "Come under the sheet with me."

After a while, Monkey says, What did you wish to-night—on the evening star?

You tell me your wish first.

I wished for this.

Your wish came true, then.

What was yours?

It won't come true.

What is it?

That he disappears.

He?

My father. That he 'dies' like yours.

(John had turned the lamp down and blue moonlight fell across them from the hatch. As always when they slept, he cradled her against him. *We should go,* she said. *Why don't we go.* He ran his hand over her hip. Everwhere's the same, he told her. It will only disappoint you, Charlotte. *What?* The world. *I'm worried about Fitz.* Fitzgibbon will recover—I'm worried about you. *I can't go back there, John, I don't want to see it in the day.* You won't have to. Tomorrow it will look like nothing happened. The tide will have come in and washed it. That's the flaw. Tomorrow everything will be the same.)

FIRSTDAY

It was, as John expected, not a new day but a flawless replication of the one before.

On *The Ruby Girl* some jokester mimicked reveille through Matlock's megaphone, and signs of life stirred on *The Cinnabar* in the forms of Fraser and the Colonel at their calisthenics. It was not yet change of morning watch but already heat lay on the water like an oily slick and, on the calm, Matlock rowed Fitzgibbon over to *The Charlotte* where Fitz went aboard while Mat and John rowed across to talk with Sutcliffe on *The Cinnabar.* "I'm not made of proper stuff for this," Fitz said to Charlotte. He hadn't changed his clothes from the night before and he looked as though he hadn't slept. "I can't face them, to say nothing of attempt to teach them. They detest me. You should see them. They're all in parade dress this morning, each one tossing back a second helping of his breakfast. We should have put for Rangoon in the middle of the night—now we're stuck, 'becalmed,' Matlock tells me, for God knows how long in his bloody harbor. . . ."

"John says *The Cinnabar* is under power. . . ."

"God, yes, *The Cinnabar* is under everything. *The Cinnabar* has God Himself for her Commander—"

" 'Captain,' Fitz . . ."

"Don't humor me."

"I only meant that even though the wind is down *The*

Cinnabar can put for home. We could say we think the children—"

"*They*'re the children's parents, for God's sake—we're nothing but employees, two more God damn servants, for God's sake. . . ."

"Fitz—"

"I don't know what to do! They've seen me weep! I've lost all my authority. . . ."

"Fitz, listen—"

"*And* I've lost my tripod . . . I suppose I left it on that bloody beach along with all my plates . . . God knows what else we left there . . . dignity, for one. If they find out I've lost those damn exposures, Charlotte, they'll stage the God damn thing all over . . . lovely. God damned wonderful. God, I need a wash. Look at me, I'm sorry, Charlotte. . . ."

"John's clothes will fit you, Fitz, why don't you have yourself a swim—?"

"Yes, why not? Bloody lovely. With the company we keep, who needs to be afraid of sharks:

'The things you'll learn from
the yellow and brown,

Will help you a lot with the white.'

"Kipling," he added.

(Charlotte's method had never been conventional, but it had become eccentric in the year that she'd known John. She would begin by writing three names of colors on the slate while stating, "This morning's colors are (whatever: one two three)." Then she would write a word and say, "This morning's *word* is (and et cetera)." A morning, for example, that began, "This morning's colors are salmon, slate and steely blue; today's word is *rapacity,*" would be remembered, she believed, as being quite a different morning than the one which started, "Today's colors are dove grey, buff and cadmium; today's word is *persuasion.*"

This morning's colors, she began:

They were seated on the deck beneath a canvas awning.

Yellow. Brown. And white.

"It sounds awfully *ordinary,*" Sloan complained.

"Today's word is: *vainglorious.* Who can tell me what it means—Jane?"

"Vain."

"Who can use it in a sentence?"

Amanda stood: "Because of the degree of pain involved in having one inscribed, a person with a tattoo on her back would be said by those who'd seen it to be v-a-i-n-g-l-o-r-i-o-u-s."

Amanda sat down amid the others' looks of absolute unstudied innocence and Charlotte's skin went prickly, all along her spine.

Sutcliffe wasn't satisfied with what he'd seen (no game to speak of, just those whatever kind of lizards those had been—he called them, erroneously, damn Jap kind of Kimono dragons:) No, he hadn't been impressed. Oh it was top-hole, all right, a top-flight sort of place to hand over to the King, (they weren't at issue over *that:*) but what the place was missing was the sort of game that they had come to shoot: it wasn't *trophy* caliber. "You know the sort of thing we're looking for," Sutcliffe said to John: alligator, pig, boar, peafowl, roe deer, monkeys, foxes, dammit, Dollar, *jungle cats.* ("Amanda, by the way, is onecrackshot of *Panthera pardus* from the middle distance—I know no other woman who can stand her ground. . . .")

So they were going, putting under steam—the Sutcliffes, Frasers, Ogilvy and Colonel Napier on *The Cinnabar*—for a day of shooting on a sister island. Both John and Matlock expressed doubts that they would find what they were looking for, but neither John nor Matlock had an appetite for sport so they didn't know how unconvincing their skepticism sounded. Stores were transferred from *The Cinnabar* onto *The Ruby Girl* and *Charlotte,* and by four bells of the forenoon watch *The Cinnabar* weighed anchor under light airs and made head-way on a course which looked Southwest by West.

"Where is he going?" Sybil asked.

Hunting.

"Head-hunting?"

No. Game.

"Is he coming back?"

Don't know.

"Will he bring a tiger?"

—don't think so.

"Who's its father while he's gone?"

The Captain.

"Who's its mother?"

Charlotte.

"Who's its teacher, then?"

Amanda.

"Is she staying at this island, then?"

—think so.

"Does she like it?"

Very much.

"*She* likes it, too. She wants to stay. She wished it."

—on the star?

"Yes. And when they shot the guns. Amanda says she has to make a wish whenever guns go off. And at the sight of blood."

—it was a lot of *that.*

"Don't cry . . . Amanda says it was the way for making a big wish. Why are we crying?"

—we didn't know.

"We didn't wish?"

Nobody told us.

"It's all right . . . Don't cry. She can wish the next time."

—never want a next time. She was scared.

"Don't be scared."

—what should she be then?

"Amanda says she has to be a quaker."

—what's *it?*

"—don't know. Thing like Amanda."

—be like Amanda, then?

"Yes—quaker.

—*Qua—ker* . . .

(Charlotte took her sketchbook with her this time, and she and Fitz and Mat and John decided not to go back to the site of the encampment of the night before. Rowing hard against the current they rounded the southern point of the harbor, hazarded the rip, and landed on an outer reach of reef, out of sight of their two ships, where the stretch of beach was deeper than the one of yesterday, but where the surf was stronger, too strong, in fact, for all the younger children to try swimming:)

They towed the boats onto the beach, and the children, free of the confines of a ship once more, broke into impromptu running games, racing, playing tag. Fitz was feeling better, "recovered," as John had said he would be, looking younger than he usually did, outside his schoolmaster's garb, dressed in John's sailing clothes. He was going to lead the Birdwatcher's Division. Mat had volunteered to demonstrate some Fancy Knots, John and Gaby were Kite-Flying, Charles the elder was put in charge of leading the Zoology Excursion, Jib was Edible Bivalve and Crustacean Gathering, and Charlotte was The Native Flora. They were, to the extreme, marshaled, careful, curious and organized. Everything, as John had said it would be, was back to being nice, and normal.

John and Mat had handed over their binoculars to Fitzgibbon, so John didn't have a pair in his possession when he climbed the hill with Gaby and the younger George.

The ground they covered was a slow incline of coral rubble interspersed with sand, *tah*-vine, beach pea and creepers. It was the headland of the point they'd rounded—a gentle slope of only several hundred feet, not steep, not very high, but the highest point of land and they'd been searching, high and low, for wind. The calm that had beleaguered them all morning persevered—an uncommon stillness lay around the island, a refusal to disturb air's equilibrium. High up, the storks were searching, too. Against the cloudless sky, trailing their long legs, one wing dipped lower than the other, permitting them to circle for a thermal, they looked like stylized kites streaming their long tails behind them, Gaby thought. She could feel a something-wrong about the air, although she didn't know enough about an island's off-shore breezes to determine the degree of its peculiarity. Whereas she was used to air being a movement that was visible when written by the tails of kites, today's air seemed erased, invisible.

Look, the younger George said when they reached the top. Gaby didn't like him; he knew nothing about kites: "I can see Mister Fitzgibbon and the others down there—"

Gaby, shading her eyes from the white glare on the water, turned around and said, "O look—you can see *The Ruby Girl* and *Charlotte*. . . ."

She looked at John who was squinting through his hands

cupped like a mask around his eyes, and mimicked him. The way he was standing he was stiller, even, than the air and she tried to locate what he was looking at that seemed so rivetting. A dragonfly disturbed her. Younger George stumbled on a ground nest made of feathers, coral rubbish, sponge and dried seasnake and was taking it apart by kicking at it. Don't *do* that! Gaby said and tugged at John to interfere. *George, come here,* John said and positioned George in front of him with Gaby. Both of you look where I point and tell me what you see, he said. He put his head beside each of theirs and pointed near *The Ruby Girl* on the horizon. What do you see? he asked. "Wind?" George answered, skeptically. He wouldn't know "wind" if it came and knocked him over, Gaby thought, What am I looking for? she asked. "A boat," John said. She squinted at him: *Éh . . .* so?

Clearly neither child had seen it. A vision is a vision—in an inversion such as this, he knew, especially over water at midday, a man could suffer an illusion. It was not, by any means, a symptom of insanity, nor the advent of a revelation. It was merely the accumulation of warm air obtaining impetus—a condition of the weather which appeared as a dark silhouette, an outrigger, dispersing into light behind *The Ruby Girl.*

O marvelous, O stupendous necessity, Leonardo wrote about The Eye—"Who would believe that so small a space could contain the images of all the universe? O mighty process! What talent can avail to penetrate a nature such as these? What tongue will it be that can unfold so great a wonder? Verily none! Here the forms, here the colors, here all the images of every part of the universe are contracted to a point. O wonderful, O stupendous necessity—These are miracles . . . forms already lost, mingled together in so small a space it can recreate and recompose by expansion. The soul is content to stay imprisoned in the human body because thanks to our eyes we can see these things; for through the eyes all the various things of nature are represented to the soul. . . ."

"merveilleux"
"prodigieux"
"l'univers"
"la nature"
"les formes"
"les couleurs"
"les point"
"les miracles"
"la personne"
"les yeux"
"l'âme"

They were painting daisies.

Because the wind was down, they could draw and paint with no interference from the sand so they were sitting in a circle on the beach in a square of shade beneath a canvas stretched on oars. Oopi was tracing outlines of shells onto her paper, but everybody else was focusing on specimens of mistletoe, fan-flowers and beach daisies.

"Who can tell me if she hears the meaning in this flower's name?" Charlotte asks, holding up a daisy. The girls stare blankly, first at it, and then at her. "Try saying it v-e-r-y s-l-o-w-l-y," she advises.

The meaning of *what?* Amanda demands.

"—it's name," Charlotte answers.

Names don't have to mean.

"—that's true: but some names mean something never-the—"

Does yours—?

"I—"

—it's a kind of pudding, I think. Charlotte. It's a kind of trifle. Lewes—what's that? Lewes . . . lose . . . loose—

D-a-y-s-e-y-e Oopi says, very slowly. Then realizing what she's said, she pipes, "Oh! Day's *eye—!*" and Charlotte, in a reflex of relief, dabs her paintbrush on the tip of Oopi's nose and leaves a round mark of vermilion. Oopi wrinkles her nose and makes the others laugh and Amanda paints a broad stroke of viridian down Oopi's cheek and says, Let's paint our faces—("Oh . . . yes . . . *let's!*")—and no one thinks to look to Charlotte for permission or approval:

(Marching sideways, crablike, arm-in-arm, Sloan and Sybil run among the soldier crabs who scurry, un-crablike, forward backward, in formation in their uniforms of blue coats and orange trousers until, in full retreat, their field-marshal gives the signal and they corkscrew, simultaneously, into a hundred different bivouacs in the pink sand.

A bone moves sideways, toward them.

What's *it?* Sloan says, stopping as they almost fall.

Jib says, "That's how you tell a hermit.

"—a hollow object moving sideways that can't move itself.

"—a crab's inside," Jib says.

"Pick it up," Sloan says.

"—might bite us," Sybil argues.

"Hit it with a stick," Sloan says and pokes into a hole in it with driftwood. Instantly a claw emerges, grips the wood—the bone begins to edge away. *Hey,* Jib says.

"—hey this is a monkey skull."

He *is?*

"—see? These here? These are the eyes—"

This hole?

"—the nose."

Mat comes over to them with a pail of clams and says, "Jesus. Where'd you find *this?*"

—in the sand.

Mat runs his knifeblade 'round the inside of the cranium and a small black crab falls out. "You two run along, now," he tells them.

—give over her monkey then!

"—go on . . ."

—*her* monkey, she found him!

"Here," Mat orders, "I'm the Captain here and you'll do as you're told—"

He holds the skull behind his back before any of the other children have a chance to see it, cups his palm around its dome and runs his fingers down the cliff-in-miniature that is its profile, thinking, *You poor bastard—how long ago and from what hell did you wash up on this forgotten beach—?*)

What did you do with it? Fitzgibbon asked him later.

"—I mean: they wanted to *paint* the damn thing. It didn't seem right. . . ."

"No, no, of course not, but: what did you *do* with it?"

"I buried it."

"—you *didn't.*"

"I *did.*"

"—and you're sure it was a—?"

"The jaw, you know. And the skull, itself, was big. Plus. . . ."

"—go on:"

" . . . its teeth was equal."

"—regular."

" . . . that's it."

"Then . . . what's your doubt?"

"My doubt is—when I got the chance to really look at it—it didn't seem to show the signs like it had been in water."

"Like it had been in water *long,* you mean?"

"—like it had been *at all,* I mean. So that made me think it *couldn't* be a—"

"—no, of course not."

"—so I went and dug it up again."

"You *didn't.* . . ."

"I *did.*"

"—and?"

"It wasn't there."

"I don't believe you."

"On my word of—"

"It's impossible."

"Yes, sir, that's what I think, too."

"—so?"

"I think those girlies dug him up."

"—so you think it *was* a—"

"I'm fairly certain, sir. I mean, the poor son of a bitch looked like he'd been *trepanned.*"

"—not bludgeoned?"

"*Carved,* sir."

"By a *tool,* you mean?"

"I mean, sir: by an *artist.* . . ."

. . .

SECOND NIGHT

Red with sun, hungry and exhausted they had returned to the two ships, where the servants had lit lanterns and prepared their suppers. By this time tomorrow, they were thinking, they'd be in Rangoon, back to their familiar, their accustomed places, streets with English names, some other English faces. The nation they had made by virtue of their journeying together would annul itself. Even if the boys remained as close as they now pledged among themselves, they'd never have that night again, nor be in the company of Matlock, nor be sleeping on this deck in this darkness under all these thousands of stars.

On *The Charlotte* the girls said they would sleep below. No whisper of a breeze had stirred since *The Cinnabar* had sailed this morning and the air contained in quarters below deck felt packed and wooly. The girls, their faces painted in bold colors and designs, stripped their nightclothes off and fanned the air with fans they made from Charlotte's watercolor paper. In the murky light they looked like dolls or demons as they kept themselves awake, and waited.

What if they don't sleep downstairs? a voice inside a green face with red and yellow markings (Sybil) asked.

Not "downstairs": *below,* she was told.

(She couldn't see what told her.)

(It's face was gone—a black-in-black—its nipples looked like hollow eyes.)

"They will," Amanda said. "They'll sleep in John's cabin the way they did last night."

"How do you know?" Nolly said.

"They don't want the servants watching them," Amanda answered.

"But what if they don't?"

"They will."

"But what if they . . . like last night, what if they—?"

"They *will,*" Amanda said.

"This is our last chance," Nolly said. Hers was the most decorated head because she'd found *aigrettes* while bird-watching with Fitzgibbon, and she wore them tucked behind her ears: her face was yellow, like a tiger's, with black markings. "You better not be wrong," she told Amanda. Then she made a noise that sounded like an animal and stole across the cabin toward the hatch.

("Did Mat show you his 'man'?" she asks.

Instead of answering, he says, "—it's so damn still."

"—hear them on *The Ruby Girl*. . . ."

"Mat's got them bunked above."

"—often wondered. Sound. The way we hear the fishers from our bed at night at home—can they hear us?"

"Of course."

"—they can?"

"Why wouldn't they—?"

" . . . I thought the air was blowing all the sound in one direction—"

"—not tonight."

"—birds aren't even—"

"—only seen it still as this but twice before."

"What does it mean?"

"—last time I was in Haiphong the day before a *tai fung* and the first time was when we were calm in open water fifteen days in the horse latitudes south of Malagazy. I've made you smile . . ."

"You're like the twins, sometimes, interchanging 'we' and 'I'."

"—the difference, darlin': 'We's my dad and I."

"—a sailor?"

"Second-best."

"—to you?"

"Hell no I'm down there around 'tenth' . . ."

"Who was the First?"

"My father's father."

"Did he have that many sons, that you come Tenth?"

"—that many wives."

"I wouldn't rank at all—"

"Oh I don't know—"

"I told you how sick I was my first time out—"

"—but never since."

"—no sense of how it works. The wind. . . ."

"—thought I saw a visitor today."

"—another boat?"

"Maung Ang and U Thet say they didn't notice anything."

"—Pandi says they slept all day."

"Did I ever tell you Marco Polo sailed through here?"

"Yes—and Battúta?"

"Later."

"—when?"

"1347."

"—past here?"

"Most likely."

"—here? Where *we* are?"

"Yes. . . ."

"—but it didn't look like this," she tells herself. "Did the stars? John? I wonder if the stars looked different too. Did they? Oh the hell with you John Dollar. Why are you laughing at me—?")

God Who sees all things, God Who watches all, even as the stars in Heaven do look down upon the earth so God watches every deed, watches as we sleep and eat, everything we do is known to Him Who is invisible yet He Who can observe our every move. The eyes of the Lord are in every place beholding the evil and the good. Proverbs 15:3. Before I was confirmed I memorized the Catechism, Father made me say it every night for three months, the Questions and the Answers. The way I memorized it was by staring at the page. At the top of the page it said, then,

THAT IS TO SAY,
AN INSTRUCTION TO BE LEARNED OF
EVERY PERSON THAT IS BAPTIZED HAVING COME INTO
HIS YEARS OF DISCRETION
BEFORE HE IS BROUGHT TO BE CONFIRMED
BY THE BISHOP IN THE LAYING ON OF HANDS

Question.
What is your Name?

Answer.
"Norris Catherine Petherbridge."

"—what does *that* mean?"

"Don't interrupt—"

"—*that* part that you just said—"

"—interrupted, Gaby, then I have to close my eyes and go back to the beginning. . . ."

"—*'years of discretion'?*"

"—shut *up,* I said!"

"Shut up, *both* of you—it means 'thirteen,' " Amanda whispers.

"It does *not!*" Nolly insists.

"—not so loud, they'll *hear* you!"

"—if it means 'thirteen' how come the Bishop let me be confirmed at twelve—?"

". . . because the 'Bishop' was your father—"

"It means the snake has bitten her," Sloan says.

"It does *not—!*"

"*—sssh!*"

"—don't bite boys and boys can be confirmed. I think they can. *Can't* they?" Oopi asks.

" 'Years of discretion' means old enough to know The Secrets," Gaby says. "That's what it means. We have it in The Holy Roman, too . . . have they come below, yet—?"

"*—quiet!* . . . think I hear them coming . . ."

Question.

Who gave you this Name?

Answer.

My Godfathers and Godmothers in my Baptism; wherein I was made a member of Christ, the child of God, and an inheritor of the kingdom of heaven.

Question.

What did your Godfathers and Godmothers then do for you?

Answer.

They did promise and vow three things in my name. First, that I should renounce the devil and all his works, the pomps and vanity of this wicked world, and all the sinful lusts of the flesh. . . .

John and she had undressed slowly, almost ritualistically, while embracing, caressing each part of the other's body as it came to be revealed. They began as dancers, standing, facing one another, as, one by one, descending, she undid the buttons of his shirt. She held the waistband of his trousers, slipping them around his buttocks down his thighs and knelt as he stepped out of them. She ran her tongue along his instep, bit him lightly on the inside of his legs until her mouth discovered his erection. John wrapped her hair around his hand and pulled her head back. Sloan thought it looked like it was hurting them, but then Nolly came and took her turn. What Nolly saw were Charlotte's fingers pressing in John's anus then John turning her around by pulling on her hair and pushing her facedown onto the mattress of the berth. He knelt behind her, put one hand into her place and slapped the bottoms of her feet. He dug his fingernails into her calves and then he slapped each thigh and then he slapped her on her rearend then he put his mouth against it. It was Gaby's turn. It went on for half an hour so Amanda saw the moment Charlotte mounted him. She saw Charlotte take him into her. Oopi saw him eating Charlotte's breasts. Jane saw Charlotte lick her palm and rub her spit along his penis. Sybil saw John's head inside her legs and saw her strike his shoulders with her fist. What Monkey watched had seemed to her a violence and when John and Charlotte reached their ecstasy eight girls in paint and feathers, naked, heard their cries of ravishment and looked at one another in disguise and made a silent pledge, mistaking the sad echo of extreme joy for a noise of an ungodly agony.

QUAKERS

Jib woke John at three bells on the morning watch. *You better come,* he said. He didn't even bother to excuse himself to Charlotte.

John could smell the wind before he hit the deck: altostratus clouds disguised the sun and made the dawn seem like a sigh in darkness. It would blow in a few hours, he could tell—real wind. In the meantime, it was quiet, still and calm.

The Ruby Girl was gone.

She had drifted, sails trimmed, on the current, half a mile to sea, under weigh as if her anchor had been hauled.

John sent up three white star rockets.

The Ruby Girl stayed silent and did not return the signal.

"Can you see anyone?" Charlotte asked, beside him. John was searching through binoculars. "Goddam him," he cursed. "Can't you see anything?" she insisted: "The boys were sleeping on the deck last night . . ." *Rum,* he said. "—they're only *boys,* John . . ." *"Rum,"* he said again: "Or *gin* or whatthehell . . . this is rummy sailing, *damn* him," he repeated. He sent up three more flares. When they went unanswered, he and Jib lowered a punt and rowed out on the current on the hope that they could overtake her.

When they were shouting distance from her he and Jib began to call. The stillness on *The Ruby Girl,* doubled by the stillness on the water, echoed back their words.

Behind them, on *The Charlotte*, as instructed, Nolly and Amanda sent up three more flares. *They're playing* Oopi said, winking toward the ship named after her through one lens of John's binoculars because her eyes were not as far apart as his: "They're playing Hide-and-Seek," she said. Let us see it, Sloan requested. "No one there," Oopi confirmed. They're playing dead.

Jib and John maneuvered 'round to port where John could see the *Girl* was dragging on her anchor. *Why don't they answer?* Jib demanded and began to shout out Matlock's name again.

They made fast to the ship's side and John secured them with a grapnel, then they boarded by her ropes.

It was orderly and quiet on the deck.

The punts were cradled in their davits.

Nothing moved.

No sound was heard except the timbers easing in their joists.

Though he didn't say it, Jib was thinking This is what John says he's never found when he talks about a "ghost ship." John signaled him to search astern while John went forward on the rail to bow. Finding no one there he raised the forward hatch and let himself below. From the forward cabin he heard a whistling in the air through the deck beams like a flight of birds, like a great disruption in the sky high overhead as if a flock of storks or egrets were migrating. As he went into the galley a cup slid down the horizontal and the ground careened. Amidships heeled, the timbers shivered, *We've collided* he judged wrongly and he ran astern as best he could. Jib called to him and he caught Jib in his arms.

Jib vomited. Behind him in the hold there were flies buzzing in an eerie light. John entered, sliding in the thin ooze underfoot, the beams and planks were splattered with their blood, now fouled and frenzied with the flies, the bunks were gashed, the sheets were scarlet mats, their blood ran everywhere as if the boat were bleeding, weeping. Not a trace. Fitz. Mat. Maung Ang, U Thet. And the boys. There were no bodies. Stench coagulated in his nostrils. By the second tremor he had made it up the hatch onto the deck, where he was hurled against the windlass. At the third he had a sense of Jib dashing for the rigging, falling overboard. Two thoughts, two "Charlottes" merging into one compelled him toward the wheelhouse but the wind was churning birds and insects in the air. In the distance he could see two sirens, Charlotte and *The Charlotte,* and the sky was black, the wall of water that the quake gave birth to rolled far out, "tsunami," devil-talk which meant *annihilation* and he lay between it and the island and he'd die before them certainly, by seconds, in another Captain's coffin while the other two would perish folded on themselves, a boat named for a woman 'round the woman, he could hear the tidal wave above the wind, the birds had fallen from the sky, the bees were stunned among the halyards, frogs and lizards fell to deck *o christ it's funny* was his last thought *that I ever said I'd never drowned*

I never found a ghost ship
and I never loved
a
wo
man
un
til
her

3

ON "THE ISLAND OF OUR OUTLAWED DREAMS"

WAKING

Monkey woke hearing the ocean. Her mouth tasted of vomit and mucus, her lips were soldered with salt. Her throat burned. Her eyes stung. Sunlight and heat punished her. There was sand in her nose. It was day and this was a desert. The ocean was coming to get her. For miles around there was waking. After an earthquake the earth is like new. It has swallowed itself. After an earthquake a new earth is born.

The air smelled like diamonds. It was sharp in their lungs. Jane lay in a hole in the sand dug by the tide 'round her bones; she was cold. Further on there was Sloan without Sybil. There was Nolly. None of them moved. Theirs was a not-life, a state of nonbeing, a coma from which they were waking, a stage in the life of a worm. Their hearts were beating, their lungs emptied and filled, but the wall they had ridden onto the shore had collapsed on their memory, none of them knew whose body this was, whose pain she was feeling, or even, most strange, if the pain was the proof that she was still living. Each one, when she was able to, wept. No one was glad to discover that she was alive. This was not life as she'd known it. This was a torture. Gradually, slowly, they moved. They were not far from each other. From where she was, Gaby could make out the shapes of some others, all orange. Things that could not swim were swimming: trees, the horizon, a bee. Colors swam. There were orange forms crawling out of the earth. Gaby tried to move and remembered her knees. Needles were turning in them, her knees had been shaved on the coral. They stung. *Basta!* she wanted to say, but her tongue was covered with sand. How many hours it took them to wake didn't matter. They woke. They woke slowly. They couldn't move. Life preservers had saved them, sleeveless orange jackets defining their species among the corpses of fishes strewn at the high water line. By noon of that day the heat raised a stench of dead fish and dried seaweed. The adjutant storks had returned with the gannets and jungle crows—carrion eaters arrived. They stalked around Oopi, testing her palatability, pecking her till she jacked herself into a sit. Her head hurt and the sun was too bright. She was confused. She was wearing one shoe. She picked herself up and felt dizzy. This orange thing was hot and it wouldn't come off when she pulled it. How long had she slept? She was scratchy and stiff. What was the name of this game? Where was breakfast? She walked down the slope to the water and squatted and peed through her knickers. Something about it suggested that it wasn't right but it felt like the right thing to do. She took off her shoe and forgot it. Something smelled awful. She noticed the fish. She walked up the beach and the birds ran at her, letting her know their opinion. They were eating the fish by the dozens, scissoring out the gray flesh with their beaks. She felt thirsty. Amanda was clutching her head in her hands and Oopi sat down in the sand next to her. "I'm thirsty," she said. "This orange thing is bothering me."

"Take it off, then," Amanda tried to say kindly. The boats were both gone. She had been sitting and staring for hours, waiting for Help.

"Can't," complained Oopi.

Amanda untangled the matted straps of the life-vest and helped Oopi slip from it. "We should try not to lose these," she warned.

"I've lost my shoes."

"I lost mine, too."

"—while we were sleeping."

Amanda put her hands to her head. "We're in trouble," she stated.

"Why? What did we do?"

"They forgot us."

"Who"

What will we do in the *dark?* Amanda was thinking.

"—a bit hungry, too," Oopi confessed.

The first thing we'll build is a *fire,* Amanda decided. Her face hurt. She'd scratched her cheek on the coral and bitten her tongue. Her skin burned. And shelter, she said. "We have to stay out of the sun." Her mind was beginning to function. A day, or two days, at the most, she was thinking, then they'll come back for us. Parents come back. Parents don't go and forget where they've left their children. She was remembering, now—her memory stirred to inform her: "Are you hurt?" she asked Oopi. No, but your face looks awful bad, Oopi told her. Flies were settling on it. "We ought to wash it, I think," Oopi heard herself saying—it turned something around in her mind. She remembered her ayah. She saw the wave coming and remembered the instant it hit her, the way she went into its jaws and its stomach. The sleeve of her blouse had been ripped on the coral so she tore it and soaked it in the tide. She dabbed it around Amanda's wound. There were sand and some coral bits in it. It was purple. It showed her bone. "We ought to wrap it," she said to Amanda. It was something her mother would say. Something else turned in her mind: *I have a mother. This is the beach where the turtles were killed. There are no boats here to take us away.* She frowned at the ocean. Her red hair was matted, and it itched her. "I need a hat," she complained. First things first, Amanda determined. She pulled herself up. "Let's find the others," she said. Oopi pointed to bodies further along down the beach. Not till then had they realized that some of them hadn't come out of the wave. There were five others, five forms in life jackets washed up on the beach with the debris from the boats. Nolly had counted them. She had good eyesight, better than Amanda's, and her reflexes were faster because she was never in doubt. Even now, while Amanda was trying to think of a plan, Nolly had been thinking for hours about all that they needed to do. She had dreamed it. At the edge of her nightmare, they gathered wood. Weaving through her unconscious they'd found clear water. They'd constructed their houses. They'd made fabric, invented the wheel, minted money. Hers was the mind that had memorized both the Questions and Answers in her Catechism, never doubting that one category existed to satisfy everything that the other one needed. She thought faster than Amanda even though she was younger because she had the Answers while Amanda quite often lost time thinking hers up. Nolly believed that for each problem there was a solution, and vice versa, a finite amount. There were no more solutions than problems—no more answers than questions. She believed in the creed, the commandments, the sacraments. She owned an enthusiasm for the Almighty which made the other girls trust her in a way that they wouldn't Amanda, because everyone knew she knew she was right.

Question.

What is thy duty towards thy Neighbor?

Answer.

My duty towards my Neighbor is to love him as myself, and to do to all men, as I would they should do unto me: To love, honor and succor my father and mother: To honor and obey the King, and all that are put in authority under him.

It wasn't an argument . . . they were all, except Nolly, in a very bad way—especially Sloan. Sloan wouldn't speak and she wouldn't stand up. She sat on the beach, clutched her knees, while she rocked back and forth. Sybil was missing. Charlotte was missing, and John, and Jib, and Captain Matlock and Mister Fitzgibbon and all the boys and the bearers and both the boats but Nolly was saying that Sybil ought to be found. Amanda was saying they needed to salvage debris from the boats before the high tide and then they should gather some wood, search for food and clean water but Nolly said, "If it were me that was lost, I'd want to know everyone was doing her best to come get me. . . ."

"Why don't we look for more than one thing at a time?" Gaby suggested.

"Sybil's no 'thing,' " Jane whispered.

"Did anybody see her in . . . when we were in the . . .?"

None of them ended the sentence: no one could answer the question.

They decided that the stronger girls—Nolly, Gaby and Monkey—should drag the supplies and debris from the boats over the high water line on the beach, while the rest of them—Oopi, Amanda and Jane—hiked up the cliff at the end of the point to try to see Sybil.

Three don't need to go, Nolly said.

"—at least *two,*" Amanda said. "That should be Law Number One. 'No one is allowed to go alone.' "

"—'go' where? Where can we go?" Jane said.

"I've been up that cliff," Gaby volunteered. "It's nothing to be frightened of. I went up it yesterday with Capitão João. . . ."

No one spoke.

Everybody had the feeling Gaby had just uttered some unlawful words.

"I'll go by myself," she said.

No one goes off on her own, Amanda repeated.

"I'll take Ruby with me—"

"Oopi's too slow. Take Monkey," Nolly said.

"—I need the Monkey, she's strong," Amanda argued. "There's a lot to be done right here on this beach before night if we're going to make shelter. . . ."

Sloan started screaming. Down the beach a body in a life preserver rolled among the waves and disappeared into the undertow then came to shore again and rolled and disappeared then came back up and rested, getting the attention of the gannets. When she failed to recognize it, Sloan began to kick it, rolling it back into the sea until they made her stop and she collapsed again on sand. It was the body of the bearer Pandi, stripped of one leg and the flesh of his remaining one, by sharks or coral. His open hip looked like a sponge, his leg looked like a jew's-harp. His face was perfect in repose except that his eyes were open and rolled back. "We have to do the Christian thing," Nolly instructed.

"What's that?" Amanda asked.

"We have to bury him. . . ."

"I don't think he was a Christian," Gaby said.

"*—nevertheless. . . .*"

"There're other things we have to do," Amanda said. "We're tired and there isn't any shovels. . . ."

"Prayer, then," Nolly said. "Unless you are too 'tired'—?"

She stood like a pilgrim in the surf beside the mutilated body and made prayer, from memory, while the others gathered in the sun, in silence, on the sand. After several minutes it appeared the undertow had ebbed, the body was too heavy for the waves to carry back so Nolly nudged it, gently, with her calves, while praying. The other girls stood watch, as if at a wake, except for Sloan who rocked and hugged her knees. Eventually they left, Amanda leading Jane and Oopi toward the ships' stores broken on the beach, while Gaby and Monkey went around the harbor toward the cliff. Sloan stayed where she was, immobile. She had given up her rocking and sat staring at Nolly propelling the torn corpse through its own wake. *They are as a sleep,* Nolly was reciting: *and fade away suddenly like the grass*

GHOSTS

Is it far? Monkey asks.

See for yourself, Gaby says and gestures, but the words come out in Portuguese.

Monkey is used to receiving answers in languages other than English, so for an instant she thinks she has misunderstood, but then Gaby says, *perdi a minha,* so she waits. After a while she asks, Are you afraid?

Sim.

"Does that mean 'yes'?"

"Yes" and "maybe."

"—which?"

Yes.

"So am I."

Both she and Gaby had lost their shoes and the beach was too hot to walk on above the tide. They looked at the rubble they had to traverse to climb to the top of the cliff and they knew that they'd never be able to make it. . . . *achchha,* Monkey murmurs. *Má,* Gaby says. She sits down on the wet sand and removes her blouse: "We'll wrap our feet." She tears it in two with her teeth. "Do you get *muito* red from the sun?"

We get gray.

Gaby stops. *"—you get gray?"*

Like an ash, Monkey says.

"Does it hurt?"

It's like holding your hand to a flame.

"—well *I* never get it."

You don't?

"Grandfather says it's because I have skin of an olive."

—an olive?

"Olivá. . . ."

"—does *that* mean?"

"—olive."

"—but what does *that* mean?"

"—it means 'olive.' "

"Ol-ive?"

"Olive!"

"—what is 'ol-ive'?"

"You don't know what an olive is?"

"No."

"You really don't know what an 'olive' is?"

"No."

"You've never seen an 'olive'?"

"It's a kind of skin?"

"It's a fruit. It's a fruit about *this* size. It's green. Very bitter. It has a big seed in the middle. *It's* green, too. When they press them, they get an oil. . . ."

"Green oil . . . ?"

"Sim."

"I know about green oil. My uncle uses this green oil on his sewing machine."

Monkey watches as Gaby wraps the wet cotton around her feet, then both of them look out to sea a while.

"How long, do you think, till they come?" Monkey wonders.

"They told João they'd be back today. If I had my kite—"

Where is João, do you think? Monkey whispers.

Gaby blinks several times but doesn't answer.

Do you want to know what I'm afraid of? Monkey asks.

"Não."

I'm afraid "today" isn't *today,* Monkey says.

And you know what else? Monkey says after a while.

I think we're dead.

"—stop talking nonsense!" Gaby answers.

It makes sense.

"—I won't listen!"

Charlotte had my hand. All four of us. Charlotte, me, Sloan and Sybil. We went in the water at the same time. Charlotte said, Don't be afraid. I won't let go of you. Then we jumped. You see? *I don't know how to swim.* I don't know how to swim but here I am. And where is Charlotte—?

"—*stop* it, *stop* it, *stop* it!" Gaby yells.

The shout echoes off the cliff and sounds like *its its its,* then continues "ITS—!"

Gaby grabs Monkey's hand. *Olá!* she whispers: *birds?*

"Hell-oooo!" she shouts into the air:

"—ITS!" comes the reply.

Gaby runs up the slope, calling at intervals, while Monkey follows the shore toward the point. The beach is littered in places with masses of jelly, dead fish and dying anemones: it is sticky in places with yellowish slime. All of the flowers have washed away.

As she rounds the point the wind changes and the waves are much higher. The beach on this side is deeper and piled with debris—fallen palms, twisted mangroves, dead storks, bloated fish, a mast, glass, canvas: *and Sybil.*

Gaby sees her from the top of the cliff and runs toward her at the same time as Monkey, but even though Monkey is nearer, her route's the more treacherous: *Charlotte is here* she wants to believe.

Charlotte and John are both here.

She cuts her foot on the coral but doesn't stop running. Her blood leaves a blush on the sand. Sybil is calling *it's over here!* waving her arm, *alive,* Monkey sees, she's alive I'm alive *we're alive* she realizes.

SOME THINGS ARE DIFFERENT, SOME THINGS ARE THE SAME

They carried Sybil between them back to the point, where they were met, on the leeside, by Sloan who runs shouting, "She *heard* us, she *heard* us, what's *happened* to *it—?"*

"Her *leg,* Sybil says. A *tree* landed on him. We *knew* it, Sloan says. We couldn't stand *up.*

"It's broken, we think," Gaby says, not surprised by the fact that she spoke like a twin.

"Amanda found *fooood,"* Sloan announces. "Lots and lots. Jam and chutneys. Fishballs. Tinned pudding, our favorite. . . . "

"Ours too," Sybil agrees.

"What else did we find?" Monkey asks.

"—any *shoes?"* Gaby hopes.

"Any . . . *one?"* Monkey asks.

"Lots of things," Sloan continues. "Lots and lots. . . ."

"—any *water?"* Gaby asks.

"—coconuts. Hundreds of them on the ground. Lots of coconut water inside." She wants to carry her sister herself, on her shoulders, an arrangement which makes them equally happy and makes them appear even more like one person.

"She's too heavy for you," Gaby frets. "don't lose her—"

"—never again!" Sybil promises.

"She's sorry," Sloan says.

"—she's sorry," the other one argues.

"She let go our our hand—"

"—she let go. . . . "

"It was lots of water. . . . "

"—it was a lot of *that."*

"Where did you go—?"

"—under."

"—but how did you come over there?"

"—can't remember."

Was Charlotte with you? Monkey asks.

"Charlotte was talking to us," Sybil remembers. "When she put on our jackets. . . . "

After that, Monkey prompts.

"—they jumped in."

—then? Monkey asks.

"—too much water. They swam."

Who swam?

"Charlotte."

You saw her?

"She held us. She carried us up on the beach. . . . "

Monkey stops.

"Don't *stop—*" Gaby tells her.

We ought to go back there, Monkey offers.

"I want something to eat," Gaby says.

Monkey considers what she ought to do.

Gaby is older than she, the third oldest after Amanda and Nolly. In declension by age Monkey is next after Jane, then the twins, and then Oopi—but Monkey's race nullifies privilege in their view; in her view as well. Hers is the role of submitter, conceding, of seeking permission, of earning their *yes.* Less than a guest at their table, hers is the part of an upstart, the bastard relation. Tacit and sacrosanct, theirs is dominion in which she colludes. To be any way other than that, to rebel, to object, to abjure the text would be outlawed, illegal:

"I'll go by myself, then," she dares.

"You can't," Gaby says, "it's the Law—"

"*—what* law?"

"—the First One, the one about going alone. Come along, *èh?* I can't go back without you—do you want *me* to get into trouble?"

No, Monkey attests. Next to Jane, Gaby's the person she likes best—after Charlotte. Her order of preference is, first, her mother; then Jane; then Charlotte; then Gaby. The rest of the girls don't count, on her list. Each of the girls has a *list,* Monkey hears them ask *who'd you like before me?* She's never been asked and she's never asked Jane. She's afraid of the answer. Today is the first day she hasn't heard two of them talking about it. Today is the first day she almost forgets who she is. Recalling the old world's too mournful if everything's going to be lost in the new.

"—Amanda is calling to us," Gaby urges.

Gaby—? Monkey begs.

"*—quê?* Hurry up—"

Don't you *want* to find Charlotte?

"*—e João, oxalá! Número um* on Grandfather's 'list'! But

what can the two of us do? Suppose we went now and found them. Suppose they were hurt. How could we carry them? What could we do for them? Do we have water? Do we have food? We don't even have shoes—*Não.* There is a right way and there is a wrong way. We must do this the right way. *Sim?*"

Sim, Monkey says, which Gaby accepts as a "yes" even though it is said as a "maybe."

"Bom . . . now, come on. Give me a race—

Gaby—?

"—what *now?"*

"This 'olive'. . . . "

"—yes?"

"It's *this* size? *Very* bitter? Bitter seed inside?"

"Yes, yes—"

"—grows on trees?"

"It does."

"All my life everyone called it 'cardamom.' "

"—it's *not* cardamom."

"—we called it that."

" 'Cardamom' is something else!"

" 'Cardamom' is not the same as 'olive'?"

"Não! Is a *passarinho* the same thing as a *rã?"*

"—a *'rã'?"*

"Bird! Frog! *Same?"*

In *this* language, Monkey thinks, *who knows?* "yes" and "maybe". . . .

"Olà: vamos. Run! I'm giving you the *adiante—"*

—headstart?

"Go! I'm counting to six and then I'm going to beat you—"

Monkey thinks: why *run?* She asks herself Why are you *running,* daughter? What about this foot of yours? What about this pain? *Is Jane watching?* I can win! Gaby runs like wind but I can win! *May* I win? No disgrace in losing by a little. *Should* I win? *Run!* Who are they cheering? *What?* GAby! GAby! GAby! GAby! *Jane is watching—!*

"Why did you slow down?" she wants to know.

"I got tired," Monkey pants.

"No, you didn't," Jane accuses and looks at her like she is going to spit.

"Who'd you like," Monkey blurts out, *"better'n me—?*

E v e r y o n e , Jane pronounces.

RECALLING THE WORLD

Just before evening the butterflies return. The girls were sitting on the sand in a formation they'd devised:

Amanda

Nolly Gaby

Sybil
and
Sloan Jane

Oopi

Monkey

—and Amanda had just said, *We need some kind of signal.*

"I'll build a kite," Gaby answered.

What good will that do us at night? Amanda was asking, when Oopi jumped up and shouted, *"Look everybody! They're back! Like before—!"* and every girl's heart stopped for a minute.

Every girl's eyes searched the lagoon—*Please, Lord, not yet,* Nolly prays: in her soul she believes fervent prayer has rendered them here, that they've been set apart, set down as chosen ones with an as-yet-unrevealed purpose, a mission at hand. It had occurred to her, waking this morning, that perhaps there were Natives here, Beings to whom they'd been sent, *she'd* been sent, to instruct in His Word. Or perhaps there was something among them—some *one* among them—who was being tested by God. If their parents came back now it was the work of the not-God, the devil. She didn't believe there was anysuch being as Devil—her father believed it; she didn't. Devil, to her mind, was the vacuum Christ leaves in an infidel's soul. *Is there an infidel heaven? Yes,* Nolly believes. It burns coal, it is sooty, impoverished. Its streets are unpaved . . . but it's a 'heaven', removed from the World, like this island. If their parents come back now it is the work of the not-God, an interference in something she needs days or perhaps even weeks, even longer, to do. *Stupid!* she shouts at Oopi, who is batting the moths with her arms, "Sit down! Don't frighten us that way!" *"—'frighten'?"* Jane asks.

Monkey likes where she's sitting because she can stare at Jane all she wants and no one can see her. Because of this, she didn't argue with the seating plan of the formation—she might have, otherwise, she tells herself, because they've left her from the circle, like a satellite, but she can watch Jane freely from this vantage so she doesn't mind. Jane looks perfect, Monkey thinks. She's still wearing all her clothes, even her life jacket. Everybody else has either lost her shoes, or her clothing has been torn, or she's discarded it; not Jane—her clothes are tidy and they've dried, salt-stiffened, as if newly pressed. Her hair is tied—as they've sat, talking and deciding on a plan and eating, Jane has plaited and re-plaited her hair in one long ever-more-fastidious braid eight times, pushing the food around on her plate with her fingers from time to time, to make it look as if she's eating. A band of perspiration has blossomed on her lip. "You're the one who 'frightens' people," she says to Nolly, "when you yell at them."

"It's all right," Amanda says. "Ruby jumped up out of order. . . . "

"It's not all right to yell," Jane says. "It's not 'all right' to make a person cry—"

"Oopi is a cry-baby," Nolly says. "Everybody knows it. Shauna always said so."

At the mention of her sister, Oopi quietens.

"I've never seen her cry till now," Jane says. "She hasn't cried all day. She didn't cry the night they killed the turtles—"

"Certain things are 'outlawed' to be said," Amanda states, "and that is one of them. . . . "

"We should make it 'outlawed' if you frighten someone," Jane insists, "If you make the other person cry—"

"Hear! Here!" Sloan and Sybil say: It's the thing they heard the Colonel say a lot and they like it 'cause they get to say the same word twice.

"That's silly," Amanda says. "We have to be careful how we make the Laws and not make silly Laws—"

"We should make a Law that says we can't kill turtles," Sybil says.

"—not kill *anyone,"* Sloan says.

"That's already Law," Nolly reminds them. "It's *God*'s law. We're making laws for just this island. . . . "

"How many have we got—?" Gaby asks. She's been drawing circles in the sand, not paying attention.

"Sixteen," Nolly answers.

"Basta," Gaby complains. "That's two for each of us. Instead of making laws, we should be making maps. We should make an exploration. We should give a name to all these different places—that place on the other side—the cliff—and we should look for things, *á-bê-cê,* there might be other people here, or *trésor—"*

Oopi jumps up and shouts, "NAKEDS!" and everybody laughs—all her life she's thought 'native' is pronounced the same way as the condition of undress: *"Borboleta,* what are *you—?"* Gaby jokes with her.

"Tell them about Charlotte, Sybil," Monkey suddenly demands.

Everybody except Gaby looks at her.

"Would you like to speak among us, Brother Monkey?" Amanda asks.

"I'm not a *boy,"* Monkey mutters.

"O? what *are* you—?"

"Stop it," Gaby says. "We are all here, that's the fact. We are all here as a family. . . . "

"—and *he's* the *brother!"* Sybil giggles.

"Stop—!" Gaby repeats.

"—what *about* Charlotte?" Jane asks.

"Sybil saw her," Monkey says. "Over there, on the other side. Sybil says Charlotte carried her to shore."

"She might 'of dreamed it," Sybil says.

"—there was a lot of *that,"* Sloan says.

"We ought to send explorers," Gaby says: *"irmãozinh portugês. . . . "*

"*She's* not going back there!" Sybil says.

"*—she's* neither!" Sloan upholds.

"—is it *nice?"* Oopi asks and jumps back up. "Is it very *nice,* the other side?"

"—you don't have to stand up when you speak," Amanda tells her. "You're supposed to stay still till 'dismiss' the same as class."

"—is that a Law?" Gaby asks.

"Number Seven," Nolly says.

"—I think we should have *new* laws. We should do what God did," Gaby argues. "We should Name Everything. We should make this map and name things—we should have a name for places—like that beach where we found Sybil—we should call it 'Sybil Beach'—"

"Here! Hear!" she's seconded.

"Maybe we should call it *Charlotte's Beach,"* Jane says.

Sim, Gaby agrees.

"Charlotte already has a *boat* named after her," Oopi argues. "If it's very nice we should name it 'Beach That's Nice.' That's what I think."

"—then what would they call *this* one?" Sybil asks.

" 'Beach Were There Was Food'," Oopi elects.

"—but what about *Charlotte?"* Jane insists.

"Should we *vote?"* Amanda offers.

"—I mean, what about *finding* her?" Jane says.

As they argue, Monkey falls into a kind of dream.

"Without fire there's nothing we can do at night," Amanda is re-stating. "We can't do anything at night until we work out how to make a fire. Help will be here, probably tomorrow—and at least we'll have the moon tonight—otherwise, I know this from the times that I've been sailing with my father, you've no idea how completely dark the night can get—"

Monkey falls into a sort of dream, a dream of darkness, of a world where names of places tell their stories. Perhaps she is recalling an old story that her father used to tell her about . . . where was it? a place he said was named Wide Open near Viewly Hill and Royal Oak and Pity Me. Walbottle, High Spem, Fallowfield . . . he used to read out placenames from the Map of England: Ruffside, Branch End, Hetton le Hole, Esh Winning, Butterknowle—the names, themselves, were foreign sounds suggesting foreign places: sometimes he read her stories of deep woods, impenetrable forests where the trunks of trees were wider than embraces. Of *snow* he read to her—feathers from the sky which turned to drops of water when they touched your skin, he told her. He told her how the leopard got its spots and how the camel got its hump and how the princess Briar Rose was wakened by a kiss, after sleeping for a hundred years. Monkey faintly hears Amanda saying something about *hats,* about how they have to guard their heads from sun or else they'll all end up stark mad and Nolly says they ought to weave umbrellas in the morning from palm leaves and Jane says quietly, "Father calls them 'Sarah Gamps'. . . ."

"—umbrellas?" Nolly asks.

"—guarda-chuvas," Gaby says.

Monkey becomes aware that she's moved closer to the circle and that twilight's closing in. *"Tell a story,"* she demands. She blushes, but it's dark and no one sees her and besides Sybil, Sloan and Oopi all begin to clamor, *Story! story! story!* so Amanda starts, *"At the edge of a great forest there once lived a poor woodcutter and his wife and his two children. . . .* They were very poor and didn't have some food to eat. 'Tomorrow,' the wife said one night when they'd gone hungry the whole day, 'let's take the children into the forest—into the thickest part, into the Lurk of it—and make a fire for them to keep them happy and give them crusts of bread and then let's leave them there. We'll tell them we're going off to cut some wood and we'll be back, but instead we'll leave them there and they'll be lost and never find their way back home and we'll be rid of them.' " She stopped. Birds in the jungle canopy had settled for the night and now the bats were flying overhead. The moon was up and Jane was staring at it, Monkey noticed. "Don't tell this one," Sybil says. "It frightens her."

"Tell 'Little Red Ridinghood,'" Sloan demands, but Amanda chants, *"Nibble nibble little rat, It's my house you're nibbling at—!' "*

"No!" Sloan and Sybil squeal, as they crawl closer to the circle—all the girls do, even Monkey—until most of them are touching one another.

" 'Hansel and Gretel' is too scary," Sybil says.

"Tell 'Little Red Ridinghood,' " Sloan repeats.

" 'Why, Grandmama, what big ears you have!' " Amanda says, and everybody giggles. *" '—what terrible big jaws you have—!' "*

(*Menaka—?* Jane whispers.

Monkey moves a little closer.

The moon is full, Jane says.

Monkey nods agreement.

It wasn't full last night, Jane says. *It wasn't even nearly full.*

It grew, Monkey agrees.

Too fast, Jane says.

It ate a lot of cheese while it was hiding from the sun, Monkey proposes.

Jane shakes her head.

Or else tonight is actually the day after tomorrow, she declares.)

"—but the huntsman was passing by the house at that same moment," Amanda is saying. " 'So I've found you!' he says to the sleeping wolf. 'I've been hunting for you a long time!' Then as he's aiming to shoot the wolf he thinks, 'That's odd . . . I wonder what he's done with the old woman—?' so he takes out his hunting knife and he cuts into the mean wolf's stomach . . . and! . . . he sees a bright red ridinghood so he cuts further and Little Ridinghood herself jumps out and says, 'O! Mister Huntsman! How frightened I was! How dark it was inside the wolf!' Then Grandmother comes out, even though she's been eaten, and she says, 'O! Thank you, Mister Huntsman! You saved us both!' and Little Red Ridinghood says, 'As long as I live, Grandmother, I promise I'll never, never, ever, leave the path and run into the forest by myself again—!' "

"—now tell the one about the Nixie in the Pond—"

"No, tell 'The Devil's Three Golden Hairs'—"

"—no, tell 'Snow White'."

Once upon a time, in the middle of winter, when the snowflakes were falling from the sky like feathers, a queen sat sewing at a window, Amanda starts.

Nolly is watching. *What is the Lesson of the Second Parable of the Lost Sheep?* she is thinking.

Answer.

"God's Joy over one repentant sinner."

What is the Parable of the destroyed Temple?

Answer.

"It is a prophecy of His resurrection on the third day."

What are the Virtues of the Parables of Jesus?

Answer.

"He employed them to teach the Truth."

"He made use of familiar things in telling them."

"He used them in a simple manner."
"They were fresh and new and vigorous. . . ."

(*You can put your head down on my feet,* Jane murmurs.
May I—? Monkey whispers. You won't mind?
—*go ahead.*
Thank you.
Pleasure, Jane recalls.)

FORGET-FULNESS

Somewhere else a man lays dreaming in a world outside his consciousness. The moon shines through this dream, white disk, disguise, an old man in a masquerade, a dog, a devil. *Old dog doesn't know he's dying*—his father would have said. *Try to teach an ancient monkey a new face*—can't be done. Strange words flood back, are left back in the flood. Strange facts: Phoenicians colonize the Rio Tinto, an earthquake ruins Troy in 1275. Words: more words: the names of winds: *shamal,* Haboob, the Bad Sammoun. There are moments, phases, like the faces of the moon, when John knows he's wakened—other moments when he feels himself a captive to these dreams. In those phases of his wakefulness he senses having been somewhere and lost its memory; he senses that he's lost a memory of time but feels no loss, feels no desire, floats, sustains no thought, sinks effortlessly into dreaming. He dreams the Governor of Qusantínan rides out to greet him. He dreams his own father and he are riding zebras through a village built of fishbones where his mother waves at them from high, inside an air balloon, aloft, shouting at them *Numbered! numbered! weighed! divided!* Logarithms: *John,* he dreams his father saying, *Every sailor dreams that death can only catch him on the desert.* What's this sand? The field of consciousness is not so small that it refuses to accept more than a single problem at a time. *John,* he dreams his father saying, *I've been thinking.* Light has got to have a speed. It's obvious. Light travels. People say, "The stars bring tidings of the future," but I'm thinking What we call a star might only be its ghost. At the very moment that we see it, John: it might be *gone.*

BELOW THE HORIZON

Nolly wakes, having dreamed that she is Noah, naming animals.

Animals, all kinds, were filing by, composite things, hybrids, halfcats, wingedtoads, horneddogs, and she was naming them. She was calling them by words she couldn't remember, until two halfboys filed by and she pronounced, "Go forth and be called *the Nigel,*" and she woke.

The sun is up—a few degrees above the horizon.

Nolly walks down to the surf, responding to a call of nature, in accordance to Law Number Eleven. Amanda's mother was compulsive about conditions, everybody knew—she was particularly opposed to Touching Things ever since Amanda's father took up with his Burmese. Amanda's mother acted as if only strict *conditions* in the household could prevent them all from catching something awful and she'd become a one-woman army against contagion. Amanda had inherited her mother's skills—

Law Number Ten. No one is allowed to peepee anywhere but in the ocean.

Law Number Eleven. No one is allowed to pong above low tide.

Law Number Twelve. Everyone will keep her knickers (a) clean; (b) dry.

Number Twelve was impossible for Oopi because she was afraid a crab would take hold of her if she went into the water with her knickers off, and Number Ten and Number Eleven were impossible for Sloan and Sybil because Sloan had to carry Sybil on her shoulders *so how was she supposed to—?*

Already, on this first day since Law-making, Nolly sees the evidence of disobedience. Someone's *pong* is on the beach. Someone else has gone along toward the cliff as far as she can see—there are footprints leading off, another set returning. When she shows these to Amanda, Amanda says, "They're mine."

"You broke the First Law?"

"The Laws weren't made for *me,"* Amanda tells her. "They're for the others. We don't have to go by them, if we don't want to. . . ."

" 'We'—?"

"—the two of us."

Nolly starts to feel the way a person feels when she's failed to recognize the devil.

"I *like* the Laws," she says.

Amanda shrugs. "They're 'Let's Pretend'—father will be back today and I had to think of something that would pass the time and so I did. If you like them, you can keep them," she says merrily. "The only thing we have to do today is wait."

Nolly squints at her.

"Did you actually *see* them?" she asks.

"I thought I saw a ship just before dawn."

"—you went up on the cliff in *dark?"*

"It wasn't dark. There was the moon. It was bright enough to read by. I found a box with three books in it in this stuff. If we had to, we'd get by all right with just the things that we could find in all this stuff. . . ."

As she speaks the others come to sit around her.

"What's its colors for today?" Sybil asks.

"We're not playing 'School,' " Amanda answers.

"—what's its *Word?"*

"R-e-s-c-u-e," someone spells.

They form a line along the sand and stare at the horizon.

Monkey wonders whether Jane will tell her secret, tell Amanda how the moon got fat by eating yesterday.

"I'm bored," Oopi says after a few minutes. She stands up. Her knickers are (a) wet; (b) dirty. Nolly tells her that she's going to get a rash if she continues to break Number Twelve.

"Aren't they going to have some breakfast—?" Sloan complains.

"—yes, yes," Amanda answers absent-mindedly.

"—she's feeling nasty," Sloan observes.

"—she didn't have a nice sleep," Sybil sympathizes.

"We ought to be prepared for when they come," Gaby says. "We ought to show them how we've managed. You ought to let me build a kite to signal."

"—yes, yes, all right: don't bother me, we need to watch. . . ."

"I'll take charge of feeding everybody if you'd like," Nolly proposes.

"Yes . . . go ahead," Amanda says, distracted.

"—and *the kite?"*

"Stupid, where will you find kite string—?" Nolly answers.

"—with permission: *I may look?"*

"Take a partner," Amanda warns.

"Law Number One," Nolly recites.

Gaby chooses Monkey and sets out to explore among the shattered crates and timber for some string.

Nolly takes the others toward the hoard of damaged goods and Jane stays with Amanda, sitting several feet behind her, off to her right side.

They stare, together, at the sun.

Gnats and chigoes pester them—land breeze has receded with the night and the sea breeze hasn't stirred above a whisper yet. "Father says this is the worst time to make landfall," Amanda says. It sounds, to Jane, like an apology. She is feeling heavy, heavier than usual, as if she'd banqueted all night. She tucks her pinafore around her legs because she doesn't like the way they look.

"Did you see the moon last night?" she asks Amanda.

"It was bright enough to read by," Amanda says again.

"It was full," Jane emphasizes.

"—that means it's springtide," Amanda says. "The tide is at its highest." She turns to look at Jane and smiles, proud of her nautical recall, hearing in her own words an authentic imitation of her father.

Jane sees Amanda's eyes glance off her ankles, so she crosses and recrosses them, hiding one first, then the other.

"What I mean is . . ." she begins.

She can't think of any way to say what she suspects to be the truth.

"I don't think they're coming," she admits.

Amanda squints.

"The moon," Jane says. "Last night it should have been *like this. . . .*" She makes an oval with her hands, between her palms. "Do you understand?"

Amanda twitches slightly.

Jane can tell she is about to make Amanda angry because Amanda stares at her the way her father stares at her, as if they wished she would evaporate.

"That wave," Jane plunges on, "it must have been two days ago. It couldn't have been yesterday or else the moon wouldn't be as full. It was *two days ago,* Amanda, and they haven't come."

Amanda turns her head and looks at the horizon.

"You're wrong," she says.

She sounds determined.

"Where are they then?" Jane asks.

Amanda nods in the direction of the open sea as if to indicate the sight of something below the horizon.

"Any moment now," she promises.

She sits, watching, chin on her knees, for half an hour, until Oopi comes with a banana leaf and puts it on her head.

"Hat," she says.

Amanda doesn't seem to hear her. Oopi ties it on her head with a length of slimy seaweed. "Gaby found some spools of string but she won't give me any," she reports. She doesn't like the way the slimy seaweed feels against her skin.

"Sybil says our dads have prob'ly shot some bears. That would be nice. Maybe they shot some tigers, too."

After a while Oopi walks away because Amanda isn't talking to her. She forgets she's not supposed to go off on her own and sets off down the beach to look for treasures and finds shells. When she leans over to collect them, the rim of her banana leaf plays in the surf. There are coral branches loose, a lot of prickly nuisance, and she decides she ought to try to find her shoes. She has no sense of the size the ocean is, nor of how it works. All she cares about is that it's got her shoes. It took both of them at different times and now it would be very nice if she could have them back again, together. Instead the ocean lets her have a metal box, half buried in the sand, which she struggles to dig out with a flat shell. The metal box is square and she hopes there are some sweets and a bottle of cool water in it. She doesn't like the water in the coconuts. She doesn't like the taste of it. She doesn't like the fact it's warm. A cool drink of ordinary water would be very nice right now, she thinks, or some papaya juice with lime in it . . . but the metal box proves disobliging. It won't open. When she shakes it, it rattles on the inside, as if it might have gingercandy in it. Single-mindedly she carries it to Nolly and says, "Open this, I think there's gingercandy in it."

"Where'd you find it?" Nolly asks. She is tearing a large leaf into strips to weave into umbrellas.

Oopi points to where she found the box. "It's mine," she adds. "Open it and I'll give you some of what's inside—"

"—*not* yours, stupid. Have you forgotten how to read? *The Ruby Girl,* it says," Nolly recites.

Oopi stares at the words painted on the box. She realizes it was wrong to bring the box to Nolly. Nolly doesn't like her, for some reason. Nolly's going to walk away and keep her box.

"—hey, come back!" she shouts. "It's mine! Stop, thief—!"

Oopi catches up with her. She doesn't like the look on Gaby's face when Nolly shows the metal box around.

"There's gingercandy on the inside," Oopi volunteers.

"Stop playing games," Nolly demands. "You know what this is. It's from your father's boat. You've seen it lots of times. You know exactly what it has inside it. . . ."

Oopi looks at it and blinks a couple of times.

Ginger she is making herself think but something else is saying *yes the smelly salts the turny kits for when the snakie bites.*

"It's the Nursie," she acknowledges.

"—the *medicine box,* you mean," Nolly tells her.

She puts the box down and steps away from it as if she doesn't like it anymore. Immediately, Oopi sits on it.

"—*still* mine," she says. "I found it."

Gaby says, "It might have washed up on the other side, where we can't see it. *The Ruby Girl,* I mean."

Nolly says, "That makes sense."

"The boys and Mister Fitzgibbon—"

"—yes, they're probably thinking—"

"—that we're—"

"—lost, or something."

"—drowned."

"We ought to go exploring."

"We don't need to ask Amanda."

"—we'll just go."

"—leave the little ones with Jane."

"—no, send Jane and Monkey *that* way and you and I can go around the other side where you found Sybil yesterday."

"—we should take two shadow sticks the same size and keep walking 'til the sun makes shadows *so* long, then we should all turn back so we don't get caught out in the dark. . . ."

"—yes, and then when they come to rescue us we'll all be together—"

"They're not coming," Jane interrupts. "No one's going to

come. Here's the proof, *The Ruby Girl* was wrecked the same way as *The Charlotte.* Everybody's drowned. . . ."

"*We* aren't!" Nolly argues.

"Everybody's drowned," Jane repeats. "*The Ruby Girl. The Cinnabar.* Everybody's drowned, but us."

"Don't say that!" Nolly yells.

"You don't believe me?"

"Never!"

"Watch," Jane says.

She sits down.

A hundred yards in front of her, Amanda sits, immobile, under her banana leaf. The tide comes in around her. Sloan puts Sybil down against a tree. They open a coconut and drink from it and watch.

Gaby goes to find two shadow sticks. When she comes back, Oopi and Nolly have sat down with Jane. A little bit away from them, Monkey's sitting by herself.

"*—anything?*" Gaby asks her.

Monkey shakes her head.

Gaby plants the shadow sticks in sand, looks at the sun, looks at their shadows and says, "*—vamos.* Let's go. . . ."

Monkey shields her eyes, looks up at Gaby.

"—think we'll find something?"

"Sim."

Monkey stands.

"Can you make fire?" she asks, as she shakes the sand from her.

"Out of nothing? *Não.* Nobody can. . . ."

". . . have you ever seen a dead?"

"Pessoa?"

"—does that mean 'person'—?"

"—yes. The answer's *'não,'* except for him that drowned man, Pandi, yesterday. Have you?"

"—yes."

". . . and also once I saw a dead shark."

"It's not the same."

"—I didn't think so. Still, it was very big. . . ."

"—which way are we going?"

"—that way," Gaby says, pointing toward the cliff. "—go and look for Charlotte. . . ."

As they pass the others, only Jane looks up but even she seems not to see them.

"—you want to be blind?" Gaby shouts. "Stop looking at the sun—*what for?"*

"They can't hear you," Monkey says.

"—crazy in the heads—!"

". . . what are they watching for—?" Monkey marvels walking backwards, watching them.

Gaby finds a piece of flotsam from *The Charlotte* and hurls it back into the surf.

". . . Deus," she swears.

DISCOVERY They walked until the shadow was as long as Gaby's forearm and the sun was sitting on their shoulders.

Gaby's feet were scored with wrinkles from the tidal rills; Monkey's feet were blistered. They had walked along a violent beach, holding to the high-tide line, chilling to the surf's spume as it fell across their sunburned shoulders. They saw crabs, and lizards. They were pursued by gannets feasting on remains of fish, they were annoyed by silver fleas.

In the distance a navy blue hallucination shimmered. They were always moving toward it, never getting any nearer.

This was the harder of the two sides of the island that they knew. The waves were thunderous and cruel. To speak, they had to shout above the din of a hundred million churning tonnes of sand and water. Anything that washed up on this shore would wash back out again, the sea was that voracious.

Monkey felt as though she'd lost her hearing.

It seemed hours since they'd passed the place where they'd found Sybil and still the shore stretched, barren, straight, unbroken. She had no sense at all that they were turning 'round a circle. She couldn't see the cliff behind them.

To their right the forest made a wall, behind which seemed to loom a welcome silence. Birds flew in and out of it, green parrots, soundless on the wing, because all other sound was drowned, as well, by this uncompromising sea.

The sight of birds delighted Gaby.

"If you could ask for one thing different," she calls to Monkey, "what would it be—?"

". . . about all this, you mean—?"

"—não não, about yourself. About your person."

"—my *pessoa?"*

"—sim."

Monkey doesn't hesitate before she answers, "—skin!"

"—what's the matter with it?"

"I'd rather have your kind. 'Olive.' "

"—eỳ! They call mine 'dark.' You should ask for skin like Nolly's, white as wheat. Skin like Sloan's and Sybil's. . . ."

"Jane has nice skin, don't you think—?"

"—for me, I'd like to fly."

"—wings, you mean?"

"Não, same flapping arms—"

She runs ahead and flaps her arms and tries to jump into the sky.

"Angels fly. You should ask to be an *angel—"*

"God make me an angel!" Gaby shouts.

Monkey holds the shadow stick as if it were a wand and waves it in a circle, joining Gaby in her chant,

God make me an angel . . .
angel . . .
God make me an angel, please—

Gaby twirls around and Monkey tries to dance with her, but her head begins to swim.

When they see what they both see they stop dead-still and take the other's hand.

"Deus," Gaby breathes.

She doesn't move.

"—está morto?"

Monkey shivers.

"—go see," Gaby whispers and gives the younger girl a shove.

Monkey inches forward. The flies are black over his buttocks, teeming at his anus. Sand and dried blood mask his legs, his back, his shoulders and his hair. His arms are pinned beneath his body. His head is turned to one side, buried slightly in the sand—the eye that she can see is swollen shut and worms have lodged under its lid.

Monkey doesn't recognize him.

As fearful as she is that he is dead, her greater fear is that he's still alive, and she's afraid to touch him.

Cautiously, from several feet away, she extends the shadow stick and prods his foot.

The flies stir like pollen in a breeze, and then resettle.

"éh?" Gaby calls. *"Está vivo, sim ou não?"*

"Sim."

"—vivo?"

"Maybe."

Going closer, Monkey kneels beside him. His skin is like a lizard's—bubbly, cracked, encrusted. Even his hair has formed a shell, a sandy crust. She touches it. Beneath its hoar she sees its color and a wave of recognition overwhelms her.

"Quem é—?" Gaby calls. "Who *is?"*

Monkey puts her finger on his neck where she believes there ought to be a pulse but she feels nothing. She lays her open hand along his neck but still feels nothing. In a rising panic she touches him with both her hands, searching for his arms, his wrists, searching for a heartbeat in his chest, searching him all over, until in desperation she puts her head down on his back and holds her breath and listens.

Gaby has come up behind her and is murmuring, ". . . *São Cristo e Maria—"*

"—quiet!" Monkey whispers.

Gaby sinks down next to her and begs, *"—não, por favor . . . não é possivel . . . não é João. . . ."*

"—listen!—hear?—Can you hear it?"

They put their heads together, foreheads touching, on his back and listen.

Gaby begins to push at him. *"João! João!"* she shouts. "—wake up!" She tries to roll him over, but he doesn't move. Together she and Monkey push against him, but there's no response. Gaby digs into the sand with her scarred knees and throws her whole weight into rolling him and there emerges the most dreadful sound of agony from him that either girl has ever heard, and they fall back, awestruck.

"—what's the matter with him?" Monkey whispers.

Gaby hugs herself.

When he makes no other sound for several minutes, Monkey crawls to him and tries to lift his head, but can't. Gaby starts to dig away the sand around his face and together she and Monkey free his features. Both his eyes are closed. The half of his face which has been buried in the sand is a different color than the half which has been pestered by mosquitoes, exposed to sun. His lips are morbid; yellow.

Monkey puts her hip beneath his head and starts to groom him, carefully removing every grain, each scale of crust.

"—what should we do?" she asks.

Gaby's sitting on her haunches, waving flies away from sores along his back.

"I'm thinking," she replies.

It's as if John's body fell from heaven instead of having been tossed up by the ocean—there is nothing else around, no evidence of all the others, no glass, no wood along this part of the beach, no remnants of *The Ruby Girl.*

"I don't understand this *oceano,"* Gaby says.

She stares down the beach toward the never-any-nearer shimmering hallucination.

"How did he get here?" she asks.

"—so far away from all the others," Monkey says.

"—what *others?"* Gaby asks. "Where are *they?"*

". . . perhaps if we kept going—"

Gaby plants the shadow stick in sand.

"Can't," she says emphatically.

The shadow is as long as her entire arm.

"—time to go back," she states.

"And leave him here—?"

"—can't move him."

"But what if—?"

"—can't lift him, *by ourselves."*

Monkey pauses with a grain of sand she's lifted from John's eyelashes between her fingers.

"One of us should go for help," Gaby states. "We'll have to make some kind of carry—like *um palanquim.* A litter."

"—which one of us is going to go?" Monkey asks, trying to believe she doesn't know the answer.

"Me."

Monkey squeezes on a single grain of sand until it hurts her.

"When will you be back?" she asks.

"Tomorrow. We can't travel in the dark."

"—but *there'll be the moon."*

Gaby funnels sand from one hand to the other.

"—I'll want a *sesta."*

"—'sesta'?"

"—sesta, sesta, I'll be tired—"

"I'll be scared."

"—you'll be *brava."*

When Monkey doesn't answer, Gaby says, "I'll leave the stick for you."

"—how will that help?—what good will it do me?"

"—keep you company."

"—so it talks? I haven't heard it talking. Can it feed me?"

"—tells the time."

"At night—?"

"—in day."

"I'm not frightened in the day."

"You'll be all right . . ."

Gaby stands.

"What will I eat?" Monkey demands.

Gaby goes to find some fruit for her and Monkey tries to think of some way to stop Gaby leaving.

"It might rain," she says when Gaby comes back with a jackfruit, some bananas, a liana from a climbing rattan and a handful of red fruits the size of cherries.

"There were no coco's," she explains.

"—I said, *'it might rain.'* "

"It won't."

"—what am I supposed to drink, then, if there aren't any coconuts?"

Gaby lifts the tip of the rattan liana and nips it with her teeth. A thin, clear liquid runs from it.

"—is it water?" Monkey asks.

"—better . . ."

Gaby aims the flow toward Monkey's tongue.

Monkey drinks, then gags.

"—bad medicine!"

"Try to put some into João, when you think you can," Gaby advises.

"What are these—?" Monkey asks, holding the red fruits.

"—they seem all right."

"Have you eaten any?"

"—they're all right."

"I don't think I'll eat them."

"This is all there was—"

"—bring me something nice when you come back."

"—a cake!"

". . . some shoes."

". . . *adeus!* I'll hurry—"

"—don't go yet! When will you be back? What time? How long a shadow—?"

"—early!"

She is walking backwards, moving off.

"—two hours, only, after dawn! Try counting to *cin-*

quenta mil . . . um . . . dois . . . tres . . . quatro . . . cinco . . . seis . . ."

She flies.

Monkey stands up, shades her eyes and watches.

Gaby runs before her own dark shadow. Every now and then she flaps her arms. Monkey thinks she hears an echo . . . *doze! treze! vinte!*

Gaby shrinks from sight into the light, the white sky opens and she sinks in it.

Monkey sits back down.

For a minute after Gaby's gone Monkey thinks she sees her shadow, flapping cormorant, stretching, racing, taking off. Then poof! as soon as it is gone the beach, the world, becomes a place entirely motherless. No love, no providence, no pity—a place entirely dangerous. Monkey owns no power to prevent the worst from happening. She has no god nor any parent who can intercede in her behalf. *What could happen?—end of world?* she asks herself. It was the End already, yesterday, two days ago, three days, however long ago it was when she was thrown into the water. Surely that was worse than anything that Death could be. She wonders where her mother is, what Ammi is doing, where she thinks her little flower is, and she grows deeply sad. She misses everything; the world. This is *not* the world, this beach, this water thunder, ants, the heat, the gnats, the shelterlessness, arbitrariness, unmanageable extreme of it. What is the reason for it? Monkey wonders, what are these birds complaining for, running up then down then back up again, trailing the surf? Why do they exhaust themselves? Why not hold still, sit and wait—?

She knew the sun would fall into the ocean where she sat. She could sense the land behind her, sense the island as a mass for the first time, as the light faded.

Please, wake up, she prayed.

She rocked back and forth and the first star came out.

She moved closer to John, lifting his head into her lap again and worked her fingers, cleaning, through his hair. Behind her, the moon rose.

Wake up, she whispered.

Please?

She shivered as the sun dropped and the dark descended.

"I'm frightened," she told John.

She imagined what he answered was drowned out by the roar of lions, boom of monsters—by the sea. She imagined what he said was, Your father told you to be brave before he left. Didn't he tell you to take care of Ammi for him? Think of all those nights when she had no one to watch over her except you, Menaka—

"It's true," she says out loud. "I *am* brave."

She imagines John tells her there is nothing to be afraid of here, on this beach, this part of the island. He'd been here several nights and nothing had endangered him—only the sea, by swallowing him. No monsters would emerge from behind them in the jungly forest, she imagined he assures her, no demons would swoop down on them from the sky. Because she couldn't really hear him over the din, their conversation sounded in her mind the way her conversations with her father do and so it didn't seem that strange when she heard her father scolding her. He was *very disappointed,* he was saying—What was she doing here, in this place, Re-mote god-knows-how-many-thousand-miles away from Ammi? All he ever asked her to do was to take care of her mother, watch over the most beautiful of women. Now she had made that most beautiful woman most bereft—how could she have done it? of what had she been thinking?—why was she so wayward, so perverse, so bad?—why was she unworthy of anybody's trust, of everybody's love—?

Monkey starts to cry.

It is a cry arising from a soulfelt desolation, a cry that cracks the heart. Competing with the ocean she can hardly hear the sound of her own anguish, but her body cramps with sobbing, she can't catch her breath. A misery made more profound because of its small depth, its youth, afflicts her. *Let me die,* she thinks, knowing all there is to know of death but almost nothing, a first flicker, of existence. She weeps unlike an infant—a baby cannot mourn. She weeps, instead, the grief of nine-year-olds, the sadness of a broken promise and the sorrow that moves in when something that one loves has gone away.

She falls asleep eventually.

Eventually, her weeping quietens, becomes the descant to her breathing and she sleeps, a dreamless sleep, a spent one, her head dropping to her chest, her arms resting, listlessly, around John's shoulders. Occasionally she stirs, almost waking to the shivers of her few remaining sobs. Once she wakes to move her legs and stretch herself around John's body. Time, she feels, is passing, though she doesn't dream. She feels John's breathing. When she wakes again she has to touch her lips, her eyes, to see if she is crying.

Someone's crying.

Someone's crying and it isn't her.

Monkey is afraid to lift her head from John, to sit up, turn in the direction of the weeping. Its sound weaves in and out through the crescendo decrescendo of the waves. The weeping is a girl, or it's a woman, Monkey thinks, and suddenly she's seized with the suspicion that the weeping is her mother's and she bolts up, half-suspecting to be greeted by those long lamenting arms but what she sees is a pale dog, the ghost of a hyena, digging for its bones, scrabbling insanely on the moonlit sand.

It stands.

Monkey claps her hand over her mouth to keep her terror from escaping. If the thing should start to make its awful way toward her she doesn't know what she will do. *Run* she suspects, leaving John . . . she searches for the shadow stick, but can't find it. She doesn't want the thing to see her so she holds still, hoping that the stillness will conceal their bodies, knowing that it can't. If the thing turns 'round and sees them, they are finished, Monkey knows.

It turns 'round.

Monkey watches, terrified, as it turns, caught in a rotating madness like a mayfly on a web. Its arms tear at the air as if night were a hanging curtain. It emits a heartrending cry of torment and despair, then runs, half-bent and stumbling, through the undergrowth into the wood.

I've seen a ghost, Monkey consoles herself.

The moon has swung around in front of her but she sits facing away from it, her back to the ocean, watching the black wall of trees. From time to time she strokes John's back as if to certify his substance. "It was a ghost," she tells him. "Did you see it?"

Yes, she imagines that she hears him answer, *yes*—I saw it, but we're safe, it won't come back.

"—you're sure?"

I promise.

"—that it's gone?"

For good.

"—how do you know?"

Because *we* saw *it* . . . but *it* could not see *us.*

SANDPRINTS

The sun came up and Monkey counted to three thousand without stopping. John hadn't moved all night although he'd urinated, Monkey smelled it.

The birds returned with daylight—pelicans flew overhead, and along the tideline scavengers on high thin legs ran behind the surf and pulled their breakfast from the dark wet sand.

Monkey was hungry.

She didn't like the taste of uncooked jackfruit and the bananas that she had were green. As a last resort she ate two of the red fruits and very quickly she regretted it. The pain was so bad she could not stand up to walk down to the water so she crawled. Lying on the water's edge in agony she found a periwinkle so she pryed it loose and ate it.

When she was able to stand up again she realized the sun had travelled a great distance. Several hours had gone by. She tried to drink from the liana and this time its salty taste refreshed her. She turned John's head and dropped some liquid on his lips but he didn't move and all it did was draw more flies. Monkey tried to keep as many as she could away from him—it became an occupation. Hours passed, or minutes, hours, morelike—still they didn't come. She waited, and then, casually, a moment came when she was finished waiting. She stood up. Without a plan, she started walking. Without thinking about anything, she laid John's head down in the sand, whispered *wait here,* and started walking toward that point where she remembered Gaby disappearing.

The sun was very hot. She could feel it like a whip across her shoulders. Hot and bright—it blinded her. She lost sight of the horizon, of the sky, the forest. The sand was hotter than the sun. She kept within the tidal reach, on wet, and all that she could focus on were her own footsteps, one after the other. She began to count and lost count several times. Each time she lost count, she forgot that she'd forgotten—she slipped into a state of boundarylessness, a place too bright, where everything except her footsteps was a single swimming brightness, a place where everything was indistinct and counting had no purpose. She didn't know if she was walking in her sleep or slowly nodding off. She didn't know how far she'd walked or if she'd walked at all. Her feet were moving, making indentations in the sand, but she wasn't sure she was connected to them. Her thoughts were disconnected—in this floating world, everything was floaty, riding high, spumy and ephemeral, and through it there emerged a distant error, smudge, a dark fleck in the hyalin, a spider on the glass, tarantula, an ambulating armour-plate advancing on black legs.

Monkey stopped and watched the black thing moving toward her. First it was an insect, then an army, then a troupe of ragged girls. They marched in syncopated disarray, led by what seemed to be their captain, a tall girl bound in dirty cloth, decorated with broad leaves, who carried something like a parasol of woven palm fronds balanced on bamboo sticks to protect her from the sun. They advanced in silence. When they reached her the girl in front signaled to halt and stepped, alone, toward Monkey. She had black oily lines smeared underneath her eyes. She moved her mouth as if to talk, but Monkey couldn't hear what she was saying. It seemed like waiting for a sound of words to be produced between the pincers of a crab claw.

Stupid! What are you doing—? it demanded.

Monkey smelled its breath, sweet sticky smell.

She blinked.

All around the edges things were swimming, growing dark.

The next thing that she knew she was sitting in the sand, held by Gaby, in the shade of Nolly's parasol, and Jane was staring at her.

". . . hunger," Jane was saying. "Drink this," she instructed. She passed Monkey a tapped green coconut and Monkey drank from it, then retched. Sloan took her hand and patted it. "It's not nice," she said. There were red welts on her cheeks and forehead—raised weals, like whipcords, wound over her shoulders, down her back and chest where she'd been stung by bees. Over these, streaky with her perspiration, Sloan had smeared the same black oily substance Nolly used as salve beneath her eyes. It had a pungent smell, like rotting fish, and flies were buzzing at it. Sloan's scalp was covered with it, too, her whiteblond hair escaping from it like a shock of ermine. "They didn't come," she said. She looked sadly serious. "The boats," she added. Monkey tried to think about the meaning of Sloan's words. "So now we've come for Captain John," Sloan said, "to help us."

"—we're doing fine all by ourselves," Nolly insisted. She put her face up close to Monkey's. "Where is he, anyway? Has he disappeared?"

Monkey looked around her.

"—John?" she asked.

"O Capitão—"

"Is he still alive?" Nolly demanded.

"John . . . " Monkey repeated.

She focused on Jane's face.

Of all of them, Jane seemed the most the same. Her dark long hair was neat and tied. She wore no paint, no decoration. Her nose and cheeks were sunburned, but she still retained her skirt and blouse and pinafore. Her eyes seemed slightly duller and a crease of disappointment, of a certain sternness, was engraved around her mouth.

"There was a ghost," Monkey began, but Jane stopped her with a look that bore no sympathy.

"Stop talking rubbish," she commanded. "If we can't find help, we're going to die."

"—we're not!" Nolly argued, shouting. She planted both her feet more firmly in the sand. "We're doing fine on our own except for you and all your mewling, Miss Suspicious, Miss Judith Iscariot—"

"How are we doing 'fine?' " Jane answered, rising to her feet, *"—how?* Do we have fire?—water?—shelter? Look at Sloan—look at you! Fishguts on your face—!"

"Shut up!" Gaby yelled. "You frighten all the rest—you make the little ones go off their heads—!"

"—little ones? How about Amanda? *I'm* the reason she's gone bonkers?"

"—if you had more *faith,* Jane," Nolly told her.

"—in what?"

"In *Whom,"* Nolly corrected.

"I'll believe in what the Captain says," Jane said. "I trust *him.* I'll believe what John says. John will save us—"

For the first time, Monkey noticed the large canvas, remnant of a sail, that Jane and Sloan hauled between them. "What's that?" she asked.

" 'The Carry,' " Gaby answered.

"—drag," Sloan explained.

"How far is he?" Nolly asked.

Monkey shook her head.

"—don't know," she testified.

"Stupid!" Nolly shouted.

"—you didn't come," Monkey argued to Gaby, "and I waited—"

"We had to make a *Plan,*" Gaby answered. She gestured with her head towards Nolly, "and it wasn't easy," she explained.

"—don't *you* remember where he was?" Nolly goaded her.

Gaby stood and looked forlornly down the beach.

"—can't see him," she admitted. "It might be half a mile, a mile from here, it's hard to say, there are no landmarks . . ."

"—it's *far,*" Monkey attested.

"You were stupid to have left him," Nolly said.

She started walking.

When she was several yards away she turned around and shouted, *"—coming?,"* and Sloan helped Monkey stand. "Is it *very* far?" she asked.

"I can't remember."

"It seems *very* far already . . . "

"Is it true, they haven't come?"

"Amanda says they'll come today."

Sloan slipped her fingers around Monkey's.

"She says that *every* day," she added solemnly.

They walked in single file about a quarter of a mile along the beach in silence until Gaby called attention to his figure high above the tideline on the sand.

"He moved," Monkey whispered.

She held Gaby's arm and blinked and tried to gather in a picture in her memory.

"We weren't so high up," she maintained.

"—who cares?" Gaby said and broke into a run.

They all reached him within seconds of each other, Sloan and Monkey coming last.

Because they hadn't seen him like this, Jane and Nolly turned their heads away and Sloan began to whimper but Gaby fell onto her wounded knees and crawled toward him, in fear.

"—I told you!" Monkey said beside her in the sand.

They were afraid to go too near, afraid to touch the sandprints until finally Gaby held her hand above one, as a test, and tried to fit her fingers to it, afraid, as if the image of a hand might hurt her. *"—É sua?"* she asked Monkey, "—Are they yours? Did you do this—?"

To demonstrate her answer, Monkey placed her foot inside a footprint.

"—eỳ!" Gaby howled.

John's body had been dragged with what appeared to be a labor up the beach, forty feet, toward the jungle. He'd been left there, on his back, his legs drawn out, his arms crossed on his chest, as if he had been coffined. All around his body the sand had been trampled and disturbed as if someone had rolled around in violent throes against him. His head was turned to one side and his eyes were closed.

"—is he dead?" Jane whispered.

Gaby pointed to the human footprints leading from John's body toward the jungle.

"Não é a sua alma fazendo uma volta . . . "

"—speak English, for God's sake—!"

Gaby took her time before she said, "It is not his *soul* that walked away from here . . . "

"So he's alive?" Nolly persisted. She could not conceal her disappointment.

Gaby looked at her.

She took the sail from Sloan and with Jane's and Monkey's help she began to make a sling around the body to transport him.

"Viva o capitão," she whispered with a kind of vehemence: *"Viva nosso João. . . ."*

JOHN He remembered Charlotte.

Maybe he was dreaming—he *was* dreaming—there she was as though they'd never parted, her voice, her touch, especially her touch. He'd waited all his life, he'd told her once—and she had laughed. Chance, the random circumstance, *she* did not believe there was one man, one preordained above, one love, for every woman. She did not believe John was the better of her two loves—his was a *different* love, she said. John had startled her. *No love is different,* he had said. All love's the same. There's better love, or worse. A man can want two women at a time, but one is better, one is worse. A man can love two women at a time, but only one refuses subjugation to the other. She'd always found his way of speaking about love unsentimental. He'd always spoken about love as though he thought it ought to be heroic—a transcendence over odds, over mortality, the ordinary. He had known a lot of women. What marked women out for him, he said, was quickness—quickness of eye, her mind, her spirit. *Touch:* he had never had a woman touch him with the calm that Charlotte had—it was almost a redemption, almost healing. She had warmth, a heat, a steadiness that he construed as a conviction, never understanding that her calm was an exposure of turned earth, a surface burial, a steady dead accreted skin of sadness, interred passion. He expected women to be nervous, quirky, exercising fluttery, flirtatious touch—he had never known a touch like Charlotte's, all-encompassing, compassionate yet startling. She was like the sea itself, an even wash across his senses, sometimes merciful, expansive, never calculating, often violent, never still. Hers was the touch of shoals and rills, a touch known only at the depth of nature where the surface of all things combines with slippery ease, seeming to be seamless. *Je te suis* she said as she embraced him, I am you, I *am* you, I am *you.* Laughing with her, loving her as he had never loved he slowly surfaced from his dreaming to be welcomed by the touch he recognized as hers. Searching, as a dreamer searches, in anticipation of the sight of her, he first saw the sky, his dream still playing out across its blue. Sand, imbued with diamond cutting edges, stars, took shape—suns, the planets, eight of them, tiny blonde bright mercury with her twin the morning and the evening venus . . . ruby mars . . . the mighty jupiter, dark craters 'round her eyes . . . ringed saturn, dark uranus, swimming 'round him in and out of mists, their eyes, their faces, eight of them, eight goddesses, impassive, staring not at him but at the serpent, their eyes fixed on the snake as they ringed 'round him, he, the sun, their manner reverent and vigilant, as if they waited for some miracle to be revealed. First one reached out and touched it with a stick and then another touched it. Waking from a foreign world John watched the serpent raise itself. His arms were held, but he could lift his head. Not knowing that his spine was broken, he woke to a pure wonder, same as they, pure wonder and amazement—and to terror unlike anything they knew, as, without a shiver of sensation, he observed with them, omnipotently and removed, the serpent's spew, his sperm, his climax, what the snake was saying, his own magnificent detached ejaculation.

4

JOHN DOLLAR

APOTHEOSIS

There was time but not a thing by which to tell it, save the passage of the sun and the phases of the moon.

John's whiskers grew.

For what might have been a week after they brought him from the *wildibeach* back to what they now called *home,* they did little else by day but look at him. For the first two days they sat around him in a circle, watching, as he slept. It was peculiar sleep—even Sloan and Sybil, even Oopi, knew it was peculiar for a man to sleep so much. He rarely moved. His wounds were bloodblack but not crusted, some of them were scaly with whitefly and fungus, others oozed, bubbly suppurations like the signatures of slugs. The flies were fervid on him, drawn by pus and blood and by his rank septicity. He stank. By rotation, four of them with leaves as switches, kept the flies and ants off him, but in the night, without fire, under the waning moon, there was little they could do except try to keep mosquitoes and the shadowy night vermin from him.

On the third day they resolved they ought to wash him.

Wisdom came to them like dreams from which they woke recalling only parts. Like a dream, the wisdom they retrieved seemed hauntingly segmental. Things they would recall seemed sensible but only in another world. Laws of nature, laws of grammar, parliamentary laws could not apply to what they found to be an alien and purposeless reality. Even their own Laws had been forgotten or discarded, dying, like an ancient language, from disuse. Occasionally one of them would wake from the communal lethargy that had moved in like a muffling fog around them and say something on the order of, *if we found the North Star then we'd know which way is North.* The lethargy that settled on them drugged them like the loss of hope, or like the tiredness that overcomes starvation victims. They fed themselves but didn't hunt for food. When something fell, banana, *coco,* fruit, they ate it. When they were thirsty they might rouse themselves to search for *cocos* or lianas but they satisfied their thirst *in situ,* never thinking to take *home* reserves. They were frightened of the jungle at their backs and so at night they huddled close to one another, sleeping in the pattern they'd adopted from the start, an intimate proximity, abreast and juxtaposed. All their searches were by daylight. They had yet to go afield by any other route except the one that wound around the cliff which they had named *the oont,* because it looked a little like a camel. Of what lay the other way they had no conception other than the dull suspicion that the shore was all the same, back and front, like lace around a dressing gown. At night they heard what Nolly said were monkey armies making war in the interior—hooting, laughing, screaming, grunting—nightly they waged tribal battles against silence. "Maybe they're telling monkey stories," Gaby said one night, waking to the wisdom with a start. Their own stories had grown lengthy—or maybe they were telling them more slowly, pausing longer between words, pausing longer in their search for them. Amanda had begun to suck her thumb. Since the first long day she'd waited for her parents to return, she hadn't spoken, hadn't said a word to anyone, as if her contract with the world had then and there been broken. Even when the young ones begged her to tell stories she remained unmoved and mute. She had been their Storyteller—the best one. Nolly told them parables of Jesus, which they didn't like as much. There were too few girls in them, in fact none, and not nearly a sufficient range of animals or spooky bits, plus Jesus spoke, in Nolly's version, with *haths* and *ye!*s and *lo!*s and *sayeths.* Gaby told good stories but they didn't have good endings and Jane told stories that got off to well told starts but ended in their middles. Without Amanda there were no good stories to be learned and they'd forgotten, in their lethargy, the myths they'd known before, forgotten Nyx, goddess of Night, forgotten stories of the eight daughters of Chaos, of Prometheus. Monkey knew no less than a hundred and one stories but she was afraid to speak them, wary of the others' ridicule. The stories that she knew had been told to her by Ammi. They differed in a lot of ways from the stories that the others told, from the stories that the others liked to hear, so she was shy to tell them. They differed in their names for one thing—her stories were about Doda and Dodi and King Ram and the goddess Parvati, forever intervening on the side of Women. Hers were stories about terrible mothers-in-law and children whose souls were held captive in mango trees and gods who were both men and beasts. She knew the stories of Ghanim Bin Ayyub, the Distraught, the Thrall o' Love and the "Tale of the Rogueries of Dalilah the Crafty and her Daughter Zaynab." The stories that she knew were less like stories that the english knew and more like lengthy stratagems exaggerated to fantastic lengths. In her stories, like the stories that Amanda told, there was greed and there were orphans, there were poor abandoned girls of rare outstanding beauty of both face and form who come to the attention of a stalwart prince—but instead of witches there were djinns, instead of wizards there were gods, and no one, not one person, ever ended in another being's stomach. She would have liked to tell her stories, if for no other reason than to exercise them, to help her not forget them, perhaps, even, to help her cry. None of them had cried for days. The lethargy that held them stopped them doing even that. They didn't weep, didn't explore, did not consider the enormous peril of their desperate condition. Rather, they acted as a group, as if something would be revealed, some message, wisdom, some solution from another source would be delivered to them. John would speak. Occasionally, one of them would shake herself to voice some half-wise thought such as, *if we could find a compass then we wouldn't have to find the North Star to tell which way is North*—but such thoughts were not the answers they were waiting for. Having agreed that they should bathe him, they were stymied by the task of doing it without fresh water.

"I don't think water from the ocean would be bad," Jane said.

"—sal," Gaby reminded her: "the salt!"

" . . . is that *bad—?"*

"In *wounds—eý!"*

"What about rubbing him with fruit?"

"—moscas."

"—what?"

"Flies!"

"I mean it would help him smell a whole lot better. . . ."

"—it *does* smell. . . ."

"My ayah used to rub her skin with lemons . . ."

"—mother used to bathe in milk. I never saw her do it, actually. . . ."

"We need to do it *right,"* Nolly insisted. "We need to do it like a kind of baptism, you know—not just wash him. . . ."

"—we need to make him *smell* good."

"—make him beau-ti-ful. . . ."

"Não. We need to clean these cuts. The way *un médico* would do. *Contra o infecçaão. . . ."*

Nolly stood up. " 'I need baptize you with water unto repentance,' " she recited. She was speaking in her Jesus voice and holding out her arms as if she were a *dhobi* with a load of linen. ". . . But he that cometh after me is mightier than I, . . ." she said, " 'whose shoes I am not worthy to bear: and he shall baptize you with the Holy Ghost and with fire—!' "

"—we don't *have* fire, Nolly, so—?"

"Eý—we don't have *shoes . . .!"*

" 'And *lo!* he saw the heavens open and the Spirit like a dove descending, And there came a voice from heaven saying, This is my beloved Son, in whom I am well pleased. . . .' "

They looked at John.

"—we don't think we *want* to baptize it," Sybil stated.

"—just bandage it up," Sloan said.

"There's dressings in the 'Nursie,' " Oopi said, to her own and everybody else's awe.

They turned, as one, toward the scattered stockpile of supplies along the beach which they had picked through, haphazardly, from time to time, in search of biscuits, sweets, a length of string. "What did we *do* with that red medicine box—?" Jane asked vaguely. The question struck a chord in Nolly and she said, " *'Question.* What is Christ's First Miracle?' "

She pointed to a battered cask, lying on its side between the tideline and the jungle.

" *'Answer,'* " she recited. " *'Christ turneth water into wine.'* "

Everybody looked at her, except Amanda.

" *'And when they wanted wine,'* " Nolly recited, " *'the mother of Jesus saith unto him, They have no wine'. . . .*"

"—what do we want *wine* for?" Oopi asked.

"—água!" Gaby said. She scrambled to her feet. *"Água de banho—por lavar!"* She clapped Nolly on her shoulders. *"—um milagre . . .* miracle!" she cried. *"O vinho* into *água . . . Bem!* You are *um génio,* a genius—!"

Nolly stared at her. No one had ever called the Savior

"genius," she was thinking, it was not a word that fit religion.

Among the things they found when they went looking galvanized by Purpose, were: a sodden rug, three umbrella handles, nine umbrella spokes, a tea kettle without a lid, the MEDICINE BOX, five silver forks, a tin of Swedish meatballs, half a bed, string, TIMBER, a tripod, poles, a hatchet, ROPE, a knife, three books, a COMPASS, broken glass, five sealed chests of linen, CANDLES, several dozen black metal rectangular objects, WINE, a flag, two chests of broken "Hyde Park" china, and a finger.

In the chests of linen they found sheets to wrap him and the cloths with which to sponge him.

The wine had turned to vinegar, which made them think that it would act more like a medicine, because of its aroma.

In a separate chest, the size of a valise, engraved with the initials E. A. S., they found items of a gentlemen's toilet—a small leather box of pearl and onyx studs and collar stays, bootblack, chased-silver brushes, gold tweezers, a razor strop, a bar of wax, shaving soap, a shaving brush, scalp oil, a gold toothpick, tooth-powder, a toothbrush, talcum, liniment, Macassar oil, toilet water, a corset, a gold sovereign, a postcard of a naked woman (front) and a naked adolescent (back), a mustache comb, silver scissors and—most startling and beautiful of all—a hinged, ivory-handled razor.

"—gorblimey," Oopi said.

"—aren't they pretty?" Sloan and Sybil whispered, afraid to touch their dirty fingers to the cut glass, silver and soft brushes.

"It's Mister Sutcliffe's," Jane said, reading, "E.A.S. . . ."

"—hé! Amanda, it's your dad's—"

"—shh! Don't tell her. . . ."

"It's your dad's stuff, Amanda—look!"

Amanda took her thumb from her mouth and sat down on the sand. She stared at the contents of the box a minute and a change came over her. She looked like she was going to speak, but then she didn't. She picked up the razor and held it, hinged under her right jaw, while she stuck her thumb back in her mouth and closed her eyes.

The medicine box was locked—secured with a padlock the size of Oopi's fist, but the welding of the hasp had been weakened by the elements to let them pry it open with a little force. Inside, on the top, wrapped in a pale rice paper, they found two balls of opium, which they examined with their noses, hoping they were chocolates, then they tossed them away when their aroma proved that they were not. Under them was a book called "Seaman's Guide to First-Aid" which Jane began to riffle through. A moth flew from its pages.

"Read the part that tells about his sleepy sickness," Oopi said.

"—Read out how to dress a wound," Nolly instructed while she removed the other items from the box. There were several rolls of cotton wool and cotton dressings, all of them damp. There was a sewing kit, scissors, tweezers, plasters and adhesives. There was a smaller box filled with a series of glass phials labelled "Iodine," "Alcohol," "Chloroform," "Camphorated Oil," *H. Virginiana,* "Gentian Violet" and "Sterile Water."

Nolly opened each phial, sniffed it and passed it to Gaby, who did the same and then handed it to Sloan and Sybil. When she came to the small bottle labelled "Sterile Water," Nolly held it up so everyone could look at it and then she laid it back inside the case. There was a box marked "Aspirin," a box of unidentified pastilles that tasted bitter, a box of salt tablets, a "Laxative," a "Purgative," an "Emetic," "Ipecac," "Bicarbonate of Soda," an unmarked jar of sticky jelly, a syringe, some smelling salts, a tin cup and a spoon and a terra cotta-colored hot-water bottle.

"—mine!" Oopi claimed and grabbed possession of it. She held it by its neck while she inspected it, then she cradled it against her shoulder as if it were a baby.

The last thing Nolly found inside the chest was a box of plain white tablets.

"*—uh-oh,*" Sloan muttered when Nolly held them up.

"—how many are there?" Gaby asked.

Nolly made a quick count.

"Forty, maybe fifty."

Gaby frowned.

"There are eight of us. Plus *him. . . .*" she said.

Nolly nodded.

"Not enough," she murmured.

"—what *are* they?" Monkey asked.

"*—stupid,* you don't know?"

"—lots of people never take them and get on fine," Gaby offered. "Grandfather—"

"—your *grandfather* was *stupid. . . .*"

"But not dead from *mosquitos, éy?*"

". . . And Father never took it," Jane put in. "He always said a person has to learn to live with his conditions. The natives never took it. . . ." Unconsciously, she looked at Monkey. "Did your parents ever give you quinine—?" she inquired.

Monkey said she didn't know.

"You'd have known it," Sybil said. "Every day for breakfast, quinine and godsliver oil. . . ."

"—two grains a day."

"—and now we don't have *any.*"

"We have *some.*"

"I say we save them all for João—he's the sick one. . . ."

Gaby held a quinine tablet up and said, "*—for João!*" and Jane began to read from the first-aid manual. " 'General Rules of Hygiene,' " she began:

". . . 'if circumstances permit, wash your hands thoroughly with soap and water before attending to wounds. Cover any exposed cuts or breaks in your own skin with a waterproof dressing . . . if a wound is not too large, and bleeding is under control, clean it and the surrounding skin before applying the dressing: . . .' "

Sloan and Sybil tore the linen sheets into strips, while Nolly rinsed John with the wine and Gaby dried him.

"... 'Avoid touching the wound or any part of the dressing which will be in contact with the wound.' ..."

"—are we going to wrap him?"

"Yes, I think we better. ..."

"—*eý,* this part's a mess. ..."

"... *'Never talk or cough over a wound or a clean dressing.'* "

"—cough?"

"—what does it say about a *whisper?"*

"Read the part that tells how we can wake him up," Oopi insisted. She sat down next to Jane and watched her read while everyone, except Amanda, helped to wash him. They cut the bloodcaked remnants of his clothing off his chest, and Sloan and Sybil swabbed his hands and cleaned between his fingers. Monkey cut the tangles from his hair.

"There's something called ... there's something here that's called 'unconscious,' " Jane read. "... 'If the victim does not respond to conversation,' " she read, and Gaby sent her an insane look, " 'test his response to other stimuli such as touch or pain to determine whether he is "conscious" or "unconscious" ... ' "

"—what is 'unconscious'?" Gaby asked. "—is it serious? What does it say to do—?"

" 'EYES'," Jane read. " 'Do they open in response to pinching skin on the back of the victim's hand?' "

They pinched his hands.

His eyelids flickered.

" 'SPEECH' ..." Jane read.

"—what 'speech'?" Gaby demanded.

" 'MOVEMENT'," Jane continued. " 'Does the victim move in response to painful stimuli?' "

They looked at one another.

"—*bite* him," Nolly said.

Instead Gaby pulled his pubic hair but nothing happened.

"Bite him," Nolly repeated.

Gaby pulled the whiskers on his jaw and finally, to their relief, John flinched.

They bound him in clean linen and built a canopy of

leaves over his head. Oopi collected his shorn hair and put it in her hot water bottle. "We should shave him," she suggested, thinking that she'd like to have his whiskers, too.

Using the tin cup as shaving bowl and foaming the brush with soap and ocean water, they lathered him. Sloan and Sybil dabbed the lather on in small swift strokes and then Jane painted him with overlapping whorls. None of them had ever used a razor, though they'd seen their fathers use one many times. When Amanda handed it to her, Nolly nicked her thumb on it, surprised to find the blade so sharp.

"We have to pull the skin away like *this*—and keep the razor *flat,"* she said, and cut the first swath through the lather.

". . . pretty," Oopi breathed.

Monkey wiped the razor clean and Nolly made a second sweep.

"—he looks nice," Sloan said. "—can we put some perfume on him?"

"When we're finished," Nolly said. She worked around his ears, beneath his jaw, between his lip and nose. . . . When she finished, Gaby wiped his face and Sloan and Sybil dabbed him twice with Mister Sutcliffe's toilet water.

His breathing sounded deeper.

"He looks bonny," Sybil said.

"—garboso. . . ."

"Handsome."

A trace of blood appeared along his jaw and bled into a line.

They stared at it.

When it seemed about to trickle off his chin, Amanda took her thumb out of her mouth and wiped his blood with it.

Her thumb glistened for an instant, then she licked it. Then she smiled, and closed her mouth around it. There was a word her mother used to use about the taste of things that came from England, as if they had arrived, imported, from the heights, from some emporium in heaven. *Di-vine,* she used to say. Try this, dear. Isn't it *di-vine?* hasn't it come straight from *heaven—?*

This time, when John awoke, he knew he wasn't dreaming. No dream could be like this, he knew. In dreams, time does not pass slowly, the sun and stars don't fix themselves precisely, and one can wake himself from fear. What this was, he knew, was not a nightmare. If anything, he thought, this wasn't dreaming, it was death. But English-speaking forms behind face masks, not devils, fed and pampered him. There were eight of them. The eyes of one above the piece of cloth she wore over her mouth, were hauntingly familiar. "Things are not so bad," she said. "You'll see. I'm making a *kite—*" She held a cross before him. Later she returned to show him a large piece of blood-colored sail. "You see?" she said. "—not so bad. This is the best. They can see a kite from this in any weather, *não?* Same as the *Charlotte.* They could see her sails from everywhere, you said. . . ." At the mention of that word, John was sure he wasn't dreaming. He remembered where he was. He could not remember where the others were. He remembered there were others. He could not remember who they were. When he spoke, they looked at him as though they couldn't understand him. When he repeated what he'd said, he couldn't hear the sound of his own voice. *Am I speaking?* he demanded. "What's the matter with him?—when's he ever going to *talk?*" one of them said. They told him things that he forgot as soon as they had spoken them. *Fire?* they kept asking. *Water?* Had there been a fire? He remembered heat. His skin had burned. He remembered making love to Charlotte in the lamplight, near a dancing candle. He remembered how to temper brass, a boatswain's craft his father taught him, strengthening by heat and quenching. He remembered water, miles of it, and chasing something, like the wind, around a promontory: *kite—*what was this apparition with a girl's breasts telling him? A *kite—?* A kite's a bird. He remembered that a kite's a kind of bird. He remembered a whole passage from Leonardo's "Notebooks" and recited to them, out loud, in some foreign language,

"mon destin" "... writing about the kite seems to be my destiny since among first recollections of my infancy it seemed to me
"mon berceau" that as I was in my cradle a kite came to me and opened
"ma bouche" my mouth with its tail and struck me several times with
"mes lèvres" its tail inside my lips. . . ."

They fed him, they were always feeding him, forcing food and drink between his lips as if he were a newborn in his cradle—this was *his* first memory, *this* was, this instant, what was happening right now—this was not a dream, it was *remembering the world.* When they bathed him, he could feel the sting of the salt water drying on his skin along his arms and on his chest, but when they sponged his legs he could feel nothing, though he knew, though he *remembered,* feeling. One of his keepers, the one with the long hair, the too-thin one with the pale eyes—she noticed first. "You can't feel this, can you, John?" she asked. *How do you know my name?* he thought. "If you can feel this, John, blink twice," she said. Feel *what? What are you doing?* He watched as her long fingers pinched his thigh and he recalled a feeling. He watched her pinch his other thigh and he experienced the same memory of sensation. He watched the blond girl, the tall one with the square-tipped fingers, draw a needle from a leather sewing kit and say, "Let me try with *this."* He watched her pierce his thigh with it. It was a strange sensation, like an amputation, he imagined, like dismemberment. A recollection stirred in him, something that he needed to recall, but couldn't. "I don't think he feels it," his tormenter said. "Even when I *twist."* She withdrew the needle from his thigh and plunged it, while he watched, into his groin next to his testicles. "No reaction," she observed. "It's like he's dead down there. . . ." John tried to move. He held his shoulders off the ground, leaning on his elbows to watch her, and his head swam and his vision blurred. He was going to stop her even if he had to hit her, he determined. He tried to lift his leg, to bar her from him, kick her if he must, but he couldn't move it. He tried to move his other leg, tried to bend its knee, but it was unattached from him, disobedient and unresponsive. Overhead there was a strange blood-colored object in the sky, the sight of which was terrifying, the sight of which inspired panic in him, made his heart beat fast. The tall blond girl withdrew the needle. With her other hand she clasped his penis, *Stop!* John shouted. She let go of him. *Get it down! Stop her!* He pointed at the object in the sky. As he looked at it, blood ran across the clouds, an ocean of it, a thick sea, the smell of blood, its memory, what he'd seen before the earthquake and the tidal wave, the carnage, a blood memory:

We have to leave! We have to get away from here—!

They gathered 'round him, thrilled.

Lift me, he instructed.

—shouldn't we just build a boat? one of them was asking.

—would it take us long to build a boat? her twin was saying.

"—just goddam *lift* me!" he shouted. "Break this camp—hide everything—we have to leave—get that kite out of the sky—do you want to get us *killed?*"

They stared at him.

It was wonderful that he was talking, that he had finally come awake so he could tell them what to do, but they'd forgotten how a grown man shouts, forgotten what it's like to be the object of his anger. They had taken care of him, now his anger made them feel that they'd done nothing right. Instead of waking gently like a god well-pleased with his creation, he unleashed a storm of anger at them—they were feeble minded, chuckle-headed, rattlebrained, dim-witted, timid, senseless, imbecilic, pigeon-hearted *shrikes,* he told them, "Es-pe-cial-ly *you!"* he shouted at Nolly "—and *you!"* (Amanda). —What day was it? he demanded; —how long had they been there? hadn't they bothered to observe how many *days?* hadn't they gone inland to find *water?* had they built a *shelter?* had they gathered *food?* Chimpanzees—*baby* chimpanzees! *defective* ones!—could have managed better than they had—had they inventoried the supplies? had they organized a search around the island, scouted all the shores? Had they done *anything* to try to save themselves? and why were they wearing these ridiculous face masks that made them look like bandits—?

He went on in what Jane's father would have called a strapping good dress-down until Gaby sat down next to him and took her mask off and said, "João, forgive—you're talking *louco."*

With her mask off he recognized her as a child that he was fond of, the granddaughter of an old man he was very fond of. As he stared at her other memories unfolded, revealed themselves within his mind, prompted by her face, her eyes. She looked so *old,* he saw—except for the animation of her eyes, her smile, her face had taken on the shades and lines of an old woman. Even the way she held herself—the way each one of these young girls had started holding herself, he realized as he began remembering the way they used to be—seemed strung on militancy, disappointment, fear, whatever base it is the skeleton adopts at its utmost rigidity. He remembered Gaby flying kites with him, her body bobbing like a cork, hardly able to contain its gravity, she was so carefree. One by one they sat down near him and took off their masks, except the oldest girl, the one he now remembered as "Amanda," Sutcliffe's daughter—her cheek had been ripped off, the skin around it had turned black, her eyes seemed not to focus and she sucked her thumb. Next to her were Ogilvy's two daughters, twins, whose names he couldn't remember—and next to them was Fraser's little girl, the one Fraser had named his cutter after. She was a redhead, like her father, and she looked extremely young, like six or seven. She was very flushed and very dirty and she carried a hot-water bottle with her. Next to her was Napier's girl, the very thin one whose name, he now recalled, was Jane. Next to her was the half-breed, Mister Lawrence's offspring, one of the half-baked loaves he'd left behind before he took his seed back to its home in England. Finally there was Nolly, the Reverend Petherbridge's daughter. He had always thought her ugly, only now she looked less so. *Your brother,* he began to say. She didn't make an effort to lean closer or to ease his pain in speaking. She had stuck the needle in her headband, over her right eye, next to a feather, where everyone could see it. Your brother, he repeated.

"—Nigel," Gaby prompted.

"Nigel's dead."

The words seemed to have no meaning to her.

"I'm sorry," he continued. "Everyone aboard *The Ruby Girl.* They died before the wave. They were killed before the earthquake—"

"—'killed'?"

". . . Matlock. Fitz. Your brother. Everybody."

They stared at him in silence. The words "dead," "died," "killed," seemed meaningless to all of them.

"È l-o-u-c-o," Gaby finally spelled.

"Not *'louco',"* he said. He leaned on one arm, suddenly aware of how his useless legs were pinning him like anchors. "There's a bluff behind me, I can't see it, I can't turn—there's a bluff there, isn't there? a headland? We climbed that headland, you and I and little George, that second day, to fly our kite, didn't we, Gaby—?" he insisted. Gaby blushes when he says her name. "I can remember things. I went aboard *The Ruby Girl* with Jib, remember? *Listen* . . . what I saw there—" He looked around the circle at their faces. *"We can't stay here,"* he repeats. "We have to go up on that headland, hide. You have to carry me. You have to do it *now.* We have to hide all trace of having been here—all the middens, shitholes, fruit pods, shells, the footprints, everything, every trace as if we'd never lived. . . ."

"—but our dads are coming," Sloan tried to explain to him.

"—and this is *home,"* her sister said.

"I like it *here,"* Oopi stated. "—I don't *want* to go somewhere again. . . ."

John looked at Nolly. He looked at Gaby, hoping she would intercede, but it was Jane who spoke first, asking, *"Are* our parents coming, John?"

"Yes," he answered.

"—when?"

How to measure Time confused him, the rules of Time, its laws, eluded him, he realized. The girls were watching him—especially the oldest ones—as if they were suspicious of his doubt. They were believers in the absolute, and here he was, half a man, a cripple in their midst, to whom they looked, toward whom they turned and watched, for guidance. If he asked again, *How many days have we—?* he would expose his own uncertainty. Answers, miracles and absolutes were what their vigil begged of him—he *did* believe their rescue was imminent, but he believed, too, in their dreadful danger, he was certain of it, but unsure of how to find the words, to make them seize it.

"The boat will come as soon as—*wind,"* he lied. "—Remember how the wind calmed us that day when we arrived—? The wind here is notorious—waiting on the wind. Soon's there's wind, we'll see them. . . ."

"—but it's *nice* and breezy!" Sloan and Sybil demonstrated, standing up, letting the wind unfurl their long blond hair.

"—muito. Plenty," Gaby affirmed. "—it tried to lift me right up with the kite—! So perhaps they're coming, *sim?* with a wind as big as this—?" She looked at John, expectantly.

"On a wind like this," he said, watching as they nodded

all around. "But a boat is very big. Much bigger than a kite—longer than your hair. It takes a lot of wind to move a boat like theirs. We could see them better from the headland. We should go up *there* . . . we should go and build a camp and watch for them. . . ."

Gaby looked at Jane and nodded but Nolly stopped them when they started to stand up.

"—why?" she asked. "Why do we have to go up there and leave no trace as if we'd never been? Nothing's bothering us here. This is *home.* We like it here. The other side is nasty. *This* is where we landed. *This* is where they'll come. *This* is where they know we'll be. . . ."

"Something else might come before them," John warned.

" 'Something else'?—what kind of 'something else'?"

"—those turtles, maybe," Oopi said. "I liked those turtles. . . ."

"There's going to be another *wave,* you mean?" Jane asked him.

"We'd be safer on the headland," John repeated.

"Why should we have to hide our footprints from *a wave?"* Nolly demanded. "Why should we—? You say my brother's dead. Why should I believe you? The same wave that wrecked *The Ruby Girl* wrecked us and *we're* not dead. If he's 'dead,' where's the proof? where's his body? where are *all* their bodies? *Ruby Girl*'s supplies washed up—so where are they? You say something killed them. Why didn't it kill us? Why should we believe you when you won't tell us the truth? *I* know what the truth is. You think you can hide it, but I know. *I* know what you're frightened of. You don't have to lie. It's the devil, isn't it? He's going to come. It was the devil, all this, wasn't it?" She'd turned it over, argued with herself ever since Amanda had stopped speaking, ever since she'd realized that she, Nolly, was in charge. She'd had to start to make sense of things—to see that there were *two* sides, a seen and an unseen, a hidden and revealed to everything. God was apparent, yes—God spoke in many ways to her, revealed Himself, but she had not *believed* before. She had not believed there was a *devil,* the hidden side, the demon that her father called the anti-christ, God's opposite, His equal. It made sense—the evidence all pointed to it, scriptures, tales, Christ in the desert, Beelzebub, Old Nick, Belial, stories that her father told about the Evil in the land, rampant in the form of opposites—whores and mothers, moneylenders and philanthropists, actors and evangelists. Before, she had believed evil defined itself by vacancy, that it existed in the nonexistence of its opposite, rather than in its *co-*existence—she had always thought it dwelt outside, beyond, *elsewhere.* Her father tried to teach her Evil is man's natural state, that one must struggle one's entire lifetime toward a state of grace, but she'd denied it. Now it all made sense. What other sense did all this make? *Something evil* was attempting to establish its own order, turning the old order upside down, killing, causing earthquakes, removing her without the aid of love from one world she had known into this foreign one. Same as Christ, the devil needs disciples, she had realized, and he wanted her. He would come for her, he would. The longer she resisted, the surer she became that he would visit. She expected any day to wake and find him standing there, demanding. She was ready.

"Tell me. Did you ac-tu-al-ly *see* him?"

Madness is the face which shows itself despite its mask.

I am a man who cannot walk, John reasons, *at the mercy of the mad.*

"Yes," he says.

She seems satisfied, transformed.

"—did he try to make you his disciple?"

"Yes. Of course."

"—what did he *do?"*

"He thrust his tail between my lips."

"—and *you—?"*

"I bit it."

"—*bit* it?"

Her eyes shine.

"—then?"

"I swallowed it."

"—and *then?"*

"He bit my legs."

Nolly's nodding, following the tale, the sense of it, receiving its accepted truth, swallowing it whole, the *alph* and *om* of it, its blacksandwhites, its goodandbad, the lovehate, heads and tails, the myth and truth:

"—and *then?"*

"He spit me out."

Nolly folds her hands into her lap and waits.

The story, to her mind, has reached the point from which one takes its Lesson:

"—and?"

"He told me he'd come back."

She waits.

"To eat me."

Nolly smiles.

BANANA DIVINATION

I went to the animal fair

("the fair")

All the birds and beasties were there

("were there")

The gay baboon by the light of the moon
Was combing his yellowy hair

("his hair.")

The monkey fell from her bunk

("—ety bunk")

And dropped on the elephant's trunk

("—ety trunk.")

The elephant sneezed and went down on his knees
And what became of the monkey, monkey, monkey, monkey,

("monkety, monkety,
monk—?")

. . .

"It's *our* slave-y!" Sybil yells when Nolly orders Monkey to cut *coco*'s.

"—and it's bringing us *bananas. . . .*"

"We *have* bananas. *Everybody* has bananas. We don't *need* bananas. We need *coconuts.*"

"We need them—"

"They'll go rotten. . . ."

"We're not *eating* them."

"—we're *asking* them."

"You're—?"

"Asking them."

"—we're asking if it's true."

"—about the Devil."

"—if he's coming."

Behind them, Nolly finds bananas scattered all about, their tips clipped like cigars, black flies and honey ants surrounding them.

"Stupid! these are *food!* we have to take them with us! now you've ruined them—!"

"—we ate *some. . . .*"

"—they made us *windy. . . .*"

"—so we stopped."

Nolly kicks up the heap of worthless fruit, and a miasma of flies and gnats disperses. The fruit has blackened from the sun, where Sloan and Sybil sliced the ends.

Big dot ● in the middle of the pulp means "NO," Sybil explains.

Big brown **Y** means "YES," says Sloan.

"Why did you do so *many—?"*

"—different answer every time—"

"—don't know when to stop."

"Stop NOW! Stupid!—stupid!—stupid!"

Marches off.

So much to do.

So many plans to carry through.

●—*42*

Y—*45*

Moot Banana—*47*

FIRE FROM THE ALTAR

When they moved to *the oont* they stopped calling the other place *home.* They started calling *the oont* "home" and they called the other place *there.* Sometimes they called the other place *back* there. More often they called it *down* there.

Since John started talking, their days had a new routine. Every day they went *downthere* and brought back more things from the wreckage. The portage was a hardship for them, the going was tangled and rough through the edge of the jungle and none of them was very strong. Sloan and Sybil were useless—at least Sybil was. So was Oopi. Since she couldn't walk, Sybil served as a lookout on top of *the oont* while the others—Nolly, Amanda, Jane, Sloan, Gaby and Monkey—threaded their way down the slope, through the vines to the place in the trees where they'd hidden supplies. They made one trip a day, in the morning, before the heat made them tired. One of them—Jane—seemed to shrink in the night, every night, and John had to goad her to eat. He tried to inform their discretion, school their selection of things to bring back, but every day they returned carrying something as useless to them as the sand that they slept on. They had carried the medicine box when they went up that first afternoon—Oopi had. It had taken the four oldest ones until dark to move John in his sling. He kept passing out and finally dropped into a lasting unconsciousness when they were halfway to the top of the cliff. Their first night on the headland was dark, unfamiliar, alive with strange sounds, and exposed. Even Nolly was silent that night, fear making a fist in her throat. There was no moon and the stars seemed like eyes. There were snakes on the headland, and mice. There were vultures.

Since they'd moved from *downthere,* they had to walk every day for their food. There were roots to be dug, nasty roots, foul-tasting ones, worse-tasting than godsliver oil, which John forced them to eat for their strength and their health. The roots were like strings. Gaby called them *catguts* and they made her throw up for the first couple of days, but then she got used to the taste. The roots tasted better unwashed, they discovered. That meant one less trek to the ocean each day, to wash them. They liked that. Also, it meant they had learned to eat dirt.

He tried to teach them to fish with their hands on the *wildibeach,* but he couldn't go with them to teach them to stalk and to hunt so they returned empty-handed, until John whittled Gaby and Nolly a spear and a trident and taught them to work in two's with Jane and Monkey, schooling the fish into seines made from canvas and linen. After that, they had fish—angelfish, perch and bass which John filleted and held out for them to eat, raw, off the end of a knife, but only Oopi would taste it. The others could not be encouraged to try the gray flesh nor would they eat the raw oysters he told them to dig. Oopi, however, acquired the taste and even brought him a shimmering jellyfish one afternoon because it looked *yum.* Except for the roots he forced on them, they lived on fruit and their constant complaint was for fire. With fire, they dreamed, they could roast—they could create, they dreamed, potable water. Moved by their hunger, they brought tea *home* when they found a box of it *downthere,* their senses inflamed by its smell. They passed it around, crumbling its leaves in their fingers, placing its dust on the tips of their tongues, in their nostrils. They carried home pots. They carried rice home, two bags of it, although one was buggy and the other was green. John berated them. *Rope,* he lectured: *poles.* They brought back potsherds. A *book,* he begged. Oh—we found a few of those, he was told. We didn't like them—one was about work and didn't have pictures, and one was in another language and had lots of kids' drawings of some hands and some legs and some feet. *Leonardo,* John lamented. That was Leonardo, *bring him!* but what they brought were trivialities instead. They didn't like to work—they liked to play. They liked to laze about and groom each other. Different girls liked different things. Each had a way of playing by herself, outside the group. Oopi liked collecting, Jane liked scrubbing things with sand. Gaby liked to frolic, John could see her *downthere* running on the beach, frisking, nearly flying when she thought she was alone. They played in groups—gambling games and games of toss. They made necklaces from John's discarded fishbones and they collected feathers for their headbands. John wanted them to build things—a stretcher for his transport, sleeping platforms—but they wouldn't. They would start and then become distracted. He, himself, longed for distraction—he spent hours making calculations about shelter, water, phases of the moon. He developed "bed" sores on his buttocks so he devised a plan for them, more work, a routine for them to rotate him six times a day. What they liked was pleasure, what he liked was preparedness. They liked washing one another's backs with sand and scratching one another's arms and legs. Sometimes, just for pleasure, they tickled John relentlessly, up and down his soles, along the insides of his legs, and fell about with childish mirth at his obliviousness. What they wanted was for John to tell them stories and renew their childhood. What he wanted was escape.

Then one morning there was smoke.

It appeared, its white tail, over the horizon while the older girls were gathering supplies *downthere* and John, Sybil and Oopi were alone at *home.* Sybil had been dozing, idly pouring sand on ants when she awoke, watching them crawl out of the avalanche, working toward her half-eaten banana. She was bored and started humming to herself. She'd lost sight of Sloan—she was *downthere,* somewhere. She'd lost sight of all of them—if John found out, he'd yell at her—but she knew John would not find out. He couldn't. She glanced at him. He was trying, uselessly, to balance, sitting, without using his arms. Near him, as usual, Oopi was searching in the earth, holding her hot-water bottle, collecting weird things. Sybil tossed a banana skin at her, signaling play. Oopi kicked sand back and started strutting, wiggling her bottom. She turned toward the ocean, to make a lewd gesture with her buttocks, but she stopped. *Hey,* she said. She pointed. Sybil turned and saw it, too. John had seen it. Like a dream realized, like a dying love restored, the sight of wisps of smoke started feelings in them that they'd lost hope of experiencing. *Jesus Christ,* John said. Sybil and Oopi couldn't lift him so he dragged himself to the cliff edge to get a better view. It was a steamship, no denying, he could recognize a steamship when he saw its signature —it was a British Navy corvette, he could tell.

Signal the other girls *home,* he told Sybil.

She waved her arms but no sign from *downthere* was returned.

"When did they signal last?" John asked.

"—don't know."

"—one minute ago? two? *five?"*

" . . . I was sleeping."

Damntheireyes, he thought. He'd asked them for binoculars, he knew there were binoculars *downthere,* instead they'd brought him *spoons.*

They watched the line of smoke hang in the offing, while Sybil signaled.

"—why should they come *home?"* Oopi finally asked. "Shouldn't we go *down?"*

"I *can't."*

"—I can," Oopi said.

"Shouldn't we go down and wait for them?"

"Not yet."

"But it *is* a boat?" Sybil asked.

"It is."

"—it *is* coming closer?"

"Yes."

"—to Rescue us?"

"I think so."

"Do you want us to go down and get them—?"

"No . . . they'll signal. They're supposed to. Nolly will—"

But Nolly didn't.

No one did.

Only once in the next hour did they think they saw a glimpse of something moving through the jungle *down-there*—the flash of something red and white which might have been the feathers of a head-dress, but they couldn't see the girls. The trail of smoke from the rescue ship hung like a mirage above the island's other shore, but still no sign of the vessel came in sight. Then the white line faded, became woolly and transparent, disappeared, and John feared the boat had changed direction.

Oopi had been laying next to John, on her stomach, but now she stood up, placed her hands on both her hips. *Hey!* she shouted. *Come back!* She and Sybil waved their arms. As they did, a great black pillar, shooting crimson, rose in the air from where they'd seen white smoke. It trailed straight up, then spread, blackening the sky.

"Something's burning," Oopi said. "—isn't something *burning?"* she asked John.

He was making his bad face, she saw.

"Ocean must be burning," she told Sybil.

"—don't be *stupid,"* Sybil said, trying to sound smart, like Nolly. "Ocean doesn't burn. . . ."

"—the forest, then. . . ."

"The *boat,"* John said. "They've set the *boat* on fire."

Suddenly he grabbed Oopi's leg and knocked her down. *Hey!* she cried and kicked him, but he forced his hand over her mouth and pulled Sybil to him, too. *Stay down!* he ordered. Oopi bit him, broke away and ran. "Oopi!" he yelled. *"Oopi—!"*

She took off down the bluff in the direction of the beach.

"—they'll see you!" he cried. "For godsake—! Oopi—! *Come back!"*

She stopped and turned toward him and saw him pointing. He was pointing out to sea when she looked she saw the dragon with black legs beating on the water. Next to it there was another, bigger, dragon with white teeth and one big eye, its wings also beating on the water. *Devils,* she recognized, two big snakie dragons breathing fire come to burn them up, and in no time she had scrambled back and thrown herself onto the ground against John's chest and he was forcing her head down with Sybil's, saying, don't watch, for godsake, close your eyes, don't watch, the two of you, don't watch, don't watch.

The outriggers came in with skill and beached themselves with ease *downthere.* John held Sybil and Oopi. He searched the jungle for a sign of all the others and prayed they used their heads once and stayed silent and well hidden. *Please,* Oopi whimpered, and he realized he was holding the two girls in a way they couldn't breathe, so he released them, though he kept his right arm around their shoulders, loosely, whispering, don't look, *shut your eyes.* They couldn't. What girl could shut her eyes against a dragon? and here they were, *two* of them, with wings, wings that fell off when the dragons came ashore, when the tiny naked people, other children, climbed down, leading dressed-up giants wearing pith hats like their fathers wore for hunting, frightened clumsy giants with their hands held high above their heads. The giants looked like men. They were dressed like men—but among the tiny people, they were bigger-looking and the children prodded them with the fallen dragons' wings. These were oars, Sybil realized, and the dragons were just boats. The giants, in their hats and shoes and knee-length socks, short pants and buttoned shirts, were *fathers,* yes, and other sailors. She wanted to stand up and call to them but her legs would not support her and, besides, John pushed her down. *It's Dad—!* she breathed. Sybil don't watch, John told her. *She has to get her Sloan!* Sybil protested. She imagined she could hear her sister weeping. Oopi's dad was *downthere,* too. Amanda's dad was *there,* and Jane's and Nolly's. There were other men, five others, and the tiny naked people—what they thought were children—pushed them with black oars onto the beach. The children hit them with the oars and gestured till the men undressed, then the children made the men sit down with their backs to one another in the sand. Oopi's dad was sitting there, across the distance she could recognize him from his red-hair and his barrel-chest. She had never seen him without clothes before. Although he was so far away his body still seemed pink and wattley to her, not like John's, whose body she was used to seeing. Sybil could see her father, too—waxy-looking, stick-thin, sitting with his knees drawn to his chin, staring toward the jungle, away from her, toward Sloan, she thought. Sybil felt abandoned, halved. The sun was high, directly over head, and Oopi couldn't understand why, with all the heat, the children *downthere* would begin to build a fire. The children carried timber from the dragon-boats—short logs, twigs and poles. They laid the poles, a dozen of them, on the sand beside the group of naked men. One child seemed to rub a stick against a stick, atop a stone. Others of the children sat around him, blowing at the sticks until a blue thread wriggled up, a snake of smoke. From it the children *downthere* soon established a whole flame, bright enough to see from such a distance. Others of the children down there had arranged a sort of pit, lined with twigs and logs, into which the fire children fed their flame. Suddenly a lot of smoke went up and Sybil and Oopi watched the children fan the fire. They watched the children bind the giants, men, their fathers, to the poles. They watched the children carry the bound men on poles to the fire pit and place the poles in other poles over the fire. They watched their fathers writhe and pop and as they watched, the wind brought an aroma to them on the hill. Their eyes watered but they watched because they couldn't stop their eyes from watching—they didn't mean to watch but once it was begun it was a thing they couldn't stop. They couldn't make themselves believe that what they saw was true and so they kept on watching, waiting for a proof, a final stroke, a termination in the horror, something, anything, a moment to arrive to signify that all hope, every hope, had ended.

What happened was that Gaby came back, leading Sloan.

They had come up through the jungle, unseen, 'round the back, and when John heard them coming he forced Oopi and Sybil behind him and he grabbed a stone, the nearest object, as their only weapon. When he saw the look in Gaby's eyes he threw the stone down and allowed her to embrace him. The smell of cooked flesh circled them—John could smell the smoke of it in Gaby's hair. He held her and he let her weep, and moments later Monkey came back, leading Jane, then Nolly followed. Only when the men down there were silenced, when their hair had burned and they were black and still, only after that, much later, did John whisper, *Where's Amanda?*

No one knew, or no one answered—they lay shocked and silenced, watching what the children *downthere* started to do next.

None of them had eaten anything but fruit and roots for many days, except for Oopi, who ate raw fish and was the first to fill her mouth with sand when she saw what they were doing. Jane, too, forced her face into the ground and ate it when she saw. Monkey crawled away and could be heard behind a rock. Gaby pressed her hands into her eyes and Sloan and Sybil hid their faces.

Nolly watched and went on watching as the bodies were torn up *downthere* and shared. She moved her lips, reciting prayers or verses, never blinking, *Take, eat; this is my body* she said once, and later she said, *Woe to the inhabitors of the earth and of the sea! for the devil is come down into you because he knoweth that he hath but a short time.*

When they had eaten, the children *downthere* squatted on the beach. Some of them walked up the beach as far as the jungle and peered into it and shook their fists at it, then walked back to their companions. The sun was going down. They wrapped the men's clothes around sticks and dipped them in something from the dragonboats and then lighted them with the fire from the pit. They mounted the torches on the boats and fitted the oars back into place and then some of them pushed the boats into the sea while others rowed. As dark fell the pit glowed and the torches looked like lanterns that the girls were used to seeing on the fishing boats back in Rangoon. They watched the torches move into the night. Not until the torches disappeared did they feel like speaking, but then the fire started talking in the pit *downthere.* It started rolling over in some places, bubbling up, glowing brighter, sparkling, then a tongue of it arose and started flying at them, flying up the bluff directly toward them. *Gaby, get the knife!* John whispered and she scrambled on the still-hot sand, fumbling in the dark among the tedious debris of shells and useless things that they'd collected 'round their camp until, near the medicine box, she found their knife. She grabbed the razor, too. She didn't know what she would do with it but it felt like a right thing when she held it. When she got to John the fire was flying up the bluff, very near to them, and when she handed John the knife, she could feel him hold it at the ready so she opened out the razor. The others drew in close to them, except Nolly, who had started speaking prayers again, elsewhere, in the dark.

The fire flew above the bluff, over the rim, and then it halted, then came forward, then descended to display itself, burning on a stick held by Amanda.

She smiled at them.

She was carrying a metal pot.

She put the pot down on the ground and stuck the burning stick into the sand beside it.

John dragged his body to the torch and knocked it down and buried it with sand, cursing, Jesus *hell* this can be seen for miles, do you want them to come *back* for us? But

Amanda knelt down by the pot and tipped it toward them showing off the breathing embers, glowing like a promise. Look, she said. She passed it 'round. Her eyes were shining. "Look," she urged. "Look what they left." She blew into the pot and made it glow. *"They brought us fire,"* she said, sounding grateful.

FLIES In the morning, in the light before dawn, they left John where he was and went *downthere.*

Gaby walked with Oopi, and Sybil rode on Sloan. They walked in silence, Nolly leading. Behind her, Amanda brought the fire. Monkey walked with Jane, who walked as if sleepwalking. The sea, as they descended, was very still; great birds, the storks and pelicans floated just above the water's surface, skimming, making furrows on the calm dark water with dipped wings. The last stars were fading and the jungle birds, nesting in the canopy, were stirring in the distance, as the light expanded. Blue smoke, a fog of it, sat on the sand above the fire pit, stationary, fixed as if it were a destination. As they neared it they imagined if they entered it they'd disappear and that would be just fine. They hadn't slept. Only John had found the peace to sleep—they'd sat around the firepot, mesmerized by pictures in its embers, and from time to time, as the pictures faded and the fire weakened, they had fed it cloth, dry leaves and feathers and their breath, giving it whatever it had called for for its life. Near dawn, as soon as it was light enough to see, they'd stood as if of a single mind, and known without exchanging words, what needed to be done.

As they enter through the veil of smoke it parts around them like a water. The world, instead of seeming more invisible, becomes a deeper blue. The sand looks blue, the ashes do, the bones. Each bone shines like a blue star on a darkling carpet. Each is clean, impartial, neutral as a star, polished by the fire, cold. Some of them are heaped together, some are splintered, jagged. Some are like small children's toys, like flutes, like children's whistles. Some are Oopi's, some Amanda's, some are Sloan's and Sybil's, some are Jane's. Somewhere, too, are Nolly's. Some are buried in the ashes, some are thrown onto the sand. Some are long and smooth and rounded at one end, some are curved and crooked. Some are bracelets, some are crowns. Some have chords of tendons drying on them. Some are ancient. All of them are sacred, all are gathered with religious care. No skulls are there. As they mass the bones they start to see that reconstruction is impossible, no daughter can rebuild a man, no remedy, no shape of an atonement can accumulate from ashes, no shape can come together from these parts, no daughter can resuscitate a bone, no resurrection is at hand, the act is final, they're alone. They mass all that they can find and wait for something to arise. When nothing does, their grief is such that it transcends the physical, becomes sublime. When there is nothing left to do within one's understanding of the world one does what can't be understood. On the sand, all over, up and down the beach, wherever they had squatted when their feast had ended, the other children left defecations, there were mounds of them, like offerings. Amanda is the first to understand their meaning. Falling with a cry onto her knees, she smears her face with some, her neck, her chest, she eats it. Immediately, elsewhere, Nolly does the same. They run like scavengers along the beach, each one, from waste to waste, covering themselves with it, they rub it in their hair, over their chests, they paint their legs and faces with it, run, rush, feel renewed, roll themselves around in sand. From the bones they gather ones that they can use for decoration. From the rest they build a sort of heap, a kind of totem, around which, in the sand, they draw a circle. Without speaking, they withdraw from it, understanding it is never to be spoken of, never to be touched, the bones, never to be broken, that perimeter, its ultimate offense, obscenity, its inviolability. They are different now. Even those whose fathers were not massacred are different. They are silent, changed, contaminated, beyond grief, ecstatic. Day is dawning. John is waiting for them. Blacked with shit and whitened with the sand, they gather things they hope will please him—pretty shells, a rock, a shrimp, a cinder. Flies descend. Flies follow on them. Flies are living in their skin.

OOPI'S TREASURES

Beauty lasts. Its memory lasts. Beauty, in its moment, fixes time, halts rationality, stops thought, transforms, amends the heart, reverses. Its power is despotic, but its kingdom is not absolute. Oopi knows some things are beautiful—she knows some things are not. One day a rock that's gray may catch the light in such a way as to define it as a thing of beauty, worth possessing, saving, owning, holding, shielding from destruction—then another day the world and everything it holds may look dis-spirited, entirely drab and beautyless. On such days Oopi will retreat into the special place she's found, a shelter in the mangroves, half a mile from *home,* where she's hidden all her treasures. Sometimes she serves tea there, an imaginary tea in cups that are invisible, set impeccably on saucers of the finest weightless frightfully transparent bone. Sometimes she goes shopping in the market there, walking through imaginary market stalls with imaginary children, choosing silks and cottons, carpets, oils and scents. Sometimes she rearranges furniture, ordering her household staff, flying into rages calculated to astonish and chastise unregenerate incompetence. Sometimes she gives lectures about How It Was O U T T H E R E In-the-Rough—how to live on snakemeat and rawfish, how to stalk a panther, how to make a knife. Sometimes she sails ships she makes from seed pods and banana leaves on the pool of stagnant water near her hideout, ships that sail from one shore on a sea of larvae and green slime to the other shore to save the children she imagines there. Dragonflies make battle on her fleet and legions of mosquitoes set upon her vessels, still she saves the children every time, a happy ending, and her boats are never swamped. Sometimes she is Oopi, lying on her back inside the mangrove shelter, staring up at green light through the canopy talking to her sister about things to hate or not to hate and why. Sometimes she is *memsa' Ruby,* mistress of the household, wife and heroine and mother. Sometimes the hot-water bottle is her sister Shauna or her ayah or her houseboy or her imagined husband "Jack." Inside it, she keeps her treasures, which they know, share beauty in, are part of—treasures she collects. These are secret treasures, things of rare and stunning beauty, needing her protection. When a treasure is too big to put inside the bottle, she hides it in the mangrove with her larger things, her bed, her market-place, her city of Rangoon, her future. Nothing that is beautiful that's hers can ever die, if she hides it, Oopi thinks. Assiduousness, more than anything—more than hope—is one thing she requires at all times. Sometimes she feels Sloan and Sybil spying on her, spying on the treasures. They are good at finding things, those two, and she likes walking with them, even though they're slow, because Sloan must carry Sybil. She likes hunting with them. What they hunt for though, are things to eat. They hunt for food. When they go with Oopi, they are always hungry. Oopi looks for shells, they search for fry, for fish to catch and cook to eat. Oopi takes her time, they act as if they're in a hurry, in a rush—they act as if they're always hungry. What they think she's hiding, and they know she's hiding something, what they think she's hiding is delicious food—not "delicious," not "delicious," really, something that's "enough," a food that could be called *enough,* when it is eaten. They are always hungry. Oopi's always hungry. Jane, alone, is one who never eats. Jane, among them, is the only one who seems the least bit sick. She never goes with them. Since the fire, since the day they walked back from the smoke, they haven't been *downthere* together. Theirs is failure of community—a failure of community that comes when grief becomes quotidian and irreversible: Jane's hair is falling out. Shared grief is nothing and it comes to nothing, sharing grief is nothing any animal is built to do. Jane's hair, once beautiful and rich, is brittle, shedding—Oopi knows because she finds it, one long strand at a time, and she collects it. Since the fire, Jane's stayed on *the oont* near John. Oopi has gone *down*—so have Sloan and Sybil, out of hunger. Monkey has gone *down* to gather food for Jane. Gaby's gone. Nolly and Amanda have, together. Since the coming of the fire, the two of them have acted strange, not like the rest of them, but like owners, Oopi thinks, *do this, do that,* like sergeants or superiors or kings. They order everyone around, using fire as a threat, or using John. Amanda keeps the fire, Nolly is in charge of John. Every day there are his bathing and his quinine rituals, his turnings, his tonsure, his decoration and his eucharistic feedings. Nolly is in charge of these, in charge of their performance and their liturgy, and excommunication from them is the punishment that she exacts when she is crossed. Oopi crossed her once by refusing to search for something *downthere* that Nolly ordered her to bring back *home* so Nolly banished her from grooming John for several days but Oopi didn't care—that's when she found her secret place among the mangroves. Soon after that, one afternoon, she felt Sloan and Sybil spying on her, spying on her treasures, she was sure that it was them, she saw their blond hair passing through the trees, she was sure she saw Sybil's pale head high above the ground, the height of a grown woman, as she rode along on Sloan's shoulders. Oopi threw a stick at them, which clattered through the twisted roots and branches of the mangrove trees and sent a shower of dark leaves and broken cobwebs after them, and she shook her fists at them, hooting like a chimpanzee, and they retreated in a flurry, into deeper jungle. They were always getting lost, those two, because they had one too many senses of direction. Often they would come *home* hours after everyone else, hungry, sharing equally in their exhaustion, though it was Sloan who bore all the burden. On the day she had seen them spying on her treasures in her hideout, Oopi glared at them especially nastily when she returned to *the oont* but they pretended to be innocent. Where has *she* been? they asked her and she put evil in her eye and said, *"It's mine."*

"What is?—*food?*—what has she got?"

They made a grab for her hot-water bottle which was, at that moment, her imaginary husband "Jack," whom she held up with both hands and shook at them while he waved his revolvers and hollered, "You lot show yourselves on our property again and you'll have *these* shouting up your arses—!" Jack, Oopi noticed, often yelled in the same voice as her father because he had some of Mister Fraser's bones in him, some of Mister Fraser's ashes, some of his hair. On that occasion, Sloan and Sybil had pretended that they hadn't followed her, pretended that they hadn't spied on her, but she knew they had, she knew that *someone* had, so each time after that she circled, circled like a dazed mosquito on her approach, circled so they couldn't follow her, ran there, so Sloan could not keep up. None of the girls went far afield—there was no where they could go. John had once exhorted them to *go* and to *explore,* but since the fire, fear defined one boundary of their world—fatigue defined the other. Since the fire, no one spoke of rescue anymore. The failure of their hope remained uncelebrated—no one would admit it had expired. John had said four words the day the girls had come back from the smoke with their skins filthed in their last act of community—John had said, *we're going to die.* Since then, he had spoken only three more times. The first time was when Gaby brought back the metal object from *downthere* and set it down in front of him. It was black and flat, rectangular, the shape of a large book. "What is?" she asked. *"Que é isto?* Can this help us?"

"Fitz's plate," John said.

"—como?"

"—'sposure. Plate. . . ."

"—o prato?"

"—parents. Inside. Pictures of them."

After that, Nolly sent everyone *downthere* to find as many as they could. *Pictures of our parents,* everybody marveled as they marched back with the blank black metal objects. *Our parents are in here,* they said as they turned them over. Only Oopi had refused to go *downthere* to look for them and was consequently banished from the ritual. Only Oopi had asked, *"Where?"* when Nolly stood the plates up in the sand around John's head like icons 'round an altar and proclaimed that they were venerable because they held the images, the spirits, of their mothers and their fathers.

The second time John spoke was when Gaby brought the book to him.

His eyes grew large and she thought he almost smiled.

"—éy, João, um livro, não? Now you'll have to read to us—"

"—there's only *one?"*

"Sim. One, only. . . ."

"There were *three."*

"There's one. You'll read to us? There are good stories, *é verdado—?"*

There were pictures in the book of many things she recognized—of birds and eyes and waves and hands and feet and arcs and squares and circles—but there were many pictures in the book whose meanings and whose purpose were obscure.

"Que é isto?" she asked, "what is this?" showing him some drawings.

John looked at her without expression. The overdose of quinine that they fed him every day had begun to turn him yellow. Nolly said it was God manifest in him—she said it was his halo, but the effect of its toxicity was befuddlement, confusion. His pain was a blunt constant—it was difficult for him to speak. The drawings that she held in front of him for him to see swam before his eyes. The lines swelled, curved, the letters designating points on diagrams resembled flies, the elegance and sense of drawing and of writing, he realized, were lost on him, he'd grown accustomed to a nonsymbolic world, it took him several minutes to remember how to read. *Proportion,* he remembered, was the object of the drawings—Leonardo's maps about perception, his attempt to understand the weight and ratio of man to nature, understand that every instance *in* the whole owns a place in the proportion *to* the whole, that the distance from the nipples to the crown of the head constitutes one-quarter of the total length of man, for instance; that such bizarre truths are what serve as the foundations of our rationality. John looked at the page of drawings of the human arm divided into equal lengths, five equal lengths from the longest fingertip to the shoulder and he couldn't remember what this expressed, what axiom, that the length of the hand goes four times into the distance from the tip of the finger to the shoulder joint—he couldn't remember why anyone would draw a human face superimposed on a human foot, what such a picture was meant to illustrate, and all he saw before him on the page were renderings of parts of men, a foot, an arm, a leg, a face, with lines drawn through them as if showing how to mutilate and where to butcher. Why had he desired such a book, why had he kept it with him all those years, what had it signified to him that it no longer signified? he wondered. He had no conscious memory of its function in his life, this book's, except the vague sense that at some point in the past it had been beautiful, and he had been so pleased to own it.

"—feed . . ." he finally said.

"Como?"

"—fire. Burn it. Go ahead."

"—a book?"

The last thing that he says, he says the morning Oopi wakes up with her face on fire, screaming that her blood's too hot. Her face and chest are red and she is sweating. Monkey starts to fan her but too soon Oopi shouts that she's too cold and she starts shivering and shaking.

"What's the matter with her?" Monkey asks John.

He hasn't said a word for many days and she and Gaby are the only ones still talking to him.

"Is she sick?" she asks.

John looks at the sky. The end can't come too soon, he thinks. Soon enough the rains will start and that will finish us.

"—aria," he whispers.

Monkey puts her ear against his lips.

Malaria, she hears and Oopi hears it too, the ghost of it, its insinuation in her bones.

Malaria, its voice, the fever, chills, hallucinations, *death,* you better pack your things and get on home before the fever kills you, girl, that's the sensible, the normal thing to do, the voice inside her says, so she goes *down,* Monkey chasing after, calling out *You're sick! You're sick! Come back! Where are you going? Oopi?*

Beauty lasts, the memory of beauty stays, a memory of beauty lingers, the laws of nature incline toward an endlessness, the laws of nature, of perspective, of proportion incline toward the symmetry among extremes of one's existence, toward a harmony among one's keepsakes and one's relics. Line them up, she tells herself—take them out and line them up so every one can go back home together. She takes her treasures from their hiding places and begins to line them up around her. *How beautiful,* she thinks. Her bones feel like hot metal and she hurts. How beautiful, *a rock,* she thinks. *A tiny shell.* She starts to shiver and she hates this cold that follows on the fever. When she curls against the mangrove trunk she wishes for a blanket. When she falls asleep she dreams a bed. Beside her head there are her pebbles, bits of hair. There is a bone. There are some shells, dried insects. Hair, a stone, some broken crockery, a button, bit of cinder. In her fist she clutches one round cinder as her fever burns. When she wakes, between her wakings and her final sleep, she looks at it. She sees that it's more beautiful than anything, more beautiful than all her treasures, how it kindles, how it glows. It's her favorite. With her fist she clutches it. In her fist she holds a Ruby when she goes.

"ROTI,
MAKHAN,
CHINI.

CHOTI
BIBI
NINNI."

Something was wrong with John.

Monkey watched him carefully, as carefully as when they'd been alone together on the beach that night—she knew his face, she knew his skin, his posture in repose, his state, the way he looked when he was conscious and unconscious, the way he looked when he was thinking—*John is sick,* she knew. "You're sick?" she asked him.

Instead of answering he closed his eyes. Nolly had colored his eyelids, one blue with gentian violet, one green with pollen, and in the center of each one she'd made a black mark like a pupil, with some ash. His skin looked yellow, especially his neck and hands. Flies swarmed on his head, as usual, but no one fanned them from him anymore. Monkey would have, but Nolly wouldn't let her near him and Monkey could talk to him only when Nolly wasn't looking. He never answered anymore. Since the fire, only Nolly and Amanda slept near him—the other girls slept removed by distance and by darkness, while Nolly and Amanda shared the fire. Their incidence of speech was drastically reduced. During the day they waited for orders *do this, do that* from Nolly and Amanda, they listened, or half-listened, to Nolly's incantations over John, her prayers, and they issued their appropriate responses, noises, only, Monkey thought, but they never talked to one another anymore. During the day, away from Nolly and Amanda, Gaby was still garrulous—Gaby was the one who talked to everything and everyone, especially herself, in two times as many languages as Nolly or Amanda knew. Monkey heard her talking as they gathered food. Monkey saw her jumping. Gaby jumped. But when Monkey tried to talk to her or stay with her or jump with her, go *down* from *the oont* with her to gather food, walk with her the way they used to, Gaby kept her distance, shrugged her shoulders, kept her silence. All of them, except Nolly and Amanda, were less and less a part of anything outside their selves, outside their silence and their hunger. At night, Sloan and Sybil, Gaby, Jane and Monkey heard the sounds and saw the shadows cast by the fire Amanda built near John which they were not allowed to witness—what Nolly and Amanda did to John they never knew but they knew that it was something outlawed, something that they owned no words for, and they could see that John was growing sick. Something was wrong with him and they were helpless. Nightly, they fell into a silent wakefulness, trying to remember words to use to comfort, hearing sounds from Nolly and Amanda that they couldn't understand, sounds they'd heard before, in animals, from parents, sounds they didn't like to hear. Only Sloan and Sybil slept together, touching. All the rest had learned to nest upon the sand alone. They must have slept each night, from their exhaustion, though they woke each morning with no sense of having slept. For a long time Jane had been too weak to gather food, strong enough to go *down* but too weak to climb back up the bluff so Nolly had assigned her other tasks to do, sweeping sand around John's shelter, stringing feathers with the thread and needle. Jane stopped speaking. Her lips were cracked and pale and blistered but Monkey knew that they were not the reason that Jane didn't speak, the reason that she didn't eat. She had started starving herself long before her blisters, long before her hair had gotten brittle, long before her fingernails began to bleed. She was lighter than a feather now, lighter than the feathers that she strung for Nolly's headdresses—her shoulders were like knobs, so were her hips, her knees, her back was knobby and her buttocks bore the bruises where she sat. *Eat this,* Monkey was always urging her. *Here—look what I've found for you.* In her desperation to find something Jane would taste, Monkey went out farther every day. She brought back berries—black ones, seedless, sweet as icing on a cake that no one else had found. Jane turned her face from them.

Monkey brought back red bananas that she had to climb into the canopy to reach, and Jane refused them. Patiently, with exquisite patience, Monkey held the food before Jane, held the smallest morsel on her finger urging, Eat. Always, Jane rewarded her. The capitulation would come after many tries, but always Jane would open, take a bit, a fleck, a grain, an insignificancy to end the exercise, and Monkey would begin again. In addition to her chores for Nolly and Amanda, Monkey hunted twice a day for food for Jane. She was going deeper every time into the jungle, though she went without misgiving. Her search kept her alert and unafraid—if she saw some fruit high up, she didn't see its distance, only its persuasion over Jane's resistance. There must be something, she believed, that would restore Jane's health, some magic spicecake born of nature, then one afternoon she stumbled on the tree that wept enjoyments. *Honey,* beads of it, pendants, tassels, rosaries dripped from the fissures in its black bark, glistening, ripe for tasting, the sheer weight of it in her hand made her feel lightheaded and its taste sent her to the ground, intoxicated. She filled a cone made from banana leaf and hurried *home* with it but Jane refused, this time, to taste. *"Roti,"* Monkey cajoled. She swirled her finger in the honey, held it up in front of Jane. *"Roti, makhan,"* Monkey coaxed, reciting words from childhood she forgot Jane couldn't understand, *Roti, makhan, chini : choti bibi ninni*—"Bread, butter, sugar: Little baby sleep. . . ."

Jane stopped taking even morsels.

During the day she languored, often sitting on the sand, her legs spread out before her with the palmsweep in her hand, immobile. At night she curled into a ragged form and didn't move, seemed hardly to be breathing. She grew dull, like a dull surface, more lightless as she grew more light, responding less and less to everything around her, not noticing that Monkey started touching her at night, putting her hand over Jane's ankles where she slept along Jane's feet—

she could barely feel the beating of the blood inside Jane's veins. Daily, Monkey pressed on in the hope of finding something that would save Jane's life, reverse its withering. She was going further and further in, not realizing it, further toward the center of the island, then one day she walked through a curtain of bright leaves and found herself standing on a mudflat shore beside a sparkling stream of sunlit water. She stood there, rooted to the spot, uncomprehending, not believing she was seeing what she saw before her, *water.* Cautiously, she took a step. Birds—parrots—different sorts of birds than she was used to seeing by the shore, flew in and out of sunlight in the trees above the water. The stream itself ran off to her left under mangrove arches and seemed to come from somewhere in the misty glade off to her right, over which there hung a sort of spray and dozens of small rainbows, from which she could hear the melody of running water. If I could bring Jane here, she knew, If I could bring all this to Jane. . . . She knelt beside the stream and let the water run around her fingers, thrilling to its race, so clear and cool. It tasted like a breath of heaven, like the story and the meaning of her life—like joy. She splashed her face with it. She could wash Jane's hair, she thought, she could renew her and restore her with this—then she stopped short as she realized she had nothing with her like a cup or like a pail with which to carry it. Anything would do—a bottle or a glass, a ladle, kettle, anything, a hollow wooden branch, but all she had was the rough sac she'd woven from the palm leaves that she carried on her back for gathering. She searched the ground for anything, a shell, a gourd, something that the water wouldn't pour through, but she found nothing. She found indentations in the mud, shallow holes into which water seeped, holes along the bank, leading to the shore, prints becoming more distinct, less deep, more recognizable, first one then the other, walking, bigger than her own, big steps, footprints of a human being.

Monkey watched the footprints weave along the shore

and trail into the jungle. "Hoo!" she called. "Hoo-*ooo!*" Green and crimson parrots panicked at the sound and darted like bright ribbons through the trees but no one answered. Monkey stood and listened for a while then cupped her hand over her brow and made a calculation from the sun— if she ran, she thought, and if she marked her way, she could get back to the hiding place along the shore *downthere* where they had stored the wreckage, all the old things, all the casks and timber, before the sun dropped from its apogee in the morning sky and return here with an empty biscuit drum she knew was there. Not stopping to consider how she'd carry the full drum back to *the oont* she set off, driven by her vision, by her love. It was love, exclusively, that drove her—not once did she consider what the water meant, what its discovery meant to any of them, all of them, except to Jane, or that she might use its discovery the way Nolly and Amanda exercised their power of discovery over John, over the fire. She had no thought but the thought of what the water meant for Jane, except she knew that for Jane's sake she had to keep it hidden from Amanda and from Nolly. She ran with ease, her feet had grown a second skin, a thick hard layer like a pair of shoes—and she marked her path as she had learned to do from Gaby. All of them had learned to do things that they'd never done before, things that marked them out as creatures, beings in the wild. Monkey's hands, too, had turned rough—she was aware of them, how rough they were, whenever she touched Jane. Her face, her hair, her skin and body must have changed, too, roughened, grown a second layer, metamorphosed into something else, though she had no image of it, couldn't see it, only saw the way the others looked and knew she must have changed as much as they had—only when she saw herself perceived through someone else's eyes did she understand how frightening she had become.

The drum she carried was more cumbersome than she had thought it would be and she had to stop to make a sling for it and then it banged against her as she walked so she had to stop and weight it with some rocks and then it was a weight that slowed her down. It was afternoon before she reached her final mark, the one before the curtain on the other side of which she could hear the stream. She stopped. What she heard was not the stream. What she heard was something singing. What she heard was not a song, exactly, more like music that an ocean mammal makes, a melancholic scheming, sound designed to bounce off underwater shores, a sound made out of need for definition of a place.

There was a woman on the far shore of the stream.

Monkey saw her through the curtain of the leaves.

Monkey put her drum down.

Watched her.

Time did not go by.

A thousand changes happened in her skin, a thousand softenings, a layer shed, a welcoming renewed itself, she tore through the leaves onto the mud proclaiming *Nnm!* her arms thrown open shouting *Mmb!* The woman froze. Monkey jumped, excited, *Rhhg!* she ran up and down, flapping her arms, ran toward the water, toward the woman *Nnm!* She couldn't wait to reach her, touch her, put her arms around her, then she realized she was running in the water, splashing, and the ground was going down, the water rushing to her mouth and she remembered that she couldn't swim, reversed, fell down, breathed water, gagged, stood up, wiped her eyes and spit and saw that she was gone, the woman, saw that, like a ghost, Charlotte had disappeared.

Monkey walked along the shore to try to find a narrows to cross the stream but each time that she tried to ford it, water washed around her throat and she lost courage. After a while she sat down in the open on the mudbank and stared across the stream into the trees on the far shore. *She's watching me* she hoped. *Watch me,* she begged. She tried to think of ways to let the woman know that she was Monkey even though she didn't look the way she used to look, even though she didn't sound, she didn't speak the way she used to speak before, so she stood up and held her arms over her head and turned around and 'round and 'round. *See?* she gestured. She spread her arms, invitingly, but no gesture was returned and she sat down again and buried both her legs in mud. It would be getting dark soon, Monkey knew, and she had to get back *home.* She rinsed the drum with water several times, standing in the stream, still looking toward the other shore, and then she filled it. She stood beside it on the bank before she hitched it to her back, and then she waved. Nothing came back, no sound, no stirring in the distant trees, no shimmer of a movement in the leaves, no sense that any thing or any one was there. When she came within sight of *the oont* it was dark and only the glimmer of the fire that Amanda built each night defined the land from the surrounding night. Monkey climbed with difficulty up the steeper slope, the one they called *the backway* so none of them would notice her. Gaby heard her, though, and was ready at the cliff edge with a rock held high to bash her head in if she had to as Monkey finished her ascent. "—*Éy?* you need to die?" she asked, before she helped to haul her up.

Most of the water had been spilled, and there were leaves and dry seeds and mosquitoes floating in it from the journey, but its existence was no less miraculous to them and its arrival was a work of magic, an illusion, a mirage, a fantasy. As Monkey unstrapped it from her back, they gathered 'round it on their knees—Sloan, Gaby and Sybil. In the dark, they smelled it—in their thirst they could taste it through their noses. One by one they stuck their fingers in it, murmuring small sounds of pleasure, then they cupped their hands and drank. Though she couldn't see their faces Monkey felt their joy.

"—we must keep this *secreto, clandestino, não falar a* Nolly—"

"—where did she *find* it?"

"—not so far," Monkey whispered. "There's a river. Careful—save enough for—"

"—river?— is there more?"

"—for *Jane,"* Monkey continued and everyone fell silent.

"Jane's 'sleeping,' " Sloan or Sybil finally said. The way they said it frightened her. She picked up the drum. "Where is she?"

"Sleeping," they repeated. "Can't you tell us where the river *is?"*

"—take us to it?"

"—tell us how to go to it?"

Monkey walked away from them and searched for Jane but couldn't find her in the dark.

She could hear the noises that she didn't like, from the direction of the fire. She was about to enter into the circle of its light when Gaby came to her and said, "Come. We hid her. If they found her. We were frightened."

Gaby led her to the largest rock and started digging through the sand beside it.

Monkey set the drum down.

It was such a shallow grave, a breeze could have exposed her.

"Desculpe," Gaby said, as they worked together to uncover her. "I'm sorry. . . ."

Monkey moaned.

"—she was dead this morning. When you left. You were gone a long time, little one. I thought you knew."

"She was *alive—"*

"Não. Os abutres— the vultures. They came. *They* knew. . . ."

The sand was hot, still hot with sun, and Jane's body was still warm but she was rigid.

"—be quick," Gaby warned. She stood up and whispered, "Those birds, I'm telling you," and then withdrew.

The birds did not come back.

Toward dawn Monkey poured the water through Jane's hair and combed it with her fingers. *Choti bibi,* Monkey said. She washed Jane's face. Little baby *ninni,* she whispered. Be good. I'm here. I will take good care of you. I'll be here when you awaken. *Sleep,* she said. Leave the world to me, she said, and finally, attempting no vengeance, as the sun rose, Jane allowed the sad brown girl to feed her, slowly, one by one, her kisses.

ANTS

Go downthere, Monkey had said.

It isn't far, she told them.

Go to where the empty casks are hidden.

Behind the biggest cask, the one with the red stripes on it they'll see a banana palm.

Walk into the jungle so the banana palm is always right behind them.

Walk while counting to a hundred and they'll see her first mark at the base of a tall tree.

They'll know which tree it is because there is a parrot sitting in it.

Then turn left.

Walk straight along, keeping to the upward slope.

If the ground goes downhill turn around and stay up on the highest part.

After a while they'll find her second mark.

Go straight but keep the sun at their left shoulder.

They'll find the tree that weeps enjoyments.

Beside it is an anthill.

Next to the anthill is a log across a slimy part.

On the other side of it turn right.

Go straight again until they reach a big red boulder in the middle of an open part.

Turn left.

After that the jungle will get thick and all they have to do is go until the jungle curtain opens.

Then they'll see the river.

But they couldn't always see the sun to tell if it was always on their left and they couldn't count except by two's. They didn't find the tree that weeps enjoyments. They found an anthill, though, and all the ants found Sloan. "—they're biting her!" she panicked, bending down to scratch and almost toppling Sybil.

"—she should run!" Sybil suggested, so she ran and that's when something happened to the ground and they went down, first Sloan, then Sybil, down into the slime, Sybil holding to a mangrove root while something pulled her legs so hard she thought they would rip off and she held *tight* and cried for Sloan to come and save her then the thing that pulled so hard slipped off and a large bubble rose beside her on the surface of the slime and she pulled up-and-out, because she thought it was an alligator.

Sloan? she called.

Nothing moved but she heard marching.

She lay with one cheek on the ground and watched the surface of the slime congeal around a dragonfly and drag it down and eat it.

SLOAN! she called again.

The leaves shook and the dense green jungle echoed SYBIL! SLOAN AND SYBIL! SLOAN!

—there must have been a million of them, it was shocking as they marched across her hand. The pain was like a thousand needles twisting in her bones. She couldn't run from them. She couldn't run like Sloan could, both her legs were broken, she was trapped, a mountain of them, they were on her eyes, her back, inside her ears, her nose, and when she took a breath she breathed ants in and felt them eating on her tongue, her throat, the words that she was forming, *Sloan-where-are-we-Sloan-she-thinks-we're-lost—*

It was easy to roll over. One last breath, a half a turn, a half a thing, an incompletion, one half of a whole, and it was over, both of them had vanished.

. . .

By day, they fooled the other two by working twice as hard but they couldn't fool them every evening when the quinine prayers were heard.

The quinine prayers were heard at sunset, at the coming of the evening star, when Nolly called the celebrants to prayer by banging on a metal pot with the broken haft of a soup ladle. Before there was the fire they had gathered around John at sunset every day as preparation for the night, as a form of comfort, a communal closure against fright. Before the fire they had slept around him, watching for the moment he would wake, attending to each movement he would make, as if his breathing had a hidden meaning and the beating of his heart owed its significance to something other than its physiology. They doted on him. What they believed he could enact for them, their transformation and their rescue, was worth the effort of their adoration. One runs from fear, one is attracted to relief, its promise of insouciance—assistance is the power of attraction that love and worship hold. To love is not to worship—but to worship is to arrive into a state of subjugation that defines conditions constituting love as well. They never loved him. They desired him to evidence omniscience, a higher wisdom than their own—they believed in his capacity to right their wrongs, to lead them, to resist their natural predilection for defiance. A state of subjugation makes its own revolt when the object of its worship fails to stimulate belief in its omnipotence. John was never possibly omnipotent. There was nothing John could offer as an ordinary man. An ordinary man was not what their belief in him, their spying on him, had prepared them to expect. Before the fire they expected guidance from him, straightforward elucidation of the secret workings of all things—but since the fire he had proven what he didn't know, he'd abdicated, mocked their dedication by refusing faith invested in him, turned away, retreated into being someone lacking in resolve, an ordinary man conceding silence in his argument with death. So Nolly dressed him, Nolly made him extra-ordinary. In addition to the quinine prayers there was the painting ritual, the rinsing and the washing, the grooming and adornment of him, his embellishment, his prettifying. She became his keeper and Amanda kept his fire. Every day they sent the others *down* for fuel and for more food for them and John. They had grown so privileged in their duties that they didn't notice Oopi went. Jane had been so worthless, so inert in her last days, they didn't notice she was missing either. Then the twins were gone. After that the balance on *the oont* was something different, every sunset brought an edge, the enactment of the ritual was charged with change, a chance for insurrection.

She was running out of quinine. The ritual around the placement of the quinine tablet on John's tongue now revolved around the placement of a single morsel, barely visible, a grain that Nolly shaved from the last tablet with the razor. Her incantation, too, was shaved. Her words were pared down, so were their responses. Everything—their spoken words, their gestures, their exertions—had been shaved, reduced to the demotic, emblematic, everything the ritual contained became symbolic of its former self, symbolic of its former symbol like a love that calls itself a love when it's grown loveless, like a love that is a war.

Nolly must have sensed their insurrection, must have known they planned to flee. She must have seen the forecast of it in the way they held themselves, just as God must have seen the change in Lucifer before he flew.

One evening during prayers the one she didn't like, the black one, lifted up the corner of the sheet and looked beneath it.

The sheet was filthy.

Without water, they survived surrounded by the sort of filth that bleeds, encrusts and stinks, but something on *the oont* around John's shelter had begun to reek of putrefaction. "What *is—?*" Gaby whispered, sitting up one night. Since the twins had gone she and Monkey slept only an arm's length from each other and stole away together before dawn each day to gather food. The fire was a comfort for them, too—they were afraid of sleeping *downthere* outside the circumference of its aura. They talked of stealing it—stealing it and taking it to live beside the stream Monkey had found, but they felt fidelity toward John. Instead of fleeing they were waiting for an intervention from somewhere. They didn't name it but they knew that they were waiting for another death, for Nolly's or Amanda's.

Then one evening at the prayers Monkey raised the corner of the sheet that hid John's legs and saw what Nolly and Amanda had been doing. Gaby saw it, too, and immediately Gaby vomited.

Nolly acted as if nothing had occurred. She acted as if nothing had been seen or done to interrupt the ritual *Have mercy on us* she intoned. She placed a morsel of the quinine tablet on John's tongue and said, "Lift up your hearts."

We lift them up, only Amanda, by herself, replied.

"Let us give thanks. . . ."

Only Nolly and Amanda prayed.

Every night they had been paring skin off him, eating morsels from his legs, his flesh, stanching his blood with a hot brand from the fire which he couldn't feel but which left him charred and rotting.

That evening Monkey and Gaby waited until Nolly said the Benediction, then withdrew and sat together until dark.

The moon was full.

Bats, like kites, flew across the face of it, flew across a yellow moon.

Soon they saw the sparks go up as Amanda made the fire.

"—we should go," Monkey insisted.

"We should *wait.* . . ."

"I know a place where we can hide until the morning."

"—so do *I.*"

"—why do we wait?"

"—so they won't chase."

"—we can't go quiet-quiet?"

"When they finish. When they sleep. After they've—"

They shut their eyes and held their ears.

When the moon grew silver and the night became more silent and the fireglow had faded, Monkey and Gaby went over the cliff edge, they went *down.*

A silver path lay on the water—white shells like blue paper lanterns lined the shore.

They kept to the edge of the jungle—walking and then stopping. They kept looking back.

They were afraid of the jungle at night but the shore was too bright and they needed to keep out of sight of *the oont.*

They were moving toward a place Gaby knew, some place not too far from the shore and when they reached the place where the casks and wreckage had been stored Monkey started to speak but Gaby stopped her. The ground was littered with the broken junk, heaps of rope, splintered timber, but from behind the cask with the red stripe there came a sound of something swinging on its hinge, the sound of something swinging on a metal hinge, the fire-pot, and then there were two torches flaming and Nolly and Amanda with feathers on their heads and painted faces, holding in their other hands the trident and a spear.

Gaby ran, pulling Monkey. "—Fly!—Run!" she shouted.

They ran together, side by side, along the shore, racing as they had once done one time before and this time, too, Monkey wanted Gaby to come out ahead, she felt that she was holding Gaby back, Gaby was faster but was holding back for Monkey's sake so Monkey veered away and shouted, "Go! Fly!" and sprinted toward the jungle but Gaby wouldn't let her go and doubled back and they both crashed into the forest through the dark ferns and the black vines only seconds before the others followed with their torches. Monkey knew the jungle wouldn't burn. She felt safe in it as long as she could hide, so she crouched down inside a fern beside a jackfruit tree. She was too afraid to keep on going, frightened of the night and of the jungle, frightened to be left alone, away from Gaby.

Gaby ran and ran.

There was nothing quiet in the way that Gaby ran—she attacked the jungle with her legs and arms, attacked it like a swimmer attacks water, and all the time she swore. She swore at *Deus* and at *João* and at Grandfather, at pigeonshit and ships, she swore at Monkey. She swore at both King Momo and King George. She swore at jungles. She made a great wild flapping, swearing, smashing noise and then she dropped onto her haunches in dead silence as she'd learned to do by watching tiny birds who used confusion to defeat their predators, birds who use a sudden silence as their camouflage.

Like a cloud, as silently, she moved across the jungle. Moonlight broke in places through the leaves and lighted up the night with eerie shadows. She was looking for her tree, the tallest tree in all the jungle, tallest tree for miles around, an ancient giant pine from which she hoped to sight a passing ship to signal if she climbed up into it. She crept with skill, fighting the temptation to whistle or whisper Monkey's name. She found the pine tree in the center of a clearing and was halfway up its trunk in no time. She had never climbed up higher than the branch she sat on but she knew it very well and she was comfortable. Tomorrow she would look for Monkey, steal the fire. She dreamed that she was stealing fire, must have dreamed it, was still dreaming, she could see the flames and see the tree on fire, smell the burning wood, she'd never seen a tree on fire, never seen the pillar that it makes, the fire racing up, how it jumps from branch to branch up up as if it wants to fly. The fire was advancing from the ground, she could see Nolly and Amanda, little people, from her perch above the earth. She climbed. The branches were so thin they felt like bamboo poles, like kite struts under her and she felt like she was standing in a giant kite. Above her, bats, like kites, were flying on the moon. A sudden great hot breath exploded under her, blew up and up and Gabriella de Castro y Ortíz opened out her arms and flew.

LOVE To love is to accept that one might die another death before one dies one's own.

Waking on the ground one morning Charlotte is surprised by violent light, a light so violent it repels her, fills her eyes with burning tears. *Dear god. This is seeing* she remembers.

When she can bear the light, she discovers she is living in a shaded glade beside a waterfall approximately her own height. Everything is smaller than she thought it was when she was blind. When she was blind she thought the waterfall must be the size of a glacier as big as Victoria Falls, as powerful. When she was blind the sound of it had roared, a constant, like a burning furnace and she used its sound to locate where she was. Now the water merely ran, no more, no less, with a ferocity of a minor millstream. Birds, too, had sounded larger, she had heard them 'round her head as if they were about to prey on her but now she sees them, tiny harmless things of untold delicacy and beauty in the brightest colors, while all the time she had imagined them as big and gray and black. The flowers, too, even things that she had touched, had turned over in her hands, are smaller when she sees them than when she had constructed them, through touch, in her imagination. The stream, too, is a narrow ribbon where she had imagined a great lake.

All the world seems smaller to her, this new world, as if, in blindness, her mind had reverted to an old remembered ratio, a previous proportion, the relation of a child's sense of herself, the relation of a young girl to an enormous world.

The distance she had wandered must be very small indeed, she now considers.

She's curious about herself.

Her hands, she sees, are covered with a latticework of cuts and scars, as are her wrists and arms, because she'd used them as her first defense when she was blind, seeing with them, fending with them, traveling on them.

Her skin had turned a florid red with sunburn and a rash and she's surprised to find she's naked while all the time she had imagined she was clothed.

Her hair is white.

She sees it hanging from her head and panics at it, thinking it's a spider's web around her.

She tries to find the berries she's been eating but she has to close her eyes to locate them. She tries to find the tiny mudfish that have nourished her and she's repulsed to see her hands expertly turn up maggots from beneath the rocks along the stream bed.

Nothing is as she had dreamed it. In her mind she'd made a different landscape—this one seems less real, somehow, a geography in miniature. She has to close her eyes in order to remember where she came from. *Over there* she thinks, and finds that she is looking down the stream. She remembers following the stream, following the stream away from all the thunder, crawling by the stream toward what she'd hoped would be a silence. Sound had been a constant threat. Now she finds that even sound is smaller. Sounds are thin and tiny, farther off. The stream seems just a whisper, but a murmur, and the silence starts to make her feel she is alone. When she was blind she had called out so others there would see her. Now she sees there are no others and the fear she'd had of having been invisible, of wandering about from place to place unseen, of having been marooned on, exiled to, a ghost existence with her senses, save her sight, intact, had been a creation of her mind, a product of imagination, an optimism in the guise of fear.

Her eyes now tell her she's alone. Still, her memory knows that there were others, others that she's heard, others that she's stumbled onto *No. Don't think of that*—and now she feels the presence of another as she stops to look around beside the stream.

It is a child.

Lying on its side, curled in the mud, its long hair caked with mud, its skin the color of it, there's a child asleep before her and it's weeping in its sleep and shivering.

She kneels down beside the child and lifts the hair back from its face and as she does the child awakes. Monkey retreats, crablike, on her hands and feet across the mud and stares at Charlotte from a distance. Charlotte bares her teeth. Charlotte thinks she's smiling but she doesn't know her teeth and mouth are red from all the berries she's been eating and Monkey recoils at the sight of what she sees as blood. Charlotte puts her hand out and says *There there. What's this? I won't hurt you. What are all these tears about?*

Hearing Charlotte's voice Monkey crawls to her and puts her head on Charlotte's feet and weeps while Charlotte soothes her, pats her back and lifts her to her arms against her breasts.

I never thought I'd *see* another person Charlotte wants to say but Monkey sobs *we . . . have . . . to. . . .*

Don't try to speak she's told.

"—have to try and help him. . . ."

Charlotte wipes her tears and tries to keep the hair from falling over Monkey's face.

Him? she asks.

"Try and help," Monkey explains.

"John," she adds.

"John," she says again. "John, John, John . . . the Captain. . . ."

She is hitting Charlotte with her fists.

"John?" Charlotte asks. *John is still alive?*

"Yes!"

—still alive?

"—yes!"

Charlotte is remembering a time, she doesn't know how long ago, before she found the stream, when she'd been searching for the others near the thunder.

"Still alive—?" she asks again.

"—yes!"

My John?

"—the captain, yes . . . !"

O you have to take me to him! Where is he! O marvelous, O stupendous necessity she recalls as Monkey leads her through the jungle. *O to see my love again! O wonderful, O mighty process.* Monkey tells her nothing, merely leads her and the world around them seems as new as certainly it must have seemed at its creation. *John* she marvels. *John and all the world the way it was before—*

As they near the shore Monkey tells her that they must stay hidden and she holds Charlotte back and points up to *the oont* while Charlotte looks with wonder at the sea. *All this looks familiar* she is thinking. *This is where we landed* she remembers. *This is where the turtles—*

"Is that ours?" she asks Monkey, pointing to the smoke up on the cliff. "Is that our signal—?"

Monkey pulls on Charlotte's hand.

"Don't go—" she warns, but Charlotte's running.

Monkey chases.

As they come upon the ash heap on the beach Charlotte stops and looks at all the bones.

She puts her foot across the circle inscribed 'round it in the sand.

"—don't cross it!" Monkey shouts, still pulling on her, frightened they've been seen by the other two.

"—but what *is* it?" Charlotte asks.

"—it's what's left. The grave. What's left. We can't go near it."

"This isn't a grave," Charlotte explains. She touches Monkey's nose. "This is just a kill left by the animals, don't be afraid. Didn't anybody tell you that—? Didn't Fitz? Didn't Matlock? Didn't John? Now come on—" She takes Monkey's hand and leans toward her and smiles her bloody smile. "Why are you so sad on such a happy day—?"

Monkey's heart is breaking, she can feel it breaking in her chest and suddenly she doesn't want Charlotte to know, doesn't want Charlotte to discover, too, what Nolly and Amanda have become, what the smoke up there, the fire on *the oont* in daylight, means they've done to John.

"—don't go," she whispers.

"Go?"

"—up there. —please. —don't. —it's too late."

The smoke looked like a cloud, Monkey remembered, pure white. When she thinks about that day she thinks about it from above as if she were the smoke, she sees the way that Charlotte took her hand and made her heart feel whole again, as if it were still possible to feel some sort of love. She always sees them from above and she and Charlotte look so small, like tiny people who appear on the shore—two tiny people, the sun at their backs, naked figures, a child and a woman, making their way on the sand toward the smoke on the hill, and they walk, Monkey sees, refusing to see what happened next: they walk and they walk and they walk and they walk and they walk, she believes.